The Roughneck & the Lady
By Erin Wade
Copyright 7/2018

Edited by Susan Hughes

The Roughneck & the Lady

Erin Wade
©7/2018 Erin Wade
www.erinwade.us

DEDICATION

To the one that has always supported me in everything I have ever undertaken. You have encouraged me and have always been my biggest fan. Life is sweeter with you. Erin

Acknowledgements

A special "Thank You" to my wonderful and witty "Beta Master," **Julie Versoi**. She makes me a better storyteller.

A heartfelt "Thank You" to **Laure Dherbécourt** for agreeing to beta read for me. She has added insight and an incredible knack for catching incorrect homophones.

Guest Beta **Kate Maxwell** is joining us for this book. Kate is from Australia. Both Laure and Kate provide a unique way of seeing things. Sometimes writers think everyone understands the words we use, but that isn't always true. When Laure or Kate tell me something isn't clear or they don't understand what I mean, I rewrite it. Their input is greatly appreciated.

Her

Watch her. Watch how her eyes light up when you enter the room. Watch her lips smile as her eyes capture yours and know she is feeling the same feelings as you.

Touch her. Brush your fingers lightly down her arm. Lean in to whisper and let your lips brush against her ear. Place your palm against the small of her back as you step aside to let her walk past. Hold her hand.

Make her laugh. It is the most wonderful sound in your world. To make her happy is the driving goal in your life. Share your thoughts and dreams with her. After all, they are all about her.

Erin Wade
The Roughneck & the Lady
9/2018

Chapter 1

Trin shoved the man to safety as the falling debris rained on them. The oil well scaffolding had buckled, sending everything tilting sideways. The last thing that registered in Trin's mind was the hand laying on the derrick deck. Just a hand attached to nothing.

"Very good." Dr. Heather Hunter watched as her patient moved his foot and then each toe as she touched it. "I believe we have one hundred percent recovery. Do you have any pain?"

"No," the man replied. "I'm as good as new. I swear, Dr. Hunter, I thought I was going to be crippled for the rest of my life. I don't know how to thank you."

"Your recovery is thanks enough." Heather glanced at the file on her desk. It had taken almost eighteen months for him to regain full use of his foot that had been severed in a railroad accident.

"I'm releasing you to return to work," she said, signing the papers and handing them to her patient.

Heather leaned back in her chair as the man left her office. She was thankful that she had chalked up more successes than failures during her career as an orthopedic surgeon.

"Doctor Heather Hunter report to the emergency operating room. Potential amputee has landed on Care Flight pad. Dr. Heather Hunter report to . . ."

Heather stripped off her blazer as she left her office in a dead run for the trauma unit. Her surgical team was already gathering in the decontamination room. Someone slipped a gown on her. She scrubbed and then slipped into the sterile gloves.

"What is it?" she asked.

"A severed left hand. Care Flight got it here in less than thirty minutes. The hand is on ice, and those at the scene had sense enough to put a tourniquet close to the end of the amputation." Lori Rogers, the nurse who headed up the trauma surgical team, filled her in as they entered the operating room.

"How did it happen?" Heather said.

"Oil field accident. He's covered in oil. We wiped him down, but there isn't time to bathe him."

"Damn oil fields," Heather muttered. "The way they keep sending young men in here, I'll be able to retire by the time I'm forty. Don't they have any safety protocols?"

"Yeah," Lori snorted. "They keep a Care Flight chopper on hand whenever they set up a new rig."

The patient was covered, with only the arm visible outside the sheet. The face was masked by the anesthesiologist's paraphernalia.

Heather quickly assessed the damage and the chances of a successful reattachment. "Hand," she commanded.

Moving with the swiftness and confidence of one who had performed the surgery many times, Heather began the revascularization process of connecting blood vessels and getting blood to the hand. When the blood flow was restored, she reattached the eleven flexor tendons that control the wrist, thumb, and fingers. She carefully reattached the ulnar and median nerves responsible for finger motion and sensation.

After what seemed like hours, she surveyed her handiwork. As if God were sending her a signal, the fingers on the hand jerked and moved. The ghastly whiteness had been replaced by a light pink color. Heather sighed as she checked the Frankenstein hand resting on the foam encasement needed to limit movement. The arm and hand were lean and muscular. "Probably under twenty," she mumbled out loud. *Some poor kid who thought he'd get rich in the oil fields and almost ended up without a hand.*

"You headed home?" Lori asked as they washed up and removed their surgical garb.

"No. I want to stay around until he wakes up. I want to make certain he can move all his fingers a little. I'll catch a nap in the on-call room. Maybe my father won't look for me there. Do me a favor. If anyone asks, I went home."

"What's his name?" Heather asked, though she was almost too tired to talk.

"Trin—"

"Heather, you were magnificent," the handsome middle-aged doctor who interrupted them gushed. "Absolutely magnificent. Your father will be so proud of you."

"Peter, all I care about right now is a place to lay my head," Heather grumbled. "See you tomorrow."

Moving as quickly as her tired legs would carry her, Heather pushed through the double doors leading from the trauma unit.

##

Chapter 2

Heather rubbed the sleep from her eyes and tried to orient her mind to her surrounds. It took her a moment to recall that she had performed an exhausting surgery and had crashed in the doctor's on-call room. She was surprised to find she was the only one in the room. A flurry of activity in the hallway confirmed her fear that all hands were on deck. She walked to her office and freshened up before jumping into the emergency room fray.

"Where are these people coming from?" Heather said as she tried to acclimate her sense of smell to the stench of blood.

"Some lunatic drove an eighteen-wheeler into a crowd at the Fat Stock Show," an orderly answered.

Before she could survey the situation further, Lori hailed her. "Heather, we have a severed leg on table three. I'm not sure you can save it. She's lost a lot of blood."

"Is the leg here?"

"Yeah," Lori huffed. "It came in beside her on the stretcher."

Heather assessed the woman's condition and then began barking orders. "Antibiotics, blood transfusion. Get her to the trauma unit. Lori, pull together as many of our team as you can. We can do this."

By the time the team was scrubbed and ready, the prep team had the woman on the table. The anesthesiologist was already doing her job.

Heather cringed at the sight of the leg. It was already turning blue. She located the main arteries feeding blood to the leg and sutured them to the arteries in the severed leg.

9

She then reconnected blood veins. She held her breath as she released the clamps on the arteries. The sutures held, and the return of blood through the veins told her she had gotten blood to the leg. She exhaled slowly, afraid to breathe on her handiwork.

She reconnected muscles, bones, and ligaments. When she finished, she glanced at Lori.

"Her vital signs are good," Lori said in answer to Heather's unasked question.

Heather stepped aside and let a young doctor suture the skin back together.

"Move her to ICU," Lori yelled. "We have incoming."

"Lori, I can't—"

"You're all we've got, Heather," Lori said with a shrug. "Peter Pan flew his ass home when we were notified this was headed our way."

"Where the hell is Dr. Hunter?" Heather yelled over the melee.

"Right here beside you, dear." Eric Hunter held up his gloved hands and took his place at the table next to his daughter.

Heather nodded to her father. "Then the amputees stand a good chance of surviving."

The father-daughter team worked side by side until the flow of injured slowed to a halt.

"That's the last one." Lori sighed as a ten-year-old boy was wheeled from the operating room. "You two make quite a team."

"Yes, we do," Eric Hunter said, beaming at his daughter. "She's damn good."

"You're no slouch yourself, old man," Heather teased.

"Come on, I'll buy you a cup of coffee," Eric said as he took his daughter's elbow.

"I'll meet you in the coffee shop, Dad," Heather said. "I need to check on a patient first."

Heather headed for intensive care and checked Trin's chart. *We need a last name on this chart*, she thought as she read the positive information recorded there. *Circulation is good. All vital signs are good. This young man is one lucky son of a gun.*

Heather walked toward the coffee shop to meet her father. She was exhausted, and she knew her father was too. Twenty years her senior, Eric Hunter was a handsome man with thick, black hair that had a touch of silver at the temples. She was certain her mother didn't appreciate him as much as she should.

"Dad,"—she kissed his cheek—"I'm glad you were here."

"Me too." Eric's grey eyes danced. "It was fun. It's not every day I get to share the trauma unit with our resident prodigy."

Heather laughed out loud. "I'm not so much a prodigy as I'm Eric Hunter's daughter. You're the one who taught me all the little tricks they don't teach in med school."

Eric patted her hand. "You make me proud." The admiration in his eyes made her proud too.

"Heather, Eric, there you are," Peter Trotter said as he walked toward their table. "I came as soon as I heard about the crash. What can I do?"

"Go home," Eric snorted. "The worst is over. The staff has everything under control."

"I'll just join you two . . . " Peter's sentence dwindled as the two Hunters glared at him.

"We're having a father-daughter discussion," Eric said. "The best thing you can do is go home and show up for your regular shift tonight at midnight."

Heather watched Trotter scurry from the cafeteria. "I do believe you made him tuck his tail between his legs," she said, laughing. "You truly are a daunting chief of surgeons, Dad."

"I never intimidated you."

"No, I idolize you. It's hard to intimidate someone who adores you."

Eric grinned. "Yes, it is."

"I've been here over thirty-six hours," Heather said, rolling her head on her shoulders. "Let's go home."

Chapter 3

Trin stared at the hand attached to her wrist. She wondered if it was functional or if it was just for looks. If it was for looks, someone was playing a terrible joke on her.

The hand looked as if it was being held in place by barbwire. The crisscross pattern of stitches was the roughest patch job she'd ever seen. Of course, she'd never seen a hand sewn back onto anyone before.

Holding her breath, she curled her fingers slightly. To her surprise, all four of them obeyed her command. *Now the thumb. Without opposable thumbs, man is just another animal,* she thought.

The thumb moved at her will too.

The last time Trin had seen her hand, it was laying on the derrick floor. God bless the saint who had reattached it. She wanted to meet him, to thank him.

"Thank you, God," Trin mumbled as the sedatives took over and she slipped into a dreamless sleep.

##

Heather Hunter opened the laptop as she pushed Trin's door open with her hip. The roughneck was sleeping peacefully thanks to the morphine and antibiotics the nurses were pumping into him.

So young, Heather thought as she studied the face with the sculpted angles and curves. The skin was flawless like a child's. *Way too young to be working in a dangerous oil field job.*

She examined the hand, gently flexing the fingers and thumb. The tip of each digit was pink and warm. She smiled when she was satisfied her handiwork was perfect. *Dad will be proud of this*, she thought as she made notations on the computer and left the room.

"Heather!" Peter Trotter said as he sprinted to catch up with the beautiful brunette. "Do you have a minute?"

"For a consultation?" Heather asked.

"No, a cup of coffee." Peter shrugged. "I thought we could discuss the fundraising ball for the hospital."

"Peter, you know I don't like to get drawn into the fundraising part of hospital operations."

"But you did promise to get involved with the Cattle Baron's Ball," Peter reminded her. "If you could just be nice to Bobby Joe or Billy Bob or whatever his name is, the hospital might be selected as the recipient of the donations this year."

"So now you're pimping on behalf of the hospital?" Heather glared. "Why don't you be nice to Suzie Mae or Betty Lou? Why your sudden interest in the hospital's finances? Have you managed to create another lawsuit against us?"

"I . . . uh, we may have a small problem." Peter gulped as he tried to steady his voice. "But you could fix it."

"I wouldn't touch one of your botched surgeries," Heather said, turning to face the man. "Honestly, I have no idea why Father allows you to practice in this hospital."

"You promised to help," Peter wheedled. "Your father said we could count on you."

"When is the planning session?"

"Four this afternoon." The self-serving smile on Peter's face made her want to slap him.

"I'll be there," she said instead.

Heather checked on five other patients who were recovering from the terrorist act at the Fat Stock Show.

Everyone was doing nicely. *Now for a conversation with Father*, she thought.

##

Dr. Eric Hunter finished his dictation and waved his daughter to the seat in front of his desk. "To what do I owe this pleasant surprise? Although it is rarely pleasant when you seek me out."

Heather couldn't help but laugh at her father. He knew her so well. "The Cattle Baron's Ball." The exasperation in her voice told Eric she wasn't happy about being involved in his pet fundraiser.

"Honey I'm on the planning committee for them every year. They're tired of my old face and requested you be on the committee. You'll have twelve months to put together a ball that will shine their boots. They donate millions to the hospital annually."

"Which we use to settle Peter Trotter's malpractice lawsuits," Heather grumbled. "Honestly, Dad, what's the man holding over you? I can't believe you would tolerate his ineptness if he didn't have something to blackmail you."

"You make it sound as if I have a deep, dark secret." Eric laughed.

"Do you?"

"No. As you know, Peter's father and I were in the war together. I was wounded and left for dead. Jarrod crawled on his stomach to see if I had a pulse. When he discovered I was alive, he dragged me onto his back and crawled back to the trench. I would have died on some filthy sand dune if Jarrod hadn't saved me. As he lowered me over the sandbags to safety, he was shot in the back. He's been paralyzed ever since."

"I know the story, Dad, but how many others are you going to allow to leave this hospital paralyzed because Peter is a sloppy surgeon?

"How long do you continue to let other people pay your debt to Jarrod? Peter's success rate is under thirty percent. He shouldn't even be allowed in a hospital room, much less given a scalpel. And the bottom line is, he doesn't care. He doesn't care how many patients he maims and cripples because he knows you will cover his ass."

"Heather!" The sternness in her father's voice told Heather she had stepped over the line.

"I know you promised Jarrod you'd take care of Peter," she argued in a softer tone, "but can't you at least put him in a position where he can't harm people who put their trust in us?"

Eric furrowed his brow. "What position would you suggest?"

"Janitor," Heather snorted.

Her father didn't dignify her suggestion with a comment.

"Finance," she suggested. "He could head fundraising and grants for the hospital. He's handsome and, until one gets to know him, he's charismatic."

"You don't like him at all, do you?" Eric watched his daughter's eyes. They always answered before her lips moved.

"I can't stand the man," she answered through gritted teeth. "I think he's a weaselly little prick."

"I'm afraid I agree with you." Eric chuckled as he pulled a thick file from the lap drawer of his desk. "Will you do me a favor? Look over these X-rays and MRIs. See if you think you can make this man walk again."

Heather looked at the folder as if her father had handed her the Holy Grail. "This is Jarrod Trotter's file?"

16

"Yes. If we can fix him, we'll be free of Peter the Butcher." Eric's shoulders sagged as he let his daughter know he agreed with everything she had said.

"I'll find a way, Dad."

Chapter 4

"You're a very lucky young lady." The night nurse cleansed Trin's arm and returned it to the soft cast that kept the wrist from moving. "Dr. Hunter is the best in the business."

"When will I meet Dr. Hunter?" Trin asked. "I want to say thank you in person."

"Let's get your hair out of that French braid. It can't be comfortable. The doctors are making their rounds now," the nurse answered. "It shouldn't be long."

As if on cue Dr. Eric Hunter entered Trin's room.

"I thought I'd drop by and check on you." Eric Hunter nodded to the nurse and opened the laptop.

"I'm Dr. Hunter," he said with a smile, quickly reading the notes on the monitor. "Are you a righty or a lefty?"

"Right-handed," Trin answered.

"It looks like you're having a miraculous recovery." Eric's eyes danced as he examined his daughter's handiwork. "Wonderful, absolutely wonderful." His voice was filled with pride.

"I wanted to thank you, sir," Trin said.

"Don't thank me—" A call over the intercom interrupted him.

"Dr. Hunter, please report to the trauma unit. Dr. Hunter, Eric and Heather, please—"

"Duty calls," Eric said, grimacing. "You can probably go home tomorrow. Congratulations. You were lucky to get the best surgeon in our hospital."

Narcissistic fellow, Trin thought as he headed for the door.

##

Father Nathan Provoost straightened the literature in the foyer of the chapel. He was biding his time as he waited for Dr. Heather Hunter to finish her surgery. He knew she always prayed in the chapel after every procedure.

At forty-two, Father Provoost was a handsome man with tousled sandy-colored hair. Politically he had aligned himself with Bishop Grant Ryker when the bishop decided to split his followers from the Episcopal Church and join them with the Anglican Church of North America.

Bishop Ryker disagreed with the Episcopal Church's practice of ordaining women priests and was deeply disturbed by the church's consecration of a homosexual bishop.

Ryker didn't just walk out of the Episcopal Church; he took the entire Fort Worth-based Diocese with him: 15,000 parishioners, 48 churches, and 58 clergies supported his conservative stand.

Bishop Ryker did what no one had ever done. He laid claim to all the diocese's buildings and assets, claiming they belonged to the Christians who were following him and not the American Episcopal Church. The rights to the assets had been tied up in litigation for over fifteen years, but Bishop Ryker maintained control over them.

Father Provoost had been wise to follow Ryker. The bishop made certain Nathan received a salary above and beyond the pay of most hospital chaplains. Of course, Nathan returned to the church coffers ten times his pay. When terminal patients with no heirs faced their maker, they were eager to leave their wealth to the Anglican Church as if they could buy their way into heaven.

Nathan had carved a nice niche for himself in Fort Worth religious and social circles. He had purchased a palatial home in the elite Mira Vista area and was a popular guest at the many social events hosted by the wealthy oil tycoons. More than one oil baron had suggested that it would be financially beneficial for him to request a daughter's hand in marriage.

The only woman to catch his eye was Dr. Heather Hunter. Dr. Hunter was pursued by most of the bachelors in their town but hadn't given any of them the time of day.

Nathan laughed to himself as he recalled her mother's constant lament that her daughter was getting too old to give her grandchildren.

Approaching footsteps pulled Father Provoost from his thoughts of the beautiful doctor. He turned as Heather opened the door.

"Father Provoost," Heather said quietly. "How good to see you."

"You look tired." Nathan moved to stand beside her. "Long surgery?"

"Yes, but a successful one." Heather walked toward the front of the chapel. "I'll only be a few minutes. I hope I'm not interrupting anything."

"No, no. Please take your time. Perhaps you can join me for a cup of coffee afterward," Nathan suggested.

"Perhaps."

Nathan waited in the hallway outside the chapel doors. He would stop anyone from interrupting the conversation Dr. Hunter was having with her God.

After what seemed an interminable amount of time, Heather exited the chapel.

"Oh," she gasped, "I didn't realize you were waiting for me."

"Coffee, remember?" Nathan gave her a slight smile.

"Yes. Did you want to discuss a patient with me?"

"No, I just wanted to visit with you," Nathan said.

"Hmmm." Heather linked her arm through the priest's as they walked to the cafeteria. She selected a table as Nathan got their coffee. He placed the two cups on the table and sat down in the chair across from her.

"What can I do for you, Father?" she asked before taking a sip of her coffee.

"I wondered if you would accompany me to the church's fundraising banquet Saturday night?"

Heather stared at him as if she didn't understand the question. "Oh, why don't you simply come by my office in the morning, and I'll give you a check?"

"I'm not asking you to come in order to get a donation," Nathan said, chuckling. "I'm asking you to be my plus-one. I'd like to spend time with you."

"Oh Father, I apologize. I misunderstood you. I'd be delighted to accompany you to the banquet."

Nathan beamed. "That's wonderful. I'll pick you up at seven."

Chapter 5

Heather scanned the X-ray and MRI of the hand. Everything looked perfect. It had been six months since she reattached Trin's hand. The MRI showed the soft tissues more clearly than the X-ray. The doctor was pleased to see the ligaments and muscles had remained properly attached and were healing with no visible scar tissue. She felt a tinge of guilt that the patient had appeared every week for the follow-up exams, but Heather had never met him. She had been in surgery every time. She was determined to be the one giving him the good news that she was releasing him to return to his normal activities. *Hopefully, he'll have sense enough to stay off oil derricks,* she thought.

"Your one o'clock appointment is in exam room number three," the receptionist notified Heather on the intercom.

Heather picked up the file and walked to the exam room to check on her handiwork and officially meet Trin Scott. A low growl from her stomach reminded her she had skipped lunch. She opened the door and quickly scanned the back of a blonde wearing tight jeans that showcased the nicest butt Heather had ever seen. The woman was watching the Care Flight helicopter land on the pad outside the window. At the sound of the closing door she turned to face Heather.

"I'm sorry," Heather said. "I thought Trin Scott was in this room. I . . . um . . ." The laughter dancing in the blonde's baby-blue eyes took Heather's breath away.

"I'm Trin Scott," the blonde said. "I thought Dr. Hunter was seeing me today. I wanted to thank him for saving my hand."

"I . . . I'm Dr. Hunter," Heather blurted out. "I saved your hand." For some reason she wanted the blonde to know she was the one to thank.

"Then I'm even more thankful." Full, red lips curved into a smile revealing perfect teeth. "Thankful for an incredibly talented surgeon and a beautiful woman."

She's flirting with me, Heather thought, *and I like it. If I had known you were so gorgeous, I would have . . .* Heather shook her head, clearing it of unprofessional thoughts, and said, "Let's look at the miracle hand."

She spent several minutes checking the flexibility of Trin's long, slender fingers. "Your hand seems to be functioning perfectly. Obviously, you've been religious about doing your rehab exercises. Have you had any pain or problems?"

"No. No pain," Trin said, ducking her head as if embarrassed. "However, I do have one problem."

"Tell me. I bet I can fix it," Heather assured her.

"I'm certain you can." Trin's smile lit up the exam room. "I'm alone and I'm starving. Would it be possible for you to go to lunch with me?"

Heather stood still, unable to think of any good reason to refuse the offer. "I don't usually have meals with my patients," she declared, trying to reestablish the patient-doctor relationship that had flown out the window the moment she first gazed into Trin's eyes.

Trin huffed. "It's not like I'm asking you out on a date, Doctor Hunter. I'd simply like some guidance to a good restaurant."

Heather felt foolish. It was clear Trin wasn't thinking the same thoughts she was. "I'd be happy to have lunch with you," Heather said. She signed the forms Trin would need to be discharged. Only then did she see the tiny check mark beside the word *female*. "I'll get my handbag and lose this hospital jacket while you check out."

##

"This is nice," Trin commented as the hostess led them to a table with a red tablecloth and white napkins.

They placed their order and exchanged smiles. Heather opened the conversation. "You're not from Fort Worth?"

"Glen Rose," Trin volunteered. "The greatest place on earth."

Heather laughed out loud as she surveyed the restaurant. "Restaurants as nice as this?"

Trin beamed. "Maybe not as fancy," she said, "but the food is just as good. Our five-star restaurant is The Loco Coyote."

"Seriously?" Heather couldn't stop the laughter welling up inside her. "Loco Coyote?"

"We have dinosaur tracks, Fossil Rim, Squaw Valley Golf Club and The Promise." It was evident that Trin was proud of her little town. "Have you ever been to Glen Rose?"

"No, I've never had any reason to visit Glen Rose." *Until now.* The thought hit Heather's mind like a grenade detonating.

"What do you do for fun, Dr. Hunter?" Trin took a bite of salad and waited for Heather to answer.

"Fun?" Heather gazed into blue eyes and tried to suppress her idea of fun with Trin Scott. "I . . . uh, I don't have much time for fun."

"You know what they say about all work and no play," Trin teased.

"What do you do for fun?" Heather asked.

"Whatever strikes my fancy." Trin's smile was sweet and honest. "When was the last time you petted a baby rhino?"

"Never," Heather snorted. "I suspect that where there's a baby there's a mother, and I wouldn't want to tangle with her."

Trin smiled impishly. "If I told you I could show you the time of your life in my little town would you let me?"

I think I would let you do anything. Heather's libido won out over her common sense. "Yes, I would."

"Are you available Saturday?" Trin asked.

"No, I'm on call this weekend. My days off are Thursday and Friday."

"I'll pick you up Thursday morning at nine," Trin declared. "Wear jeans and flat-heeled boots in case we do some walking. We'll stop for lunch around noon."

Their conversation was interrupted by the ring of Trin's cell phone. She pulled it from her pocket, "Excuse me, I must take this call."

"Yes, I know that... I can't this week. My doctor won't release me to go back to work." She winked at Heather.

"I don't know... The rig is supposed to be delivered to the Clear Creek site Monday."

Trin listened for a long time as a male voice hummed on her phone. Heather couldn't make out anything the man said.

"I'll take care of it, Dad," Trin finally answered. "You know my feelings on the matter... Let's talk tonight. I'll be home in time for dinner."

"Surely you aren't planning to return to that dangerous job?" Heather said, astounded that someone could almost lose a limb and still return to harm's way. "You may not be so lucky next time."

Trin smiled and handed the waitress a credit card. "Would you give up practicing medicine, Dr. Hunter?"

"No," Heather huffed. "It's in my blood."

"Oil is in my blood," Trin said.

Chapter 6

If I had placed an order with the good Lord, this is the weather I would have ordered for today, Trin thought as she walked up the steps to Dr. Heather Hunter's home and pressed the doorbell.

"Oh my God!" Trin gasped as Heather opened the door. A glorious cloud of long, black hair tumbled onto the doctor's shoulders, curling around her beautiful face. A red blouse brought out the chocolate color of her eyes.

Heather laughed. "I beg your pardon?"

"You are stunning, Dr. Hunter," Trin managed to articulate.

"If you're going to spend the day showing me the time of my life," Heather teased, "please call me Heather."

"Heather," Trin breathed the name. "Heather."

Heather caught her breath. She was surprised at how musical her name sounded on Trin's lips. "Will I need a light jacket?"

Trin surveyed her long-sleeved blouse and light-colored jeans then raised her eyes to gaze into Heather's. "No, the day is just perfect." *And getting better by the minute*, she thought.

"I've never ridden in a Jeep before," Heather commented as she fastened her seatbelt.

"I have your favorite Starbucks coffee." Trin beamed as she handed Heather a cup.

Heather sipped the coffee and was surprised to find it was perfect. "How did you know my favorite?"

"Your father told me." Trin backed her Wrangler from the drive and headed for the interstate.

"You asked my father what my favorite coffee is?" Heather leaned back in the seat and studied the profile of the blonde beauty beside her.

"I couldn't think of anyone else to ask, and I figured he owed me one," Trin explained.

"Owed you one?"

"He let me think he did my surgery." Trin glanced at Heather. "If I had known you did my surgery, I would have insisted on you seeing me for my checkups."

"My father is just as good as I." Heather's attitude was snippy.

"Oh, I wasn't questioning that," Trin said. "I'm just saying that our friendship would be much farther along than a first date if I had met you sooner."

Heather wrinkled her brow. "You think we're on a date?"

"If we're not, please let me live my fantasy for today," Trin said, her smile showcasing the dimples in her cheeks.

"Okay," Heather agreed as she relaxed and sipped her coffee.

The ride was delightful. Trin did a running commentary, calling Heather's attention to points of interest and providing the names of rivers as they drove over bridges.

"We're going to Fossil Rim Wildlife Center," Trin informed Heather as she turned off the main highway and drove along a blacktopped, two-lane road. "I've arranged a Behind-the-Scenes Tour of the rhinoceros who make their home here."

Heather tilted her head and watched the blonde. Trin's enthusiasm was contagious. "Will I be allowed to pet a baby rhino?" she asked.

"Yes. There are two black rhinos here." Trin seemed as excited as a child at the prospect of introducing Heather to the rhino herd. "They also have four southern white rhinos and a two-month-old calf. She's so ugly she's cute.

"Fossil Rim participates in the Rhino Foundation's Southern Black Rhino Sustainability Program. There are currently less than 5,000 black rhinos in Africa and only three northern white rhinos in the world. They are working to prevent the extinction of the two species."

"That's appalling," Heather said. "I've heard that poachers are relentless in their efforts to get the rhinos' horns, but I had no idea they had almost depleted the species." Heather looked around at the pristine reserve as Trin parked the Jeep.

"Poachers are so brazen that they have even broken into zoos and reserves to kill rhinos and remove their horns," Trin explained. "Fossil Rim has tight security for their rhinos. That's why I had to arrange for a Behind-the-Scenes Tour for us."

"I'm glad you did." Heather linked her arm through Trin's and allowed the blonde to lead her wherever they needed to go.

Trin spoke to someone who seemed to be in charge and followed the woman to a tram parked in the barn.

"The rhinos are kept close to the main part of the park, so we can keep an eye on them," the employee explained. "My name is Dani. I'm the main keeper of our new baby."

"Dani has a degree in zoology," Trin explained. "She specializes in biology, fertility, and reproduction of rhinos. She has been a godsend to Fossil Rim's breeding program."

Dani drove the tram through three different heavily locked gates attached to thick pipe fencing. She pointed out several cameras that monitored the area where the rhinos roamed. A mother rhino with a baby raised her head and watched as the tram approached.

"Don't make any sudden moves or sounds," Dani cautioned. "She could turn this tram into rubble if she becomes upset."

Although she was in awe of the mother and calf, Heather was also a little apprehensive about the closeness of the larger animal.

"Is this safe?" She moved closer to Trin, who caught her hand and assured her the rhinos were docile unless threatened.

Dani stopped the tram and walked to the back to retrieve some alfalfa to feed the mother and baby. The adult cautiously approached the handler, and the baby followed his mother.

"He is so big," Heather whispered, "but looks tiny compared to his mother."

"Rhino babies weigh between 65 and 85 pounds at birth," Trin murmured. "They stay very close to their mother, sometimes only leaving her side after three years."

The mother and baby ate the alfalfa from Dani's hand. "Do you want to feed them?" Dani asked.

"Of course." Trin stepped from the tram and offered Heather her hand. "If we're lucky, they'll let us pet them."

The baby was standoffish but swished his tail when Heather talked to him. After half an hour, he decided the beautiful brunette posed no danger and moved closer to her.

Heather giggled. "I love his little tail. It seems so incongruous with the rest of his body. It's so stumpy, and that little tuft of hair looks like God just threw it on as an afterthought."

Trin watched the doctor as she slowly won the baby and mother's trust. The baby moved close enough to touch Heather.

"Let him touch you first," Dani said.

The baby inched closer until he was against Heather. She was surprised by his strength and clung to Trin's arm to keep from falling when the baby rubbed against her.

They spent almost an hour feeding the pair of rhinos and touching them. Dani explained that rhinos were extremely thick-skinned—basically covered in armor—and couldn't really feel the strokes of the two women petting them.

They spent the morning touring the wildlife reserve and observing the herds of black and white rhinos that were thriving at Fossil Rim. Heather noticed the heavy security protecting the animals. Cameras, electric fences, and guards on horseback constantly monitored the location of the rhinos.

"Are they in danger here? Surely no one would harm them here."

"Poachers have broken into zoos and reserves all over the world to kill them for their horns," Trin explained. "Rhino horns are more valuable per ounce than gold. To Asians they are a sign of wealth. Can you imagine killing an animal to get bragging rights?"

"Are you hungry?" Trin asked as she laced her fingers through Heather's.

"Starving," the brunette admitted. She was surprised at how comfortable it felt to hold Trin's hand. She stared as she realized the strong hand holding hers was the same hand she had sewn back onto the woman six months ago.

"Amazing isn't it?" Trin smiled as if she were reading Heather's mind. "If not for you, I would be offering you a stump to hold. Not very romantic."

Heather squeezed Trin's hand. "I don't think that would bother me at all."

As they followed a winding path through trees, Trin pointed out smaller animals that cavorted around Fossil Rim. The trees opened to a clearing that was home to the most unique restaurant Heather had ever seen. It seemed to cling to the cliffside as it dangled over the valley below.

"It's called The Overlook," Trin explained.

"It's lovely," Heather said, inhaling the mouthwatering aroma coming from the restaurant.

True to its name, the restaurant seemed suspended in midair overlooking the valley.

They ordered lunch then sipped iced tea as they watched giraffes cavort in the pastures below.

"How large is the Center?" Heather asked.

"Two thousand acres."

"How do you know so much about the place?" Heather watched the blonde's eyes dance as she talked about the haven for endangered animals.

"I grew up around here. When I turned sixteen, I volunteered for any job they would let me do just to be here. I fell in love with the rhinos and do my own little personal crusade for them.

"Look, Heather!" Trin's eyes sparkled with excitement.

She looked in the direction Trin indicated and watched in wonder as a heavy sheet of rain moved across the pastures. It was as if God were drawing a curtain across the land. On the left the sun was shining brightly. On the right a heavy rainstorm was sweeping across the wildlife refuge. Heather had never seen anything like it. When the storm hit the Overlook, sheets of water cascaded down the thick glass walls that surrounded the restaurant and provided a panoramic view of the wonders roaming the land.

"This rivals the man-made wonders of the world," Heather murmured.

Thunder rumbled across the valley, and lightening knocked out the electricity. As the rainstorm darkened the Overlook, Trin took Heather's hands in hers and whispered, "*You* rival the man-made wonders of the world."

##

Heather leaned her head back against the Jeep's seat and dozed as she held Trin's hand in her lap. She couldn't remember having a nicer day in her life. She had laughed, petted a baby rhino, and witnessed one of God's more spectacular weather displays. Their day at Fossil Rim had been awe-inspiring, stimulating, and educational.

Dinner at the Loco Coyote had been fun and the food delicious. Trin truly had shown her the best day of her life. Deep inside she knew the real reason the day was incredible was because she was with the woman sitting beside her.

##

"Wake up, princess." Trin's warm breath tickled Heather's ear. "I have returned you to your castle safe and sound."

Heather's next-door neighbor turned on her security lights, washing the front yard and Heather's driveway with bright light.

"What's with your neighbor?" Trin chuckled. "Is she landing a jet in the street?"

Heather laughed and squeezed Trin's hand. "Would you like to come in?" she asked, her voice low and hopeful.

"I'd like that more than anything in the world," Trin replied, her blue eyes sparkling in the light, "but we both know where that would end. I don't think either of us is ready to go there yet."

"When will I see you again?"

"Is tomorrow too soon?" Trin leaned closer. "I have business to transact here in the morning, but I'll be free around one. Do you still have tomorrow off?"

"Yes."

"There's a Gal Gadot movie playing at the Dinner Tavern on Seventh Street." When Heather didn't respond, Trin wrinkled her nose. "You know, Wonder Woman. You gotta love Wonder Woman."

"I've never seen a Wonder Woman movie," Heather admitted.

"You have to get out of the hospital more often," Trin said, laughing. "I'm just the woman to help you do that."

Heather ducked her head to keep Trin from seeing the look of happiness on her face. "You'll get no argument from me."

They sat in silence for several minutes. "I won't walk you to the door," Trin mumbled. "I don't want to give your nosey neighbor the satisfaction of seeing who's with you. And I'm not certain I could turn around and walk away."

Heather opened the door and left the Jeep before either of them could change their minds.

Chapter 7

Heather glanced at herself in the mirror before answering the door. She couldn't hide her excitement at seeing Trin again today. A broad smile covered her lips as she opened the door.

"Mother, what are you doing here?"

"Is that any way to greet the woman who brought you into this world?" Melody Hunter whined. "I thought you'd be glad to see me."

"Oh, of course I am," Heather said. "I just . . . wasn't expecting you."

Melody studied her daughter. "Obviously you're expecting someone. You're certainly dressed to impress."

"I'm going to a movie with a friend," Heather explained.

"A special friend?" Melody's eyes lit up. "What's his name? I do hope he comes from one of the moneyed families."

"Just a friend," Heather said, her exasperation clear. "A woman, Mother."

"Oh." Melody's drawl dripped with disappointment as she pushed her way into Heather's home. "Dear, you need to be spending time with the eligible bachelors who are vying for your attention, not some girlfriend from college. Neither of us is getting any younger, and I want a grandbaby."

Heather ignored her mother's comment. "Why did you drop by, Mother?"

"I want to visit with my daughter," Melody ran her gloved hand over the Bombay chest in the living room. She raised her eyebrows when she saw nothing on her gloves.

"Disappointed, Mother?"

"Just checking to make certain your maid is doing her job," Melody said.

"You know I don't have a maid, Mother. I'm quite capable of cleaning my own home."

The doorbell rang and both women turned to look at the door as if it were an unwelcome intruder.

"My friend is here." Heather's lips curved into a slight smile. "Would you like to have lunch tomorrow and discuss whatever you came for today?"

"Not tomorrow, dear, I have bridge club. I'll call you." Melody walked to the door with Heather close behind.

Trin took a step back when the door opened exposing two stunning women. Melody Hunter was a more mature, but beautiful, replica of her daughter.

Melody didn't try to hide her scrutiny of Trin. Her eyes came to rest on the sky-blue eyes steadily gazing at her. The tall blonde was not easily intimidated.

Heather made the introductions.

"It's nice to meet you, Mrs. Hunter," Trin said.

"Likewise, I'm sure. You went to college with Heather?"

"No, ma'am," Trin answered. She didn't volunteer any information, letting Heather handle her mother.

"Trin is my Humpty Dumpty," Heather said, laughing. "I put her back together after she was injured in an accident."

Melody took a closer look. "You don't look injured."

"I'm a walking testament to your daughter's skills as a surgeon," Trin said. "You must be very proud of her."

"I'd be prouder if she would give me a grandchild," Melody said emphatically.

"And waste the knowledge and skill she has mastered as one of the best orthopedic surgeons in the country?" Trin's shocked expression made Heather chortle.

Heather pulled the door closed behind her and locked it. "Mother was just leaving."

Melody turned up her nose at the sight of Trin's Jeep Wrangler. She turned to look the blonde over one more time.

"What do you do for a living, Miss Scott?"

"I'm most at home in the oil fields." Trin lifted her chin. "What do you do to justify your existence?"

Melody overcame the desire to slap the impertinent blonde, as her daughter giggled at Trin's question. "You're that roughneck Heather reattached the hand to."

Trin flexed her fingers. "Yes, and everything works perfectly, thanks to your daughter."

"Really, Heather." Melody growled as she walked to her car.

"I apologize for my mother's rudeness." Heather wrinkled her brow as she watched Trin.

"No apology necessary," Trin said with a shrug. "I'm just pleased that she was so impressed with me."

There was a moment of silence in the car, and then both women burst out laughing.

Heather was amazed that Trin could turn her day from sad to happy with a single comment. She suddenly didn't care what her mother thought or said. She only cared about being with the woman beside her.

"I'm afraid Mother puts too much emphasis on money," Heather explained.

"And I'm just a poor roughneck not fit to date her daughter." Trin grimaced.

"My mother's opinion," Heather said. "Not mine."

36

Suddenly, Heather's phone rang, demanding her attention. After a brief conversation, she ended the call "I'll have to take a rain check on Wonder Woman," she said. "That was my dad. I'm needed in the trauma unit. I'm sorry."

"No problem." Trin changed lanes and took a left, heading for the hospital. "I'll have you there in no time."

True to her word, Trin pulled the Jeep up to the emergency entrance in less than ten minutes.

"You may be faster than an ambulance." Heather leaned forward, brushed her lips against Trin's, and hurried into the hospital.

"Your father is already operating," the nurse informed Heather as she scrubbed. "We have two more amputees. It's your call on which one to save."

"Prep them both" Heather hissed. "We'll try to keep them all in one piece. Give me the one with the weakest vital signs first. They're in the most danger."

"The cavalry is here," Lori Rogers announced as Heather took her position at the operating table.

Eric Hunter welcomed his daughter. "About time you got here." Heather grunted a reply and went to work.

The two worked silently as they battled to put the wounded patients back together again.

"I'm finished with this one," Eric announced as Heather connected the last vein in a leg she had just reattached.

"Same here," Heather said. She led the way to the table that had the third patient. "My God, she's pregnant!"

"Why didn't someone tell us she's pregnant?" Eric demanded.

"Just do your jobs," Lori commanded. "Her vitals are still good. If you two will stop jaw-jacking and get to work, she'll be fine."

Both doctors chuckled as their head trauma nurse pulled operating tools to both sides of the table. "Her right leg is severed below the knee," Lori informed them, "and her left hand is missing three fingers. The limbs are on ice so tell us when you're ready."

"Can you take the leg?" Eric asked his daughter.

Heather nodded and began the process to start blood flowing to the severed limb. The surgery she had just finished had taken six hours, but she knew this would take longer. Her top priority was to get blood to the limb quickly. To keep the limb alive, she rerouted an artery from the woman's left leg to the severed limb. Once she was satisfied the blood flow was adequate to sustain the limb, she began the daunting task of reattaching the bone, blood vessels, tendons, and nerves.

The surgery took sixteen hours. As Heather turned over the task of suturing the skin into place to her assistant, she staggered.

"Go home. You've been on your feet twenty-two hours," Eric said, his voice hoarse and filled with exhaustion.

"You too, Dad," she answered. "I'll sleep in the on-call room. I don't think I can make it home."

"There's a long, tall drink of water waiting for you in the family waiting room," Lori informed Heather.

Heather tried to clear her sleep-deprived brain to figure out who would be waiting for her at this hour. When she walked from the scrub area, she spotted Trin leaning against the wall, watching for her. The blonde moved to her side and slipped a supportive arm around her waist.

"I thought you might need a ride home," she whispered into Heather's ear.

She relaxed, letting Trin bear her weight as they walked to the car. She fell asleep on the way home.

##

Erin Wade
The Roughneck & the Lady

A thin sliver of light slipped through the shutters and fell across Heather's face. She rolled over and looked at her clock. It was two in the afternoon. She lay still, trying to determine how she had gotten into her bed. Then she realized she was naked.

Trin. Trin brought me home and put me to bed. She was there for me at the hospital. Heather bolted upright and listened for any sound in her home. She was greeted by silence.

She lay back, enjoying the feel of the sheets around her. She drifted in and out of sleep as dreams of Trin Scott danced through her mind.

Unable to stay in bed any longer, she stumbled to the bathroom and turned the shower to hot. She inhaled the steam that swirled around her and then relaxed into the soothing heat of the water.

She towel-dried her hair as she walked to her dresser for a pair of panties. She decided to go braless and pulled a soft T-shirt over her head.

Coffee! Coffee would save my life. She chuckled to herself as she shuffled into the kitchen.

A note written in beautiful, flowing handwriting lay beside the coffee pot. "Just push the on button," it instructed.

She smiled as she read the rest of the note. "I hope you get some rest. I will be out of town for a few days. Please call me when you feel like talking."

She poured a cup of coffee and sipped it as she wondered where her phone was. She found it in her purse and placed her finger over the number that would bring Trin Scott into her life.

"Hi! I was hoping you'd call," Trin said. "Are you okay?"

"I'm fine," Heather answered. "Except I really wanted to see Wonder Woman."

39

Trin's laughter spread a warm, happy feeling throughout Heather's body.

"When will you be home?"

"Two days," Trin said. "I'll be back Monday night. "Maybe we can catch a late dinner."

"Why don't you let me know when you're an hour away, and I'll have dinner ready when you arrive."

"That's the best offer I've had in days," Trin said cheerfully. "I checked with your dad this morning, and all of your patients are doing well."

"That's so thoughtful. Why did you do that?"

"If you're feeling the way I am," Trin replied, "I knew you'd call me first and then the hospital. I knew you would want to know how your patients were. Was I right? Did you call me first?"

Several seconds passed before Heather responded. "Yes. Yes, I wanted to hear your voice," she said, sighing.

"Good." The low, sensual way Trin said the word made Heather weak. "I'll see you Monday. Call me anytime you can talk. I want to hear your voice too."

Chapter 8

"I'm telling you, she's cavorting with that . . . that woman roughneck," Melody screeched at her husband as he read the morning paper.

"The woman is an extremely nice person," Eric said in Trin's defense. "I got to know her while she was in the hospital. She's good for Heather."

"What part of 'she's a woman' do you not understand?" Melody raised her voice another octave. "She makes her living in the oil fields.

"Heather must marry someone who fits in our social circles." Melody's face was getting redder as she complained about her only daughter. "Someone with our values and sophistication and . . . and wealth. That nice Hunt boy who follows her around like a lovesick puppy would be perfect. Or Father Provoost. He'd be a real catch. All the women are after him. He's also the hospital chaplain, very highly regarded."

Eric lowered his paper, cocked his head, and stared at his wife. "What are you talking about?"

"That roughneck." Melody's voice dropped into its normal range as she realized she had finally gotten her husband's attention. "She is obviously a lesbian.

"For the past six months, your daughter has spent every free minute she has with that oil field worker. No matter what I want your daughter to do, she turns me down because she has plans with Trin."

A wry smile crossed Eric's face. Heather was always "his daughter" when Melody was displeased with her.

"I forbid it." Melody's voice started to rise again. "I absolutely forbid it."

"She's thirty-four," Eric pointed out. "You can't forbid her to do anything."

"Then I'll disown her."

"Go ahead," Eric snorted. "She's as wealthy as we are."

Melody sputtered as she tried to think of something she could hold over her daughter. She knew her husband was right. Heather had always been a headstrong girl and was now an impossible woman.

"You have to find a way to stop her from seeing that woman," Melody insisted. "She's trying to turn our daughter into a lesbian."

Eric folded his paper and wondered what universe his wife inhabited. "One can't make someone a lesbian, Melody," he said, shaking his head. "It's just the way some women are born. They can't help that they're drawn to the same sex."

He could tell his wife was preparing to hyperventilate and tried to head off her dramatic scene.

"Heather was Father Provoost's date for the diocese fundraising banquet," he reminded her. "I wouldn't be too quick to label our daughter a lesbian."

"Yes, he would be perfect for her," Melody said, arrogantly lifting her chin. "His lineage goes back to Bishop Samuel Provoost, one of the first Episcopalian priests consecrated as a bishop in the U.S. He was the first bishop of the Episcopal Diocese in New York."

"His lineage?" Eric snorted again. "Our daughter is a woman, Melody, not a flipping racehorse.

"Heather is representing the hospital on the committee for the Cattle Baron's Ball," Eric said in an effort to change the subject. "Maybe she'll meet someone there. God knows there's enough money represented on that committee to buy a dozen hospital wings."

Melody fanned her face with her hand as she moved toward the liquor cabinet. "I need a little brandy in my coffee," she mumbled as she filled her half-empty cup.

"I'm certain Heather will see that this is the most successful Cattle Baron's Ball in history," Eric reassured his wife. "You know she strives to be better than anyone else. It should be interesting."

"At least she won't be in the company of that woman," Melody groused. "You know, the Winfield heiress is chairing the committee this year. Maybe Heather will fall for her."

Eric wrinkled his brow. "So, it's not Trin's sex that is upsetting you; it's her lack of wealth and position."

"If she must be with a lesbian," Melody slurred, "at least she can be with a woman of means."

##

"You know I don't mind dressing up and going somewhere fancy." Trin kissed Heather chastely.

"I know. I just like having you to myself." Heather leaned back in Trin's arms and looked up at the taller woman. "I don't need anyone else right now."

"Chinese takeout it is," Trin said, her eyes sparkling as she held the brunette.

Heather located her cell phone and called the familiar number. "I have a movie for us to watch too."

"Chinese cuisine, a movie, and you." Trin wiggled her eyebrows. "Sounds like the perfect evening to me. What movie did you get?"

"*Wonder Woman*," Heather said, giggling as Trin pulled her back into her arms. "We never got to watch it."

"Oh, I don't know," Trin said with a serious look in her eye. "Alone with you and Wonder Woman? I'm not sure I can be held responsible for my actions."

"Wonder Woman turns you on?" Heather teased.

The look of desire that crossed Trin's face astounded Heather. "No, you do," Trin said, her voice deep and sensuous.

"Trin, I . . . I don't know—"

"I'm sorry." Trin's smile faded. "I know we agreed to just be friends, and I'm okay with that."

The ringing of the doorbell dispelled the awkward moment as Heather went to the door and paid the pizza delivery man. The rest of the evening was spent cheering for Gal Gadot as she breathed life into the Wonder Woman legend. After the movie ended, Trin stood and stretched. Heather couldn't pull her eyes away from the blonde's flat stomach and toned arms. Trin smiled when she caught Heather checking out her physique.

"Let me help clean up our mess," Trin said as she scooped up the carryout boxes and took them to the kitchen. She rinsed out the containers and placed them in the trash compactor.

Heather leaned against the doorframe and watched Trin as she bent down to place glasses and silverware into the dishwasher. *She truly has the nicest butt I've ever seen*, she thought.

"I need to go," Trin said as she walked toward Heather. "You have an early surgery in the morning."

"When will I see you again?" Heather asked.

"Whenever you want." Trin bent down and lightly brushed her lips. "Good night, friend."

##

Heather relaxed for a minute before tackling the paperwork on her desk. She hoped it would be a quiet day so she could finish her notes and dictation. She checked her iPhone when Trin's message dinged in. "Have to leave town early in morn. Dinner tonight?"

"Early dinner. I have reception with Mother," Heather replied.

Heather smiled when the phone rang. She knew Trin wasn't patient enough to continue texting. "Hello," she said in her sexiest voice. A low moan greeted her.

"You know you're killing me," Trin grumbled. "What reception is Melody dragging you to?"

"Oh, one of her pretentious causes." Heather's voice was soft and silky. "Save the Gecko or something like that."

Trin chuckled. "What time should I pick you up?"

"Let's meet at the Regatta. They have their crab cake special tonight." Heather checked her watch. "I can be there by 5:30."

Trin agreed and ended the call.

Heather walked to the window and looked at the Care Flight helicopter that had brought Trin into her life. She was glad it hadn't taken off today. Every time the chopper lifted from the ground it meant someone was near death.

She thought about where her relationship with Trin was going. She wanted the roughneck more than she had ever wanted anything in her life. Therein lay the problem. Trin was a roughneck.

Her mother had been extremely vocal about her dislike of Trin and her vocation. *Mother is determined that I will marry a wealthy man and have children*, Heather thought. *Something I've never wanted.*

I want Trin. The thought burst into her mind before she could stop it. She had heard her mother's petty arguments about Trin too many times to count. *I'll probably have to hear them again tonight. She gets nasty when she drinks.*

If Mother would give her a chance, she would see how intelligent and funny Trin is. Trin is everything anyone could want: beautiful, cultured, warm, thoughtful, and a hard worker. Hard worker! People like my mother have no

45

idea what hard work is and turn up their noses at people who actually work hard for a living.

Heather wrestled with her options: stay with Trin and face her mother's disdain for the rest of her life, or lose Trin and die inside. The choice became clearer every day. She just couldn't bring herself to make it.

Chapter 9

"Hey, pretty lady." Trin leaned against Heather's back and whispered in her ear. "You have impeccable timing."

Trin inhaled deeply. "God, you smell good, and you look gorgeous. I love your dress. You look like Cinderella going to the ball. I envy Prince Charming."

Heather couldn't stop herself from leaning back against Trin's firm, warm body. Momentarily, Trin was the only thing in her world. Then, her thoughts were interrupted when something hard pushed into her shoulder blade. "Are you wearing a gun, Trin?"

Before she could respond, the hostess motioned for them to follow her to their table.

They ordered drinks before sharing the events of their day.

"I had one minor surgery this morning," Heather said. "After that, I saw patients and waited impatiently until it was time to meet you."

Trin's blue eyes sparkled. "I know what you mean. All I did today was picture you in tight jeans."

Heather's happiness was interrupted by the ringing of her cell phone. "Dr. Hunter," she answered. "Is my father there? I'm sure he's on duty tonight. . . Do not give the patient to Dr. Trotter."

Concern flooded Trin's face. "Do you need to go to the hospital?"

"No, they called the wrong Dr. Hunter. Dad's on call tonight." Heather shrugged. "Sometimes having a cell phone on one's person at all times is annoying."

Trin agreed. "But for those who are hovering between life and death, it's their only lifeline."

"That's why we carry them," Heather said, sighing.

"Where are you going in the morning?" Heather realized that they always discussed her work and the hospital, but Trin rarely spoke of her job.

"Odessa," Trin said, avoiding Heather's gaze.

"It's dangerous, isn't it?" Heather asked.

"Not really," Trin replied. "The hardest part for me is being away from you."

"The old Texas Side Step." Heather cocked a brow. "You can't avoid my questions that easily. You're wearing a shoulder holster," Heather insisted. "There's a gun in it."

"That's why one usually wears a shoulder holster," Trin teased. "It's nothing. I always wear it when I travel."

"I'm surprised they let you on the plane with it."

"I have a concealed carry—". Trin's explanation was cut short by the ringing of Heather's phone.

Heather glanced at the phone. She rolled her eyes as she answered. "Hello, Mother... No, I can't pick you up. I'm having dinner then going straight to your reception... Yes, I will be arriving in my own car... Yes, I am dining with Trin. Goodbye, Mother."

A scowl covered Heather's face as she placed her cell phone on the table.

"She doesn't like me, does she?" Trin asked.

"It's not you," Heather said. "It's her pompous ideas. She doesn't see the goodness and kindness in people. She judges their worth by the size of their portfolios. I'm ashamed to admit that my mother is a very shallow person."

"But you're so wonderful," Trin noted. "Someone did a good job of instilling all the right values in you."

"My dad. I honestly don't know how she tricked him into marrying her. He's such a good man."

"I'm glad he did." Trin chuckled. "Otherwise you wouldn't be the woman you are. The woman I . . . care about."

Although they had become close friends over the past year, Trin still felt as if Heather might bolt and run at the slightest hint of an intimate relationship. She often had to stop herself from saying, "I love you."

Heather gazed into Trin's eyes and thought about completing the sentence Trin had started, but she let the chance slip away.

##

Melody Hunter admired her reflection in the mirror. Few women her age were as beautiful as she. She was stunning, and she knew it. She had always used her looks to her advantage.

She'd learned early in life that it was a rich man's world. Eric had opened the doors into that world and she had charged through, making friends of the rich and powerful. She had made certain that Heather went to all the right schools, graduated with honors, and had become an outstanding doctor. In Melody's mind she was responsible for Heather's successes.

One level of Texas society she had never managed to force her way into was the old money, like the Van Cliburns, Moncriefs, and Carters. Tonight's reception would change that. She was cohosting the event with Lucinda Winfield. Lucinda was from money so old that it came over on the Mayflower. Lucinda's husband, Scott, was the Texas Railroad Commissioner. The commission was responsible for regulating and overseeing the oil and gas industry in Texas. Melody had met Lucinda at the River Crest Country Club and had wrangled an invitation to be included in a golf foursome with Lucinda, Marty Lucas, and Marion Barrett. Marty and Marion's ancestors had been the first to discover oil in Texas. They had more trust funds and portfolios than most kings. After the golf game, the four had joined Kristy Cullinan Carter for lunch. Kristy was from a long line of oil tycoons and had married a Carter whose great-grandfather had founded the *Fort Worth Star-Telegram*, WBAP radio, and WBAP TV. Kristy's ancestors had founded Texaco Oil Corporation.

I am finally getting my due, Melody thought as she pulled her Bentley into valet parking at the River Crest Country Club. *Heather is so impressive; the women will love her.*

I'm glad she isn't letting that roughneck drop her off. I would be mortified if my new friends saw Heather with her.

Heather stepped from her car and smiled at the valet as he greeted her. She took a deep breath, knowing she was about to become the star player in her mother's dog and pony show of name-dropping and one-upping others who Melody considered inferior.

She was thinking about Trin as she walked the country club halls in which she had grown from a gangly youngster to a confident woman. She wondered if Trin would feel at home in the exclusive club. *Probably, Trin's at ease anywhere.*

She gave her name to the two young ladies checking guests as they entered. The slim one smiled as she found Heather's name on the list. "Thank you for attending, Dr. Hunter."

Heather nodded, drew herself up straight, and walked into the lion's den. She spotted her mother on the far side of the room. She wondered if she dared have a glass of wine before being put on display. She knew why she was here. She was just something else for Melody to show off to her rich friends.

Too late, Heather watched as her mother closed the distance between them. "Darling," Melody drawled, "please, join us." She slipped her arm through Heather's and leaned in close. "You may have the opportunity to meet Lucinda Winfield's daughter tonight," Melody whispered. "She's chairing the Cattle Baron's Ball this year. She is a much better catch than your roughneck."

Melody smiled and patted Heather's arm as if she had just whispered motherly terms of endearment to her daughter.

Heather was gracious as her mother introduced her to the Winfields and Carters. She found that if she tuned out her mother, the other women were interesting and entertaining.

If she were able to meet the younger Winfield woman tonight, that would be good. She had some ideas about the Ball she wanted to discuss with her.

##

"I know, Dad." Trin spoke with her father on her cell phone as she waited for the server to return with her credit card. "I'll be careful, but even the authorities have ruled sabotage on the rig collapse last year. It almost cost me my hand. I need to be in Odessa for the erection of the new rig. I don't want anyone else to get hurt…

"I will… Love you, too. I'll report to you as soon as I check out everything."

Trin thanked the server, signed the check, and was standing when her cell phone rang. She looked at the dark, blank screen and jumped when it rang again. Then she realized it wasn't her phone ringing, but Heather's. The brunette had left her phone on the table in her haste to get to her mother's reception on time.

Trin answered the phone when she saw it was Eric calling. "Heather?" the male voice asked.

"No, Dr. Hunter. This is Trin. Heather accidently left her phone on the table when she went to attend her mother's reception at the country club."

"Oh, hello, Trin," Eric Hunter said, sighing. "I hate to ask you to do this, but can you get the phone to her? We're prepping a man to reattach his leg. I need to know Heather is standing by if I need her help."

"Yes, sir. I'll get it to her as quickly as possible."

"Thanks, Trin. Have her call me as soon as you give her the phone. I won't go into surgery until I know I can reach her."

"I will, sir."

"Please hold it here," Trin instructed the valet as she jumped from her Jeep. "I won't be long." She jammed her hands in her pockets and headed into the country club.

Heather felt the air around her change. It suddenly went from suffocating to electrifying. She didn't know how, but she knew Trin was near. Then, their eyes met across the room.

Heather couldn't stop the wild pounding of her heart as she watched Trin move toward her. She wore a pair of fitted designer jeans with a matching jacket and a red pullover sweater. Her high-heel boots added another two inches to her already impressive height. A cloud of blonde hair bounced on her shoulders with each step, and her dangling earrings reflected the ballroom lights. Trin was the most gorgeous woman in the room.

"Hey," Trin said with a smile. "It seems fate wants me to see you one more time before I leave town. You forgot your cell phone. Your father needs a call from you. He's about to go into surgery."

Heather couldn't stop grinning. The sight of Trin set her entire body aflame. She held Trin's hand as she took the phone.

"There she is, over there." Melody's shrill voice rose above the attendees' conversations. "Please remove her from the premises."

Two bulky security guards followed Melody as she pointed Trin out in the crowded room. One of the men reached for Trin's arm.

"Don't touch me," Trin growled. Both men stepped back.

"Mother, what is the meaning of this?" Fury swept Heather's countenance. "Have you gone mad?"

"Mad? Mad?" Melody shrieked.

Oh dear God, she's drunk, Heather thought.

"Mother, we need to leave. Where's your purse?" Heather said, looking around for her mother's belongings.

"I'm not leaving," Melody mumbled, her words slurred. "Your girlfriend needs to leave. She isn't fit to lick your shoes. She doesn't belong here."

"Then neither do I." Heather gritted her teeth to keep from screaming at her mother.

"If you walk out of here. . ." Melody narrowed her eyes and glared at Heather. "You're sleeping with her, aren't you?" She screamed.

Heather was aghast at her mother's behavior. The ballroom was silent as those in the room ceased all movement to listen. "No! I've never slept with her." Heather looked at Trin, who had remained motionless during the sordid scene. Suddenly it became clear to her what was important in her life. "I've never slept with Trin, but I would if she wanted me to."

Melody looked as if she would explode. Her face went from flame-red to dark purple, and Heather knew her mother would start hyperventilating any minute. She grabbed Trin's arm and hurried from the reception. *Let her new friends take care of her.*

"Please drive me home," Heather said, thankful to see Trin's Jeep in front of the exit. "I'll get my car tomorrow. Right now I just want to get out of here."

After Heather called her father to let him know she was available if he needed her, they drove the rest of the way in silence. Trin parked the Jeep and walked around to the passenger side to open the door for Heather.

"Would you like to come in? I'll make a fresh pot of coffee," Heather said.

Trin nodded and followed her inside. As Heather closed and locked the door, Trin placed her hands on Heather's shoulders and gazed into her eyes.

"I do want you to," Trin said.

"Want me to . . .?" Heather whispered.

"Sleep with me." Trin lowered her lips to Heather's. It was no chaste, friendship kiss. Trin's lips were both soft and firm as they moved against Heather's, searching, asking, pleading.

Heather opened her mouth and ran her tongue over lips that tasted like strawberries. Trin tightened her arms around Heather, pulling her against her body. "There are no words to tell you how much I want you," Trin murmured against her lips. "How much you consume me. How much I crave you. How much I want to make love to you."

"I want that too." Heather moaned as Trin deepened the kiss. She gasped when Trin pulled down the zipper on the back of her dress.

"Let's start by getting rid of this," Trin mumbled as she slid the dress down Heather's arms and let it pool around her feet.

Heather slipped off her high heels and took Trin's hand to lead her to the bedroom. She slipped off Trin's jacket and then slowly unzipped Trin's jeans. In one easy motion, Trin pulled her sweater over her head and dropped it. They stood facing each other, wearing only their panties and bras.

"There is something I have been dying to do to you," Trin said, her eyes dancing as she thought about her fantasy.

"You can do anything you want to me." Heather kissed between Trin's breasts.

Trin eased her onto the bed then pulled back to observe her. "I have always wanted to do this," she said as she slid her hand to the back of Heather's neck, caressed her cheek, and gently removed her earring as she kissed her.

It was the simplest, sweetest move Heather had ever experienced. She loved the gentle way Trin caressed her cheek as she moved her fingers to release the earring and held it in the palm of her hand. She did the same to the other earring.

Then, as if she could no longer control herself, Trin gathered Heather into her arms and kissed her. It was a demanding kiss, one that sent liquid flames shooting through Heather's veins and pooled in her lower stomach. She gasped as the kiss was broken. She was frantic to reestablish the searing connection with Trin. "Please," she whispered as Trin kissed down her neck to the pulse point and sucked gently. Trin's lips left a trail of fire as they moved to breasts that were tingling with anticipation and desire.

"Suck me, baby," Heather pleaded.

As Trin's mouth captured one breast, her hand began to caress the other. She squeezed and stroked as her tongue circled the nipple. Heather's brain ceased to function. All she was aware of was the warm lips and a searching tongue that seemed to be everywhere on her body.

Trin removed the remainder of their clothes as Heather arched to her, wanting more of her—more of her kisses, more of her touch, and more of her soft, warm breath whispering words of love in her ear.

Heather had no idea when Trin had gotten on her knees between Heather's legs. Trin sat back on her heels and watched the woman she loved. She firmly grasped Heather's waist and slid her hands down to her hips, where she slid them under the writhing body and clutched the soft cheeks, lifting them from the bed.

Heather couldn't take it anymore. "Please! Oh God, please do something to me. Make me know you've been here."

"Oh, you're going to remember me long after I'm gone," Trin promised as she lowered her body onto Heather's, pinning her against the mattress.

Heather couldn't stop screaming Trin's name. It was a chant invoking all the pagan gods that had ever ruled over love and sex. A cry for release and more.

Trin groaned as Heather raked her nails down her back and dug into her hips. "Harder," Heather commanded.

##

Heather snuggled into Trin's side as the blonde fought to catch her breath. "Oh God, Trin, I never knew anything could feel so good." She gave into the tremor that ran through her body. "I want you again," she murmured.

"In my world, whatever Heather wants, Heather gets." An impish smile played with Trin's dimples. "We may need a safe word. I can't seem to get enough of you."

"Take whatever you need," Heather whispered into her neck. "Do anything you want. I realized tonight that the only thing that matters is that I'm with you."

Trin took her time exploring every inch of the gorgeous body beneath her. Heather returned the passion, touching and caressing Trin until the blonde brought them both to a frantic frenzy of cries and promises they knew would be kept.

Much later, they lay on their backs, letting their heart rate return to normal. "Are you okay?" Trin asked as she stroked Heather's stomach.

"For the first time in my life, I'm absolutely perfect," Heather said, sighing. "No one has ever made love to me like that. It was like wrapping my legs around a tornado—wild and raging and satisfying. Do you know you growl when you reach a certain point? It's very animalistic and so damn sexy. I just wanted to clamp my legs around you and suck you in."

"Umm, you're something," Trin murmured. "No one has ever made me lose myself like that."

Trin shifted and pulled Heather onto her shoulder, sliding her arm under her. She could feel the dampness on her shoulder as silent tears fell from her lover's eyes.

"Did I hurt you, baby?" Concern filled Trin's blue eyes. "What's wrong?"

"My mother," Heather sobbed. "I can't believe she said those awful things about you in front of all those people."

Trin snickered. "It's okay. She got me into your bed, didn't she?"

Heather laughed. "I guess she did. I wanted to show you that I loved you no matter what my mother thought. Honestly, when you started moving your hands over my body, I completely forgot about my mother. All I could think about was getting you in—" Soft lips cut off her sentence as Trin pulled her on top of her and began to stroke her back.

"It's almost daylight," Heather whispered in her ear. "We have just enough time."

##

Heather propped against the headboard and watched her lover as she towel-dried her hair. "I can't believe you can make love to me all night and then leave me all alone," she said, pouting.

Trin sat on the bed beside her and leaned in for a sweet kiss. "Believe me, if this wasn't a matter of life and death, there's no way I'd walk out that door."

Trin's eyes sparkled. "Are you going to remember I was here?"

"Oh God, yes." Heather sighed as she let the feeling flood her body. "Definitely, yes!"

Trin kissed her one more time.

"Call me when you land in Odessa," Heather said. "If I don't answer, leave me a message. I may be in surgery."

Trin touched Heather's face with her fingertips as if memorizing its beauty. She kissed her, slowly imprinting on her brain the feeling of Heather's full, soft lips. "I love you," she whispered. Then she was gone.

Chapter 10

Trin repeated her call sign to the tower as she waited for permission to take off. The tower radioed the instructions, and she revved up the plane's engine. The small jet shot down the runway and lifted into the air.

"We should be there in an hour," she informed her copilot and best friend, Swede Southerland. "The local sheriff is meeting us at the airport. He has photos he wants us to look at to see if we can identify them."

"Have they been arrested?" Swede asked.

"No, they're persons of interest. The sheriff is hoping we saw them at the rig where I was injured."

"You lucked out on that, my friend," Swede declared in a serious tone. "You're lucky you were Care Flighted to a hospital where the best orthopedic surgeons in Texas are in residence."

"I can't argue with that," Trin said, suppressing the smile that wanted to cover her face at the thought of Heather.

"You know the purpose of our task force is to catch the guys who caused that accident," Swede said. "They're getting more and more brazen. The commissioner is afraid they'll blow up a well in a residential area to get media attention."

"I know." Trin took a deep breath. "I don't know why lunatics are always drawn to supercilious politicians and their campaign promises to end fabricated problems."

"Those two we arrested last month were from California," Swede added. "Someone's bringing them in from out of state. They know they can't incite Texans to do their dirty work."

"I'm sure there is an organized movement to cause trouble for the oil companies," Trin said. "I hope we can trace it back to the root of the problem and eliminate the troublemakers."

"How long do you think we'll be here?" Swede said as he looked out the window of the plane. "My wife is due any day."

"I'd like to visit the rigs that have been vandalized and interview the men who were hired in the past sixty days. Maybe we can shake something loose," Trin answered. "We should be able to head back home late tomorrow evening.

"Have you picked a name for the baby?" Trin asked. "Do you know if it's a boy or a girl?"

"No, we want to be surprised." Swede's fair complexion turned red. "It doesn't matter whether it's a boy or a girl. We're going to name it after you either way."

"Me? Why me?"

"If you hadn't pushed me from the path of the falling debris a year ago, there'd be no baby. I'd be a dead man. You saved my life, Trin. Reba and I owe you more than we can every repay. It almost cost you your hand."

Trin shrugged. "You would have done the same for me."

The tower at the small airport contacted them over the radio, and Trin requested landing instructions. She could see the sheriff's car parked beside the runway.

Chapter 11

"I'm certain you will like the Winfield's daughter," Melody said, harping on Heather as they walked to their table.

Heather wasn't listening to her mother. She was thinking about Trin and how lonely the past two nights had been without her. She tried to hide her smile when she saw her father roll his eyes.

"Here we are," Eric said as he pulled out the chair for his wife. "Looks like we're seated with the Moncriefs."

"I was hoping we would be with the Winfields," Melody whined. "After all, Heather is co-chairing the Ball with her."

"Mother, please don't embarrass us with another performance like the one you put on the last time we were with the Winfields." Heather was still appalled by her mother's behavior and the way she had treated Trin.

"That was all your fault for showing up with that dreadful woman," Melody glowered.

Before Heather could respond, a tall, handsome man approached them and extended his hand to her father. "Eric, it's good to see you again, and this must be your lovely daughter."

"Yes." Eric beamed. "Heather, this is Scott Winfield. He and I are stepping aside this year and turning this affair over to our very capable offspring."

Scott Winfield's handshake was firm, and his smile was genuine. "It's a pleasure to have a doctor of your caliber on the committee, Heather."

"Thank you," Heather said. "I'm looking forward to working with your daughter. I understand she's a real mover and shaker."

Scott laughed. "She is that. She should be here soon. The driver just called to tell me they're on their way."

Melody pushed her way between Heather and Scott. "I'm Melody Hunter," she said. "Heather's mother and Eric's wife."

"Yes. My wife mentioned you were at the reception earlier in the week." Winfield's smile stopped at his lips. "It's nice to put a face with the name."

Heather wanted to hide. She was certain Lucinda Winfield had given her husband a blow-by-blow description of her mother's behavior and her own hasty departure from the benefit reception.

Winfield pulled Heather's arm through his. "Lucinda has been dying to visit with you," he said. "Do you mind if I steal her for a few minutes, Eric?"

"I could go with you," Melody said.

"I have explicit instructions to bring only Dr. Hunter to our table," Winfield said with a half smile as he walked away with Heather.

Lucinda Winfield was one of the most gracious women Heather had ever met. She laughed and talked about how she was looking forward to seeing what the younger generation would do to breathe new life into the Cattle Baron's Ball.

"Our daughter has some of the most outlandish ideas," Lucinda said, laughing. "But knowing her, they will be a big success. I'm sure you have some ideas too."

"I do," Heather said, "but I want to discuss them with her before I start spreading them around."

Lucinda's eyes twinkled. "Not only are you beautiful," "you're also very wise. I'm certain the two of you will cook up something wonderful."

"Darling,"—Scott touched his wife's arm—"I'm going to get things started by welcoming everyone and thanking them for coming."

Lucinda smiled and turned to Heather. "Please, join me at our table?"

"I really should stay close to my mother," Heather said. *To keep her from getting drunk.*

"It won't be for more than a few minutes." Lucinda motioned toward the chair next to hers as Scott Winfield spoke into the microphone.

"Ladies and gentlemen," Scott Winfield said, his baritone voice resonating through the room. "We're going to get a few things out of the way while we're waiting on my daughter. She should be here any minute."

A soft murmur ran through the crowd as the door to the ballroom opened, and the most beautiful woman Heather had ever seen glided toward Scott Winfield. Stilettos added to her already impressive height. She moved effortlessly in heels most women would avoid. Her black fitted evening dress hugged a perfect body that exuded sex appeal. Long blonde hair nestled on her shoulders and curled around a face angels would envy. Her eyes . . . her eyes were mesmerizing. Heather tried to breathe but couldn't. It was accurate to say the woman had taken her breath away.

"Here's my lovely daughter now," Scott said. "Many of you already know her, but for those of you who don't, I'm very proud to introduce my daughter, Trinidad Scott Winfield."

Beautiful red lips parted in an earthshaking smile that took in the entire room as Trinidad Winfield looked at the attendees. "Thank you so much for coming here tonight to support the annual Cattle Baron's Ball," she said into the microphone.

Heather closed her eyes and clenched her thighs as the silky-smooth voice filled the room. If honey had a sound, it would sound like Trinidad Winfield.

Lucinda touched Heather's arm, pulling her from fantasies of Trinidad. "She's introducing you, dear."

Heather listened intently as Trinidad continued to talk. "Dr. Heather Hunter is . . ."

As she moved to stand beside Trinidad, Heather fought the desire to simply touch the woman. Trinidad Winfield was to women what the Silver Ghost was to the Rolls-Royce: one in a million and beyond gorgeous.

Trinidad's sky-blue eyes filled with merriment as she reached out and took Heather's hand. "I'm confident that Dr. Hunter and I will work well together and sit you folks back on your heels." She looked amused as she laced her fingers with Heather's and raised their clasped hands above their heads. "So, don't let us down. Start thinking tonight about how much money you can donate to the Cattle Baron's Foundation instead of giving it to Uncle Sam. I just want to add that neither Dr. Hunter nor I are politicians, so you can rest assured that your donations will be used for the purpose they were intended."

Laughter rippled through the crowd as they stood and applauded the two new chairwomen.

Still holding Heather's hand, Trinidad led her from the ballroom and into a nearby meeting room. She closed and locked the door.

"I'm going to kill you when I get you home," Heather said as she fell into the arms Trin held out to her. Their kiss was electrifying, igniting a desire neither could ignore. "Dear God, I've missed you. I've been so worried about you."

"You're not angry with me?" Trin asked.

"I'm furious." Heather kissed her hard. "You're going to pay for this little stunt for the rest of your life. Right now, I just want to get you home and in my bed. All I can think about is getting back into your arms. My God, you're gorgeous!"

Trin chuckled. "I'm looking forward to it—both your bed tonight and paying for the rest of my life."

A gentle knock on the door pulled them from one another. "Trin, darling, it's Mom," Lucinda Winfield said softly.

Heather wiped the lipstick from Trin's face before the blonde opened the door a crack. "We'll be right out, Mom."

"I wouldn't bother you," Lucinda said, wrinkling her nose, "but everyone is asking for both of you. I told them you were discussing some ideas with one another before floating them out to the committee."

Trin chuckled. "I love you, Mom. Just give us a few minutes. We need to touch up our makeup."

Melody was sitting alone at the table with a half-empty drink in front of her. She was congratulating herself for matching the Winfield woman with her daughter. They seemed to hit it off immediately.

Melody was having visions of being on the inside of the Winfield circle. All she had to do was get rid of Trin Scott. Surely Heather could see that the Winfield woman was far more sophisticated and fit better with doctors and lawyers than the roughneck ever would. She downed the last of her drink and looked around for her husband.

As they mingled with the guests, Heather prayed that her mother was sober. Her father stood talking to a group of men Heather recognized as the finance committee of the Cattle Baron's Association.

65

Trin introduced Heather to her friends in the oil and gas industry, and Heather introduced Trin to her friends in healthcare. Most of the town's doctors and administrators were attending the kickoff function.

Peter Trotter pushed his father's wheelchair around the room as he networked with other guests. Jarrod Trotter was an attractive man and greeted everyone with a ready smile and kind remark. Eric walked across the room to greet the two of them.

Heather excused herself to join her father and the Trotters. "Uncle Jarrod," she said as she leaned down to kiss the elder Trotter's cheek. "I'm so glad you could make it tonight."

"I wouldn't miss it for the world," Jarrod said. "When I heard that you were co-chairing the Ball, I told Peter we had to be as supportive as possible."

"I want you to meet my co-chair," Heather told Jarrod waving Trin to join them.

"Trinidad Winfield, I would like you to meet Peter and Jarrod Trotter and of course, you know my father."

"My, aren't you a lovely young lady," Jarrod said, grinning at Trin. "It's a joy to meet you."

Eric suggested that everyone join him and Melody, so the group headed toward their table.

"Eric, dear, please get me a fresh drink," Melody said. She held out her empty glass to her husband. "Jarrod, it's good to see you out and about."

Jarrod acknowledged Melody's comment with a nod.

"Uh oh!" Trin cringed. "Here comes trouble."

"There you are." With an air of familiarity a painted blonde slipped her arm through Trin's. "I've been looking for you."

A crooked smile twisted Trin's lips. "Roxie Royce, this is Dr. Heather Hunter, her father, Dr. Eric Hunter, and her mother, Melody Hunter." Trin didn't make eye contact with Heather. "Roxie is the treasurer for the Cattle Baron's Ball.

"Heather is the orthopedic surgeon who reattached my hand after the oil rig accident," Trin added.

Roxie looked at Heather then Trin. "I suppose I have you to thank for how well her hands work." Her lascivious grin was directed at Heather.

Melody took the silence in the group as an invitation to make an impression on someone important. "Roxie Royce? Your family owns the international import business Royce International, if I'm correct."

"Yes, I do." Roxie tightened her hold on Trin's arm. "That's not all I own."

"Surely you aren't insinuating that you own me?" she said, scowling as she pulled away from Roxie. "I haven't seen you since my accident."

"I'm here now," Roxie said sensually, "and ready to make up for lost time. You look ravishing, darling."

"I'm here with Heather," Trin said as she moved closer to the brunette. "We've been friends for over a year." She pulled Heather's hand through the crook of her arm.

"We'll talk later." Roxie glared at Heather. "When no one else is around." She tossed her head in a haughty manner and slinked away.

"That was uncomfortable," Heather murmured.

"Yes, it was," Trin said.

Melody was beginning to put two and two together. "Dear, did I understand you to say that my daughter has performed surgery on you?"

"Yes, Mrs. Hunter. I'm the roughneck you find so unacceptable."

##

Trin fell onto the bed beside Heather. "You're killing me," she said, gasping for air.

"I've just begun." Heather's voice was low and husky. "How could you spend a year with me and not tell me who you really are?"

"Does it matter?" Trin gazed into the eyes of the woman leaning over her.

"Not one iota." The honesty in Heather's voice made Trin love her even more.

Trin pulled herself up to lean against the padded headboard. Heather straddled her, so their breasts were touching. Trin inhaled sharply as Heather moved against her. She pushed away from the headboard, so Heather could straighten her legs.

"Oh, that feels so good," Heather moaned as she nibbled Trin's full lower lip. "Tell me, Trinidad Scott Winfield, how long would you have let this charade go on?"

"No charade." Trin chuckled. "It isn't my fault that your hospital admittance people didn't get the correct name when they admitted me. Everyone calls me Trin, and your admittance personnel picked up my middle name instead of my last name.

"It gave me the opportunity to pursue you without all the trappings of the Winfield name. When you finally came to me, I knew it was because you loved me for me and not because I'm a Winfield."

"And Roxie Royce? Why does she have the hots for you?" Heather scowled.

"Because I'm a Winfield," Trin whispered as she nibbled Heather's ear. "And because I'm very good in bed."

"I don't know." Heather bit Trin's lower lip until the copper taste told her she had drawn blood. "I'll need some convincing on that."

Trin pulled her tighter against her breasts as Heather tightened her legs around Trin's waist and locked her ankles behind her. "I'll need time to show you just how good I am," Trin murmured against lips that were already swollen. "I'll probably need at least a lifetime."

Chapter 12

Zara Reed Palava waited patiently outside Dr. Hunter's office. She wasn't a patient woman, but Dr. Heather Hunter was worth the wait. She flipped through a popular movie magazine that was nothing but a long list of whores and their pimps. She wondered how women could sell their bodies and souls for the opportunity to make a movie. *How can anyone crave the adulation of simpering fans so badly that they would strip themselves of all dignity to get attention?* she thought.

"Dr. Hunter will see you now, Mrs. Palava," the receptionist informed her.

"*Miss* Palava," Reed corrected her.

"Of course, Miss Palava." The receptionist motioned for Reed to follow her.

Heather looked up as Reed entered her office. The woman was beautiful in a dark, seductive way. Her red lips parted in a smile as she locked eyes with Heather.

"Dr. Hunter," Reed said, extending her hand to Heather whose handshake was as firm as her own. "Thank you for seeing me on such short notice."

"Please, sit," Heather gestured to the chair across from her. "Tell me how I can help you."

"My mother . . . she was in a horrible accident, and her arm was severed above the wrist. The doctor who attended her is not as well-trained or accomplished as you. To save her arm, he sewed it to the artery in her leg. It is thriving and doing well."

Reed smiled again, and Heather was surprised at how beautiful she was. "Of course, a hand on a leg is useless,

70

but her surgeons are hesitant to try reattaching it to her arm."

"What hospital is she in now?"

"She's in an Iranian hospital," Reed said, wrinkling her brow. "We have tried, without success, to get her to the United States, but her doctors won't release her to travel. They say she might not survive the trip.

"Her doctors tell me that you have accomplished miraculous things in the operating room. That you have a very high success rate in cases like this."

Heather studied the other woman for a minute. "I do, but I can't practice medicine in your country."

"Please, Dr. Hunter. Money is no object. My family is exceedingly wealthy. We have cleared all the political hurdles to get you into our country, and I have signed letters from the hospital requesting you do the surgery.

"I'm also authorized to commit the funds needed to build a new trauma wing here at your hospital." Reed smiled as if she had closed the deal.

Heather grimaced. "As tempting as that might be, I believe I would be in great danger in your country. I'm a lesbian. I believe your men stone women like me."

Reed narrowed her eyes as she surveyed Dr. Hunter. She had expected a much older, more experienced doctor. She had also hoped Dr. Hunter would be a man. The last thing she wanted to hear was that the gorgeous brunette sitting across from her was a lesbian.

"My father is Dr. Eric Hunter," Heather volunteered. "He is also an outstanding orthopedic surgeon. You might like to speak with him."

"Has he performed the operation necessary to save my mother's hand?" Reed asked.

"No, but I'm sure he could—"

"You are the only one we will pay such a price for."

"Money isn't the issue," Heather said with a sigh. "Sexuality, and the laws of your country regarding it, is the issue."

A light rap on the door prevented the conversation from continuing. "Come in," Heather said, grateful for the interruption.

Trin opened the door and peeped around it. "Am I intruding?" she asked.

"No, darling." Heather stood and walked over to her lover. "We're just discussing the dangers of being a lesbian in Iran.

"Zara Reed Palava, this is my partner, Trin Winfield." Trin shook hands with Reed as Heather made the introductions.

"Zara Palava . . ." Trin paused, her forehead wrinkled in thought. "Are you . . .?"

"A princess?" Reed chuckled. "Yes."

Heather looked from Trin to Reed. "I think I missed something."

"Zara is Hebrew for princess," Trin explained. "This is Princess Reed Palava of the house of Palava."

Reed shrugged. "I prefer not to use my title in the U.S. It seems so pompous."

Heather nodded and raised a perfectly arched brow at Trin, who took the hint.

"I'm here to take Dr. Hunter to lunch," Trin said. "Would you like to join us?"

"I don't wish to intrude," Reed said, pulling the strap of her purse onto her shoulder as she got to her feet.

Heather insisted. "Nonsense. Trin often has dealings with the Iranian government. She might help you find a solution to your problem."

Reed ran her eyes from Trin's fashionably booted feet to the top of her beautiful blonde head. She could see why a woman would turn into a lesbian for a woman like Trin Winfield.

Chapter 13

"What brings you to Dr. Hunter's door?" Trin asked as the server placed their drinks on the table.

Reed explained her situation and concluded with, "Perhaps you can convince Dr. Hunter to visit my country."

"I don't think so," Trin said as she squeezed Heather's hand. "You must know she would be in danger. Her name is all over the internet, and it's no secret that we're a couple. Honestly, I will do everything I can to keep her from putting herself in harm's way."

Reed watched the blonde. It was obvious from the way her eyes sparkled when she looked at Heather that she was deeply in love with the doctor.

"You said your mother's hand is thriving," Heather said. "It will be fine, as long as there are no complications. When she can travel, bring her to me. I'll be happy to perform the necessary surgery."

"We will protect you," Reed said with a look of desperation in her eyes. "My father is head of the royal guard. We will have a regiment guarding you always. You'll go from the plane to the car, to the hospital, perform the surgery, and then head back to the car that will deliver you to our private jet and back to America. You'll be protected every step of the way."

Trin leaned back in her chair and glared at Reed. "You know as well as I do that one word from Iran's Supreme Leader would result in the arrest of Dr. Hunter. I'm sure you also know his policy on homosexuality."

"Lesbian women are no longer stoned in our country," Reed pointed out.

Trin shrugged. "That is true. However, your laws do call for a hundred lashes. Tell me, Princess, how many women do you know who have lived through a beating like that?"

Reed hung her head. She knew the Winfield woman was right. Women found guilty of homosexuality were often beaten to death. If they didn't die from the flogging, they were horribly deformed or paralyzed.

"Now that we've settled that," Trin said, "let's discuss your current trade mission to the U.S."

Reed tilted her head and raised her eyes to meet Trin's. *I'd take a beating for you*, she thought.

"You seem to know a lot about the politics of the world," Reed said. "Who are you, exactly?"

"Trinidad Scott Winfield," Trin replied. "I work in the oil fields."

"Winfield?" Reed paused for a moment. "You're Scott Winfield's daughter. You're much more than a roughneck."

Heather slid her hand onto Trin's thigh and let her fingers fall on the inside of her leg. Trin stiffened as she gazed into the dark eyes of the woman she loved. "You're evil," she whispered.

"I really must be getting back to the hospital," Heather murmured, her voice husky. She cleared her throat. "Where's your car, Reed? We can take you to it."

##

"You aren't considering her proposal, are you?" Trin asked as they watched Reed get into her Mercedes.

"No, I won't go to any country that won't provide equal rights for men and women." Heather frowned. "But I will go to bed with you, if you'll take me home."

"Best suggestion I've heard all day," Trin said as she pulled Heather's hand into her lap. "So, you don't really need to return to the hospital?"

"No, but I desperately need some time with you."

##

Trin lay still beside the woman who fulfilled all her fantasies. They had teased and made love for hours before falling asleep. If Heather's soft breathing was any indication, she was in a deep sleep.

Although they both still maintained their own homes, she had moved into Heather's home months ago and couldn't imagine falling asleep without the brunette beside her. She fought the urge to crush Heather against her, to feel her softness.

Heather was everything Trin had dreamed of and more. An accomplished doctor and a lady in every sense of the word, Heather was a breathtaking, hard-loving goddess behind closed doors. Sometimes Trin would come undone just thinking about the brunette and how she made love to her. If Heather's schedule allowed, they often disappeared during the day and made love until they wore each other out and exhaustion pushed them into a sated sleep.

Heather stirred in her arms and moaned softly. Trin remained still until Heather was sleeping soundly again.

Trin thought about the conversations she'd heard at work when married women talked about how bad their sex lives were. Some people thought sex just happened. In a way, it did, but good sex required effort on the part of both partners. One couldn't just phone-in lovemaking. One had to put everything they had into making love to their partner. Trin hated lazy lovers. She'd encountered a few in her lifetime, and they always left a lot to be desired.

There wasn't a lazy bone in Heather's body. She made love just like she lived life. She gave everything she had, and Trin did the same. They were a perfect match. Sometimes Trin felt as if she had been swept into a raging vortex of arms, lips, and breasts. *God, I love her*, she thought.

"Are you going to play possum all night?" Heather's silky, sexy voice sent a thrill through Trin's body. "Or are you going to do something that will hold me all day tomorrow?"

"What did you have in mind?" Trin shifted and pulled Heather beneath her.

Heather nibbled Trin's lower lip and lightly trailed her fingernails down Trin's back. "Oh, I don't know. Something that will shake the Balcones Fault Line should do the trick."

"I know just the thing." Trin kissed her passionately as Heather wrapped her legs around Trin's lower back and began to grind into her. Making love to Dr. Heather Hunter definitely wasn't for sissies.

Chapter 14

Heather shifted in her chair as she studied the new X-rays and MRIs the hospital had performed on Jarrod Trotter. She closed her eyes and trembled as she thought about the things Trin had done to her the night before. She exhaled slowly when she realized she was holding her breath. She picked up her cell phone and tapped a message to Trin. "Still holding."

A message returned immediately. "I can come over for a refresher, if needed."

"Tonight," Heather typed back.

"Can't wait. Love you," Trin replied.

Heather was still thinking about Trin when she called her father's office. "Dr. Hunter, this is Dr. Hunter," Heather said with a giggle as her father answered the phone. "Do you have a minute?"

"For you, always," Eric replied. "I'll come to your office. Peter is looking for me. Maybe he won't look there."

Eric hurried to his daughter's office and locked the door behind him. "That should keep him out."

"Dad, I can't find anything wrong with Uncle Jarrod," Heather said as she motioned for her father to join her at the computer.

"There's a small piece of lead lodged right here," she said, pointing out a dark spot on the X-ray, "but I can remove that with my eyes closed. Even if we don't remove it, it shouldn't impede his mobility. I can't figure out why he can't walk."

"He refuses surgery to remove it," Eric said. "He says he can live with the pain and doesn't want to take any chances that might make it worse."

"Has he done physical therapy?" Heather asked.

"Yes, he has worked hard to keep his legs from atrophying."

"His paralysis could be psychosomatic," Heather said. "There's no physical reason for him to be a paraplegic. Have you suggested counseling?"

Eric frowned. "Many times. He isn't very receptive to ideas that will improve his condition."

"Do you mind if I try to convince him to see Edith Grey?"

"Not at all. She's one of the best with PTSD and other war-related problems. If you're okay with it, I'll turn Jarrod's case over to you," Eric said.

"I'd love to see if I can help him," Heather said, beaming.

"On another note, your mother would like you and Trin to have dinner with us Friday night."

"Dad, you know how awful she was to Trin. How can I expect her to socialize with Mom?"

"Is it Trin or you?" Eric asked.

"Mostly me." Heather sighed. "If she weren't my mother, I would hate her for the way she tried to humiliate Trin. I honestly don't think Trin cares one way or the other, and she would do anything I asked of her. I just . . ."

"As a favor to me," Eric interjected.

"Okay, but not Friday night. Trin has to go to Odessa again on Wednesday. She won't return until Sunday around noon, and then we have the Cattle Baron's meeting Sunday evening. Maybe next Friday we can plan dinner. Let me discuss it with Trin"

Eric nodded. "I'll let her know."

##

78

Across town, Trin was reviewing blurry photos of the terrorists who had bombed a gas well in Johnson County. The idea that the thugs would attack the economic foundation of her state and the people who lived in neighborhoods surrounding the wells infuriated her.

Missy Smart, Trin's secretary, opened the door to her office. "There's a Reed Palava to see you."

Trin frowned. "Does she have an appointment?"

"No," Missy said. "But she says it's extremely important."

Trin agreed to see her and got to her feet as the woman was ushered inside. "Reed, what a pleasant surprise."

"Thank you for seeing me without an appointment," Reed said. "It's greatly appreciated."

Trin motioned for Reed to sit and then took her seat behind her desk. She waited for the other woman to explain the reason for her visit. Trin had learned at an early age to let others do the talking. One never learned anything with their mouth open.

Reed got straight to the point. "I'm certain you are aware that your father is heading up the oil leaders' delegation traveling to my country later this year to negotiate an agreement with our Minister of Petroleum."

"I am," Trin said.

"What your delegation hopes to accomplish can happen if you will help me," Reed said.

"How can I help?"

"If you'll talk Dr. Hunter into operating on my mother, I'll make certain your delegation gets what they want."

"How can you do that?" Trin asked.

"My family is extremely influential in my country," Reed explained. "My uncles and brothers hold high offices in our government. Not to mention my father's position. They will do whatever is necessary to help my mother. Accomplishing your father's goals would mean billions of dollars in the coffers of Winfield Oil and Gas. And it would greatly reduce the US trade deficit."

"Princess," Trin murmured, her voice soft and compassionate, "I understand your concern for your mother, but you must understand my fears for the woman I love.

"Just last month your government flogged a lesbian to death. Surely, you don't think I would want Heather to risk such a fate?"

Trin looked down as she clenched her hands. "There isn't enough money in the world to tempt me to encourage Heather to put herself in harm's way. If anything happened to her, I don't know what I'd do."

"You could turn to me," Reed whispered.

"What?" Trin furrowed her brow, certain she had heard incorrectly.

"I said, 'I'm sorry you can't help me.'" Reed's voice was loud and clear. "I do understand."

"I could send our company's private jet for your mother," Trin suggested. "We could pick her up and take her directly to the hospital, where Heather would be waiting. She would have the best care possible."

Reed shrugged. "Let's see how well she recovers over the next few months. Perhaps she will regain the strength for such a trip."

Trin stood, signaling their meeting was over. She walked Reed to the lobby. "I'm sorry I couldn't help you. I hope you understand."

"I do," Reed said. "I hope you understand that I must do everything I can to help my mother."

Chapter 15

Heather leaned back against Trin's softness. The blonde was reclining against the arm of their sofa, and Heather was sitting between her legs. Heather glanced at the gun and holster Trin had placed on the coffee table when she slipped off her boots.

"Reed Palava paid me a visit today," Trin said.

"Why?"

"Trying to buy my influence to get you to go to Iran and operate on her mother."

"I wish we could find a way to help her," Heather said. "I wouldn't feel safe in her country. I don't trust them."

"Neither do I. And selfish as it may sound, when it comes to choosing between Reed's mother and the woman I love, there's no contest. Reed's mother will lose every time."

Trin tightened her arms around Heather and kissed behind her ear. "I love you, Dr. Hunter."

"I hate that you're going to Odessa in the morning," Heather said. "What exactly do you do in Odessa?"

Trin sat silently for several minutes. She knew that Heather would only worry if she knew why she was going to Odessa. "I'm a geologist. It's my responsibility to locate new petroleum deposits and acquire leases for Winfield Oil to drill. We own about seventy percent of the leased petroleum property in Texas."

"And that requires you to carry a gun?" Heather raised one eyebrow.

"I'm also the Texas coordinator for ten five-man teams of investigators whose sole purpose is to keep terrorists away from oil and gas fields."

Heather stiffened and inhaled sharply. "I knew you weren't a roughneck," she said. "What you do is double the danger."

"Not really," Trin assured her.

"Don't lie to me, Trinidad Winfield." Heather turned to face the blonde. "Tell me the truth or don't talk to me at all."

Trin could see her happiness with Heather slipping away.

"As you know, my father is the Texas Railroad Commissioner. The Railroad Commission has the responsibility of regulating and working with the oil and gas industry in Texas. Contrary to popular opinion, I don't report to my father. I report directly to the president of the United States."

"Your hand . . . was that an accident or an attempt on your life?" Heather whispered.

"It was no accident," Trin admitted. "But it wasn't a direct attempt on me. I just happened to be in the wrong place at the wrong time."

"So, the collapse of the derrick was sabotage?"

"Yes."

Heather rubbed her face with both hands, trying to think. She desperately wanted to make some sense of what Trin was telling her, but it all came back to the fact that she was insanely in love with a woman who walked on the precipice of death.

Heather caught Trin's face between her hands and pulled it to her lips. She intended her kiss to be gentle but found Trin had other ideas. Trin's lips were like silk as she slowly moved them against Heather's. Her tongue fought a dual with Heather's as they devoured one another. Without breaking their kiss, Heather moved to her knees between

Trin's legs and unbuttoned the blouse Trin was wearing. Soft, warm lips kissed their way down Trin's neck. Their progress was achingly slow as Trin arched her back to get closer to Heather. Heather unfastened the front-hook bra and kissed between Trin's breasts. She captured Trin's nipple with her lips and circled it with her tongue.

"Do you know what you just did?" Trin said as she tried to catch her breath.

"Uh-huh." Heather sucked air between her lips and Trin's nipple. "I hit the On switch."

"You know there's no Off switch." Wanton desire dripped from Trin's words as she flipped Heather onto her back and took control of the warm, willing body beneath her.

Trin was drifting in and out of sleep when Heather snuggled into her and hugged her.

"You do know I must fly a plane to Odessa in the morning, right?" Trin whispered into her ear. "I should get some rest."

"You'll be flying the plane?" Heather pulled back to gaze into Trin's blue eyes. "You have a pilot's license?"

"Yes." Trin's answer was simple and modest.

"Is there anything else I don't know about you?" Heather asked as she rested her face against Trin's chest.

"I'm sure there's a lot we don't know about each other," Trin said, her words measured. "But I'm hoping we have a lifetime to learn."

Chapter 16

Heather cringed when she was informed that Melody was headed her way. She closed Jarrod's file as her mother pushed open the office door.

Like a dutiful daughter, Heather stood and hugged her mother. "What brings you to my office, Mother?"

"Trinidad Winfield," Melody barked.

"What about her?" Heather was in no mood to listen to any of her mother's derogatory remarks about the woman she loved.

"Are you going to marry her?"

"We haven't discussed that," Heather replied honestly. "She hasn't asked me, and I certainly haven't asked her."

"Why not?" Melody scowled. "You're both women. Either of you could ask the other."

"Why has Trin suddenly gone from being unfit to lick my shoes to being good wife material?" Heather glared at her mother.

"Please, Heather," Melody said with a snort. "She's a Winfield. Anyone would want to marry her."

"Mother, I don't need to marry someone to validate myself. I'm an excellent doctor. I'm very wealthy and have my pick of men and women. Why would I want to rush into marriage with someone I'm just getting to know? Trin and I are quite happy with our current arrangement."

"And what arrangement is that?"

"Mother, I'm a grown woman. I'm quite capable of taking care of myself, and I no longer answer to you. My personal life is none of your business."

Melody changed the subject. "Your father said you'd bring her to dinner Friday."

"Not this Friday," Heather said. "She's out of town until Sunday. I haven't even had time to ask her if she's free next Friday."

"Surely you can reach her on the phone," Melody insisted. "I need to know. A dinner party doesn't just happen overnight. It takes planning, caterers, and the guests need invitations, and—"

"Dinner party?" Heather gasped in disbelief. "I didn't agree to a dinner party. I thought it would just be the four of us. I thought you wanted to get to know her better."

"She's a Winfield," Melody snapped. "That's all I need to know about her. She's the crème de la crème of Texas society. My friends will be so impressed and probably a little jealous that I will have her in my home."

"Let me resolve that little dilemma for you right now," Heather said, scowling at her mother. "Neither Trin nor I will be at your little dinner party—ever."

"Don't you raise your voice to me, Heather Hunter!" Melody screeched. "You may be a god in this hospital, but I know you are far from perfect. You and your father—"

"Mother stop it!" Heather said. "Just listen to yourself. What is wrong with you?"

Melody stood and leaned over Heather's desk to get in her face. "You and your father think you can ride my coattails up the social ladder without getting your precious, skilled hands dirty, but—"

"Mother, listen to yourself," Heather said, shaking her head. "Dad and I aren't social climbers. We never have been. Why are you so obsessed with being in specific social circles?"

Heather walked around her desk to stand before her mother. "Why can't you see people for their goodness and kindness instead of their money and position? Why don't you want to get to know how sweet and wonderful Trin is instead of using her to impress your so-called friends?"

Melody's demeanor changed as a mask of sweetness slipped over her face. "You're right, darling. It should be just the four of us for dinner. I'm sorry. I'm just so proud that you are with Trinidad Winfield. That's all. I promise it will just be Daddy and me. Where is Trin?"

"Odessa," Heather replied.

"Um, yes, the Winfields own several oil fields in the Permian Basin," Melody said.

"Mother, what exactly do you want out of life?"

"Recognition, adulation . . . all the things that come easy to you and your father. I want people to say, 'A dinner party isn't complete if Melody Hunter isn't here,'" she huffed.

"I want you to be introduced as my daughter—not me as your mother or Dr. Hunter's wife."

Heather cocked her head and studied her mother. "I don't know how to respond to that." Her tone was gentle and filled with empathy.

Before Melody could reply, Heather's cell phone rang. "I must take this call, Mother," she said, her heart pounding at the sound of Trin's ringtone. "I'll let you know about next Friday."

Melody nodded and walked from the office.

"Hello, baby," Heather whispered into the phone.

"Oh God, I miss you," Trin responded. "I hate being away from you."

"I know. I miss you too."

"How many lives have you saved today?" Trin teased.

"None, so far. How many oil wells have you drilled?"

"Touché." Trin couldn't keep the smile off her face. "I don't really want to talk about frivolous things. I just did that to keep from blurting out how much I adore you and want to be with you."

"We do have a mutual attraction with strong feelings," Heather purred. "Is there any chance you can return earlier than you thought?"

Trin inhaled deeply. "No. Things aren't looking good here. I have a lot to do and not much time to do it. I definitely want to be home Sunday."

"I bet Swede hated leaving his new baby and wife," Heather said.

"Um, I didn't have the heart to make him do that," Trin admitted.

Heather gasped. "You're there alone? Aren't you in a dangerous situation?"

"The local sheriff is excellent. He's a good man to have backing me up, and he knows the territory. I'm waiting on him now."

"Will you be able to call me tonight?"

"You can count on it," Trin said, chuckling. "God, honey, I can't even begin to tell you how lonely it is when I'm away from you."

"What do you miss most?" Heather said sensuously.

"Um," Trin cleared her throat. "Your lips, your warmth, the way you—"

"Doctor Heather Hunter, report to the trauma center immediately." The announcement blared into Heather's office.

"I heard that." Trin sighed. "I'll call you tonight. Love you."

"Love you too. Please be careful," Heather said as she headed out the door. "Call me."

Heather wandered through her home, straightening perfectly placed pictures on her wall, moving a vase a bit to the right or left. She tried to think of anything that would make the time pass faster. She had slept without Trin for the past two nights, and she was going crazy. She wasn't certain she could make it through the day and another night. She had volunteered to be on call for the weekend to occupy her time, but her father had insisted that it was his turn. Sometimes she thought he stayed at the hospital to avoid her mother's constant nagging.

She carried her cup of coffee into her home office and turned on her computer. She had never Googled Trinidad Scott Winfield, but she had a sudden desire to know all there was to know about the woman.

Heather watched as photos and headlines about her lover filled the screen. She clicked on Wikipedia and started reading. Trin held a doctorate in geology and owned several patents that were heralded as lifesaving technologies. She and her father held a patent that had brought fracking into the twenty-first century and was praised by ecologists and the oil industry.

Trin was a licensed pilot and held a black belt in karate. An excellent marksman, she was the director of the president's anti-terrorism team to protect oil and gas fields in Texas.

She had spent two years in Afghanistan serving with an elite team whose assignments were highly classified.

Trin's name was linked with several socialites, an extremely popular singer, and two A-list actresses. It was obvious she could have her pick of women.

Heather took her empty coffee cup to the sink and made a spur-of-the-moment decision. A quick call to the airline and she booked a ticket to the Midland-Odessa International Airport. She hugged herself as she thought about surprising Trin.

She called Uber for pickup in half an hour and tossed the few things she would need into her overnight bag. She pulled on her boots just as the Uber driver pulled into her driveway. She locked her door and almost ran to the car.

The more she thought about surprising Trin, the more excited she became.

The car trip to DFW Airport took about the same time as the flight from DFW to the Midland-Odessa Airport would—a little over an hour. She called her father to let him know where she was going. As usual, Eric encouraged her to have a good time but be careful.

As she waited for her boarding call, she realized she had no idea where Trin was staying. She called the blonde and breathed a sigh of relief when Trin answered the phone. "Honey, I'm really in the middle—"

"Where are you staying?" Heather interrupted.

"Wyndham Garden in Midland," Trin answered. "I'll call you tonight."

The flight was quick, and the cab ride was fifteen minutes. She tipped the driver and entered the Wyndham.

"I need the room number for Trin Winfield," she informed the registration clerk.

"I don't believe Ms. Winfield is in her room," the clerk said. "I'll check." She called Trin's room, waited for several rings, and then hung up. "No, ma'am, she hasn't returned."

"I'll just go up and wait for her," Heather said, holding out her hand for a key card.

"I'm sorry, but I can't give you a key to her room," the clerk said. "That's against the law, but you can wait in the club with the other woman who is waiting for her."

"Other woman?"

"The floosy-looking blonde." The clerk nodded toward a door that led from the lobby. "Or you can wait by the indoor pool. I'll have someone bring you a drink. Coffee? Wine? Soft drink?"

"A glass of Merlot would be nice." Heather smiled as she slid a tip to the woman.

"You're much more beautiful," the clerk blurted out.

"I beg your pardon?" Heather said.

"You're much more beautiful than the blonde waiting for her."

"Oh, thank you. You're very kind." Heather glanced into the club area as she walked toward the pool. Roxie Royce was sitting on a barstool flirting with a scantily dressed cocktail waitress.

Heather was surprised at how quickly the server appeared with her wine. She tipped the woman and took a sip of the Merlot. She settled into the cushioned chair and placed her glass on the poolside table. The pool was designed so one could observe the lobby through the thick glass forming the wall between the hotel and the pool area.

Heather looked up as two men and a woman entered the lobby. The men were dressed in Odessa Sheriff's Department uniforms. Heather couldn't take her eyes off Trin and her bouncing blonde ponytail.

The three were deep in conversation when Roxie joined them. Trin frowned and motioned for the blonde to sit down in the lobby. She moved the men to the far side of the room and continued their conversation.

Even from a distance Heather could tell Roxie Royce was furious. She watched as the woman tapped the toe of her stiletto on the floor, a dark scowl on her face.

Trin walked the two men to the exit and shook hands with them as they left. She turned and looked at Roxie. A huge grin crossed Roxie's face as she walked toward Trin with open arms. Trin sidestepped Roxie's attempt to embrace her. Heather moved to the entrance between the pool and the lobby for a better view of the two women.

"Roxie, what are you doing here?" Trin demanded.

"Your secretary told me you were here," Roxie said seductively. "I thought you might like some company. You know, for old times' sake."

"No," Trin growled as Roxie tried to grab her arm. "I told you, I'm with Heather."

"The whole town knows you're sleeping with her," Roxie snarled. "But I've noticed you haven't put a ring on it."

"Our relationship is none of your business," Trin said.

"Since I'm here, we might as well enjoy each other's company," Roxie insisted. "Let me buy you dinner? You used to like spending time with me."

Trin hesitated. "No, I'm very tired. I've been out in the field all day. The only thing I want to do is shower and call Heather."

Trin pushed the elevator button and blocked Roxie's attempt to follow her into the car.

"Fine, go call your prissy doctor," Roxie said, spitting out the words. "I don't need you anyway."

The elevator door closed in Roxie's face, and Heather watched her storm from the lobby. Then she picked up her overnight bag and walked to the registration desk.

"Room 310," the clerk said with a big grin. "You are too much a lady. I was hoping for a cat fight."

Heather laughed out loud. "Miss Winfield is certainly worth fighting for, but it wasn't necessary."

"I bet you'd win."

"I just did," Heather said with a smile. She thanked the clerk and walked to the elevator.

Heather tapped on the door to room 310.

"Dammit, Roxie, I told you I want nothing to do with you," Trin bellowed as she threw open the door. "I'm not interested in you . . . Heather! Oh God, Heather!"

Trin caught Heather's hand and pulled her into the room, into arms that were aching to hold her. "How did—"

Soft lips cut off her questions as Heather sank deeper into the strong arms of her lover.

"I'm sorry," Heather gasped as she tried to catch her breath. "I missed you so much. I couldn't spend another night without you."

"Honey, you have no idea how good it is to see you."
Trin kissed her again. "Did you bring the . . .?"

"Of course." Heather kissed the pulse point in Trin's
neck. "That's why I'm here, silly."

"I just left the oil field," Trin said, her breathing
ragged. "Let me shower. I'll be quick."

When Trin walked from the bathroom, Heather was
leaning against the headboard thumbing through a *Key
Magazine*. She wore a black negligee.

Desire darkened Trin's eyes. "Dear Lord, you're
gorgeous." She dropped her dressing gown and slipped into
the bed. "Is there any special reason you flew to join me?"

"Mm-hmm." Heather kissed down Trin's neck,
stopping between her breasts. "This is strictly a booty call,
Miss Winfield. A pure, unadulterated demand for sex."

Trin groaned as she pulled Heather into her. "I'm
always happy to comply with your demands, Dr. Hunter."

Trin ran her hands down Heather's body then wrapped
her arms around the brunette, crushing her against her. The
feel of the silk gown and Heather's softness overwhelmed
her senses.

Later, Trin gasped for breath as she fell onto her back.
She was certain her heart would burst through her chest.
Heather's soft moans excited her all over again. "Is this
what you had in mind?" She nuzzled Heather's hair and
nibbled her ear.

"You're just what the doctor ordered," Heather assured
her.

Chapter 17

"Please let me go with you," Heather pleaded as Trin buttoned her white shirt. "I'll wait in the car."

"It's not like I'm running into the grocery store for a loaf of bread," Trin said, frowning. "It'll be dangerous.

"I won't be gone long, honey. The sheriff and his deputies are making a raid on a farmhouse we've been surveilling. We're certain it contains explosives and detonators. I don't want to put you in harm's way."

"If things go wrong," Heather argued, "you might need my services."

"I have to admit your services are the best I've ever had," Trin teased, "but—"

Heather playfully slapped at her arm. "Please take me with you?"

"Okay, but you must stay in the car!"

Heather watched as the deputies fanned out around the old farmhouse. The windows were covered in years of dirt, and nothing could be seen inside the structure. Heather was positive it was deserted. Trin eased onto the rotted front steps and carefully moved to the front door, tapping on it with the barrel of her Glock.

"Hello," she yelled. "If anyone is in there, come out. You're surrounded by law enforcement officers."

Seconds later, a shot ripped through the door and sent Trin flying from the porch. She landed on her back and lay sprawled on the ground. Her gun landed ten feet behind her. Heather screamed and jumped from the car. Before the deputies could stop her, she was at Trin's side, kneeling in the dirt.

Another shot kicked up dust beside Heather's leg. "Don't move or you're a dead woman," a raspy male voice called out.

"Be still," Trin hissed. "What are you doing here?"

"I thought you were hurt."

"I am, dammit, but I'm okay. You're a sitting duck."

"You're not bleeding."

"Bulletproof vest," Trin whispered. "They need to think I'm out of the fight."

Heather threw herself across Trin and began to wail. "She's dead. You've killed her."

Another shot slapped the ground beside Heather. She flinched as Trin cursed.

"You, the brunette, come in here," the raspy voice commanded.

Heather didn't move.

"Get your ass in here, or I'll shoot you too."

"Damn," Trin whispered. "Damn."

"I'm countin' to ten then I'm gonna shoot you too."

"Stand up and pull me up with you," Trin directed. "Continue carrying on about how injured I am."

Heather bit into her bottom lip until it started to bleed.

"What are you doing?" Trin whispered.

"Making you look wounded," Heather replied as she wiped her mouth on the front of Trin's white shirt.

Heather moved to her knees. "She's still breathing. Can I bring her with me?" she called out to the unseen shooter inside. "I'm a doctor. I might be able to save her. If she dies, you'll get the needle for sure. She's a federal agent."

After a long silence, the voice instructed her to bring Trin with her.

Struggling under her weight, Heather pulled Trin up putting her arm around her own shoulder so Trin could lean on her.

"You're heavy," Heather complained.

"You've never complained about my weight on you before," Trin muttered, unable to resist the observation.

"I should drop you in the dirt," Heather said as she struggled to drag Trin to the porch.

"It must look like I can't support myself," Trin whispered.

The door opened, and Heather stared into darkness.

"Get in here," the voice commanded.

Heather pulled harder as she dragged Trin into the farmhouse and dropped her on an old tattered sofa.

The man waved his gun at Heather as he inched closer to Trin. "Move away from her."

"She's losing blood," Heather said, trying to draw his attention away from Trin. "Please, just let me stop the bleeding."

"I don't care if she bleeds to death." The man's sardonic laugh sent chills down Heather's spine. "If you want to save her, you need to get us out of here."

"They'll shoot you the minute you walk out that door," Heather warned.

"No, they won't. This place is full of explosives. Everyone will die if they set this stuff off."

Trin groaned as if in agony. "Use my cell phone. Call the sheriff."

When Heather took a step toward Trin, the man waved her off with his gun again. "No you don't, missy. I'll do it."

He leaned over Trin and reached for her phone. "Hey, you're not bleeding—"

Heather never saw Trin's hand move. She only saw the man grab his throat and stagger backward as his gun clattered to the floor. In one swift move, Trin had the gun

95

in her hand and was opening the door for the other officers to enter.

The man writhed on the floor, gurgling as he struggled to breathe. "He'll need to go to the hospital," Trin said. "He won't die, but he'll never talk above a whisper. We can still get the names of his partners from him."

"Nice work, Trin." The sheriff watched as his deputies pulled the man to his feet and handcuffed him.

"Whatever you do," Trin advised, "don't flip a light switch. It's probably wired to the explosives."

"By golly, you're right," the sheriff said as he examined the switch just inside the door. "Get him out of here, fellas, and send in the bomb squad."

Heather slipped her arm around Trin as an officer returned her gun. "Careful, honey." Trin cringed. "I think I do have a broken rib. Kevlar stops the penetration but not the impact."

"We definitely don't want Kevlar in our bedroom," Heather quipped as she helped Trin remove the vest.

"Oh, you're something," Trin said, groaning as she bent to kiss the brunette.

##

"We should call everyone and cancel the Cattle Baron's meeting tonight," Heather said as she finished wrapping Trin's ribs. "You're lucky nothing is broken, but this internal hemorrhaging shouldn't be ignored. Your entire torso is black."

"It's just a bruise," Trin argued. "Besides, my . . . uh, girlfriend is a doctor. She'll know what to do."

##

Erin Wade
The Roughneck & the Lady

Trin and Heather sat in silence as the sheriff's deputy drove them to the airport. He helped Trin climb the plane's steps and waited until she settled into the cockpit.

"Ma'am,"—the deputy tipped his hat—"I just want to say we weren't too sure about you at first, but it's been a pleasure working with you."

Trin's grin reflected her appreciation and her pain. "Thank you. Please let me know if you get anything out of him."

At the direction of the tower, Trin taxied the plane to the end of the runway. Heather was continually amazed and proud of the woman she had fallen in love with.

After they were airborne, Trin put the aircraft on autopilot and turned to face Heather. "I'm in no shape to convince you, but I want to say something. We don't need to discuss it right now. I just want you to give it some consideration."

Heather held her breath as she waited for Trin to continue.

"Back there, when I was searching for a word to describe what you are to me, girlfriend seemed so trivial and flippant. We've known each other almost a year and a half. I'm not trying to push you into anything, but . . ." She bowed her head as if searching for the right words. "I would like to take our relationship to a higher level. Maybe get engaged." She groaned as she inhaled deeply. "Jesus, that hurts."

"Since you insisted on flying this plane," Heather said, "I can't give you anything for the pain, but as soon as we're on the ground, I'm knocking you out."

Trin gasped. "Don't make me laugh. It hurts too much."

97

They sat in silence as they approached the Alliance Airport where Trin stored her plane. "Are you going to answer me?"

"You asked me to consider it." A smile played on Heather's lips. "I'm considering it."

Erin Wade
The Roughneck & the Lady

Chapter 18

Heather pulled a chair beside Trin's bed and turned on her Kindle. She sat in silence as she watched her lover sleep. She had heavily sedated Trin and placed ice packs around her torso to lessen the swelling and hemorrhaging. The two hours they had wasted getting home disturbed Heather, but Trin was stubborn and had insisted on getting back to Fort Worth.

News of the arrest of the terrorist was all over the television. There was video of Heather helping Trin from the deputy's car to the plane as the commentator noted that she was Trin's longtime girlfriend. Trin was right; they were a little old to be calling each other girlfriend. Still, she was having trouble reconciling her love for Trin and the deadly lifestyle the blonde lived. It had been difficult enough to think of the dangers of being a roughneck on an oil rig, but add the law enforcement aspect of Trin's career and there was double the danger.

She watched Trin's face. It was relaxed in sleep. The dark eyebrows were perfectly arched, and her lips formed a perpetual smile. Her full lower lip twitched in pain when she moved her shoulders.

Heather stood and bent over Trin, whose long blonde hair fanned out around her perfect face like a halo. There was no doubt about it—Trin Winfield was the most gorgeous creature Heather had ever met. A wave of desire swept over her, and she leaned down to gently kiss Trin's lips.

"What was that?" Trin mumbled, her eyes fluttering open.

"Just what the doctor ordered." Heather laughed. "How are you feeling?"

"Better, but I suspect it's because you have me doped up."

"Slightly," Heather admitted. "I rescheduled the planning meeting for tomorrow night."

Trin frowned and Heather thought she was displeased. "I'm glad one of us has sense enough to make good decisions for me." Trin groaned as she tried to move.

Heather relaxed and began removing the ice packs from Trin's torso. "We need to leave these off for a while."

Trin nodded. "Is there any chance of me getting food? I'm starving, and something smells heavenly."

"That's always a good sign," Heather said, stroking Trin's arm. "I've cooked my famous homemade chicken noodle soup."

"From scratch?"

"Definitely from scratch. You need to stay flat on your back until I bring it to you. Then I'll help you sit up."

"Yes, Dr. Hunter." The laughter in Trin's eyes was replacing the pain.

Heather lay still beside Trin. The warmth of the other woman was enough for now. Just lying close to her was soothing and reassuring. Heather suddenly realized she couldn't imagine her life without Trin Winfield. When Trin moaned and scooted closer to her, Heather suppressed the desire to throw her arm and leg over Trin's body and pull her in tighter.

"Are you awake?" Trin whispered.

"Yes." Heather's soft reply made Trin reach out to embrace her.

"Damn, that hurts." Trin gasped as she let her arm drop back to her side. "How long will this be painful?"

"We're going to start walking this morning," Heather said, her voice still soft and warm. "Most of the stiffness and awful soreness will dissipate as you move about."

"Will I be functional tonight?" Trin asked.

"I think you'll be okay to run the planning session tonight," Heather informed her.

"I'm not thinking about the planning session," Trin said with a seductive smile. "I'm thinking about later . . . when we're home alone."

##

"I want to apologize to all of you for rescheduling this meeting," Trin said as she glanced around the table. All of the committee members were present: Reed Palava, Roxie Royce, Father Provoost, Peter Trotter, local TV anchor Dixie Dancer, and Heather was her co-chair.

Reed spoke up first. "No apology necessary. You're a hero. After what you did to capture the terrorist, the least we could do is reschedule the meeting."

Trin laughed. "The only thing I did was get shot. Not a very heroic thing."

Reed continued. "According to the sheriff in Odessa, you and Heather captured the terrorist threatening to detonate enough explosives to level things for miles."

Roxie stood and began passing out sheets of paper. "I'm glad you're okay, Trin, and thank you for your heroics."

Trin watched as Roxie walked around the table, distributing her handout.

"Reed, I didn't realize you were going to be working with us on the Ball," Trin said to the dark-haired beauty.

"I thought she could be of some assistance," Roxie said. "Her family has made a large contribution to kick off the fundraiser, and she has a lot of good contacts."

101

Trin nodded and scanned the handout Roxie had given her. It was their beginning financial statement. It showed a $250,000 donation from the Palava family.

Trin lifted the statement as if toasting the other woman. "Thank you, Reed."

The committee spent the next hour discussing various fund-raising ideas.

"I want to do something we've never done before," Trin said. "Something that will get this town talking and generate news coverage."

"How about an auction?" Reed suggested.

"What would we auction?" Trin asked

"Ourselves," Reed said, laughing. "Local and national celebrities. Auction off an evening with Trinidad Winfield. I know I'd bid on that."

"So would I," Peter Trotter chimed in.

"My family has ties to several actresses and actors who would donate their time," Reed added. "We could fly the winners to New York to the latest hot play or musical. We need to stipulate that the evening will include dinner and a musical or play in New York, and that the evening ends when the function is over. We wouldn't want anyone to think they were bidding on anything more than a nice social evening."

"I'm certain some of the people Dr. Hunter has made whole will be happy to do her a favor," Roxie added. "Didn't you reattach the leg of that football star two years ago? You know, the quarterback that just won the Most Valuable Player award in the Super Bowl."

"Trigger Carter," Peter said. "He'd donate an evening of his time just to make Heather happy. He'll probably bid on her too."

By the time the evening was over, they had made a list of over 150 celebrities they would ask to be part of the auction.

"Let's pull the A-list from this group and narrow it down to fifty," Trin suggested.

"I bid $50,000 right now for Dr. Hunter," Reed said nonchalantly.

"$100,000," Peter chimed in again.

"$150,000." Father Provoost's quiet bid silenced the planners.

"Well, that settles it." Roxie's sly grin bothered Trin. "Dr. Hunter is definitely on the list."

"How about it, doc?" Roxie winked at Heather. "Are you willing to participate for a good cause?"

"I suppose so," Heather said, her commitment lackluster.

"And you, Trin," Roxie added. "Will you allow yourself to be auctioned off for an evening?"

"Sure, if it will help us add another trauma wing to Heather's hospital." Trin's shrug was followed by a grimace, as the painkillers Heather had prescribed began to wear off.

"We should conclude the meeting," Heather said. "Trin needs to get home and put ice on her injury."

Trin adjourned the meeting, and everyone crowded around her and Heather, trying to make one last point.

Heather felt a firm tug on her arm and turned to face Nathan Provoost.

"Father, I am so glad you're working on our committee," Heather said.

"Bishop Ryker asked me to help," the priest said. "Scott Winfield suggested that it would be good community relations for the church."

"I'm sure it will be," Heather said. "I hope you don't mind."

Nathan scowled. "I've been trying to reach you. You haven't returned any of my calls."

"I'm sorry," Heather said, forcing herself to smile. "I've been incredibly busy."

"Yes, I saw you on the TV news." Nathan shuffled his feet. "They . . . um, called you Trinidad's girlfriend."

Heather's gaze held Father Provoost's. "That was a mistake. They had incorrect information," she replied.

A relieved smile lit the priest's face. "Oh, thank God. I couldn't imagine you as a lesbian."

Heather stood quietly as Trin joined them. "Father, I'm not Trin's girlfriend," she finally said. "I'm her fiancée."

Trin smiled from ear to ear and cupped Heather's elbow as she led her from the meeting room.

"So, you'll marry me?" The pain in Trin's side stopped her from dancing a little jig. "You really will marry me?"

"Of course." Heather laughed. "Did you ever doubt it?"

"I was beginning to wonder." Trin groaned as a stabbing pain pierced her side.

"Someone has to take care of you," Heather whispered, caressing Trin's face and longing to ease her pain. "Let's get you home."

Chapter 19

While Trin recuperated, the committee met at Heather's home weekly. Those approached about the auction agreed to help, and Dixie Dancer had secured the cooperation of all the TV and radio stations to promote the affair. Everyone was excited about the auction.

As promised, Reed had produced four top A-list actors and four A-list actresses for the auction. All had agreed to attend the Cattle Baron's Ball, so they could be auctioned to the highest bidder.

Roxie produced several Cowboy cheerleaders and players for the auction, and local celebrities donated their time.

Father Provoost had asked the diocese's permission to withdraw from the committee, but Bishop Ryker insisted that he participate with the city's wealthiest leaders. "This will be a feather in the church's hat," Ryker explained. "Happy parishioners mean large donations."

Everything was moving ahead as planned, and Heather was pleased with the committee's progress.

"We'll see you all next week," Heather said as she walked the members to the door and bid them goodnight.

Trin followed Heather into their bedroom. "I believe Father Provoost has a crush on you," she said. "He watches your every move. He can't keep his eyes off you. Have you two ever . . . ?"

"No. We've always been friends. He's the hospital chaplain, and I admire him. He's extremely good with people who are grieving and have lost loved ones. I've attended functions with him but never a date or anything like that."

"Hmm. I think he admires more about you than just your bedside manner." Trin wrinkled her nose.

"And I think you're trying to stir up trouble," Heather said, nudging her fiancée. She immediately regretted the playful contact as pain flashed across Trin's face.

"Oh honey, I'm so sorry!"

"It's fine," Trin said, though her weak smile contradicted her words. "I'll be glad when I'm back to normal."

Heather laughed. "Whatever that is for you."

"Oh, don't make me laugh," Trin begged.

Trin was reading the reports her father had given her when Heather finished her shower and returned to their bedroom. She immediately closed the file and placed it on the nightstand.

"That's just one of the many little things I love about you," Heather said, leaning over to kiss her.

"What?"

Heather flashed a glorious smile. "The way you stop reading or whatever you're doing and pay attention to me when I enter the room."

Trin took her hand and pulled her down on the bed. "There's nothing I'd rather do than pay attention to you, honey. Besides, you do the same thing when I enter a room where you are."

"How are you feeling?" Heather asked. "Have the pain meds kicked in?"

"Yes. I was fighting to keep my eyes open until you came to bed. I don't like to fall asleep without you."

Heather slipped beneath the covers and scooted as close to Trin as she dared without hurting her.

"You can come closer," Trin mumbled as she fell asleep.

Heather delighted in the soft warmth of the woman sleeping beside her. She'd thought she had a full life, but she realized how empty it had been without Trin. Trinidad Winfield filled every crevice of her world. *I'm content to simply lie beside her.*

##

Trin walked the four blocks to the hotel where they were meeting and readied the room for her committee. She pulled out her phone to text Heather and realized she had a voice mail from the brunette.

She frowned as she listened to Heather's message telling her she had a hospital emergency and would miss the meeting. Trin had been looking forward to the meeting all day but only because Heather would be there. Loud voices outside the door poured into the room.

"Oh, look, gals. It's our favorite party girl," Roxie said. She was obviously drunk and had brought a group of equally inebriated friends. Reed was at the back of the group.

"Roxie, only the board members can meet in here," Trin said, trying to herd the noisy group back into the hall. Reed slipped around them and stood next to Trin.

"Are you with them?" Trin snapped.

"No! I'm just trying to get in for the meeting."

"Oh, come on, Trin. You know us," someone in the group slurred. "We're your friends. We'll be quiet."

"You can wait in the hallway," Trin said. "Just keep the racket down. We need to work."

The partiers started shushing one another, making the hall sound like a den of snakes. Trin rolled her eyes and closed the door.

They started the meeting without Heather and quickly concluded their business.

"That was fast." Roxie swayed as she stood up and collected her computer bag and purse.

Trin glared at her. "Since you had no financial report for us, we didn't have much to discuss. We can't make informed decisions without financials."

"Oh, is Trinnie Winnie mad at Roxie?" Roxie mocked her.

Trin shook her head and slid her laptop back into her computer bag. "You need to grow up, Roxie. This is no place for a bunch of drunks."

Roxie opened the door, and the group of partiers swarmed inside as the committee members hurried out. "Come with us, Trin," one of them called. "You used to party with us."

"In college," Trin huffed. "We're adults now, with responsibilities. I'm going home."

"What's wrong?" Roxie snorted. "Are you afraid the good doctor will get mad at you, or worse yet, cut you off? You're so whipped, Trinidad Winfield."

Trin leaned into Roxie's face and sneered. "Every night, Roxie. Every night."

The silence in the room made Trin turn around. Heather was standing behind her.

Heather had overheard the bulk of the conversation. She quickly assessed the situation. She slipped her arm through Trin's and tiptoed to kiss her cheek. "Looks like I've missed the meeting."

A miserable expression clouded Trin's face. She knew she shouldn't have used their private life to torment Roxie. "We've adjourned."

"Good, because I'm dying to get you home alone." The sensual tone of Heather's voice was earthshaking.

Roxie shot her a "go-to-hell" look and stomped from the room.

##

"What was that all about?" Heather asked as she pulled her car from the parking garage.

"Roxie being her most obnoxious," Trin huffed. "I wish we could replace her on the committee."

"You can't do that. She's my mother's new best friend."

"Seriously? Your mother doesn't like me, but she's friends with Roxie?"

"Oh, my mother adores you now that she knows you're someone important."

"The only person I want to adore me is you, honey." Trin reached across the seat to massage Heather's neck and shoulders. "How was your day?"

Heather leaned her cheek down to rub it against Trin's hand. "Successful. Two patients have two hands and a thumb back where they belong."

"Heather, please discourage your mother from getting mixed up with Roxie. She can be trouble."

"How?"

"Her family has always managed to make it go away, but she's been arrested for hard drugs and marijuana more times than I can count. That's just one of the many reasons I stopped associating with her."

"I'll talk to Mother, although I doubt it will do any good. She is so taken with Reed and Roxie it's disgusting. She never introduces poor Reed as Reed Palava. She always calls her Princess Palava."

Heather's stomach reminded her that she had skipped lunch to do surgery. "As much as I hate to, do you want to pick up dinner at a drive-through?"

"I made a casserole after you left for work this morning," Trin proudly announced.

"What kind? Not that I'm picky. I just want to know what I have to look forward to."

"Chicken and broccoli. We can pop it into the oven while we shower."

"Umm, have I told you lately that I love you?"

##

Trin placed the casserole in the oven and joined Heather in the shower. The hot water felt good on her back.

"Let me wash your hair," Heather volunteered. "I know it still hurts to raise your arms above your head."

"It feels better every day," Trin said as Heather shampooed her hair. "I should be a hundred percent in a few more days."

"A few more weeks, maybe. Your bruising is almost gone entirely, but your muscles are still sore, and you have some inflammation."

Trin wrapped her arms around Heather and pulled her against her. "You feel so good," she whispered.

Heather hugged her and Trin yelped.

"Maybe I'm not as healed as I thought," she said, chuckling.

Chapter 20

Father Nathan Provoost sat on the front row of pews. He thought about praying. Then he thought about a good stiff drink. He checked the time on his iPhone and decided to leave for the day. There was a shot of Jack Daniels calling his name.

He removed his collar and walked the three blocks to the bar and grill. The nice secluded table in the dark corner was a perfect place to drown his sorrows.

How can a woman as gorgeous and feminine as Heather Hunter be a lesbian? And then place her with Trinidad Winfield, who has done so much good work in the church. God must have a twisted sense of humor.

By his third drink, Nathan was beginning to question the existence of God. He tried to recall if God had ever answered any of his prayers. *Nope!* He definitely had not.

The entire world was unraveling. Women priests, homosexual men promoted to bishop. Father Ryker raging from the pulpit against women marrying women and the abomination of the LGBT elements in society. Worst of all, the woman he worshipped had informed him she is in love with another woman.

Suddenly, his stomach heaved. He barely made it to the men's room before he threw up. He washed his face with cold water and wondered at what point love turned into hate.

Who am I kidding? I could never hate Heather. She's too beautiful, too perfect, too good.

Too unattainable, another little voice hissed.

Nathan returned to his table and ordered another drink as a plan was forming in his mind. He would have Heather Hunter. God be damned!

##

"How would you feel about opening an office in my building for the Cattle Baron's Ball?" Trin asked Heather as they dressed for the day.

"We need to establish one someplace," Heather said. "Just to handle the huge volume of mail we're receiving. Reed's idea for an auction was pure genius."

Trin secured her shoulder holster and reached for her gun on the top shelf of their closet. "Everyone wants to attend. We'll discuss another location for the Ball at the meeting tonight. Roxie tells me we've already oversold our original ballroom."

All thoughts of the Ball left Heather's mind as she watched the blonde secure the Glock in her holster. "Why are you wearing your gun today?"

"Swede and I are visiting the Joshua wells today. There has been some minor vandalism on a couple of them. Dad wants me to check out the damage."

Heather slid her arms around Trin's waist and hugged her tightly. She was pleased when the blonde embraced her without flinching. "Your body is almost healed."

Trin moaned softly in her ear. "Umm, maybe we should try it out tonight."

"Just to make sure." Heather raised her lips to Trin's.

##

Trin shut out the babble from the conversations around her as she surveyed each member of her committee. She often wondered what made people volunteer their time for community projects. She knew that most of her members had ulterior motives for being there.

Reed was there surreptitiously trying to convince Heather to fly to Iran and perform surgery on her mother.

Peter Trotter was trying to curry favor with Heather.

Father Provoost hoped to secure donations to build a gym onto the church.

Dixie Dancer was trying to increase her TV station's ratings.

Roxie's ultimate goal was to break up Trin and Heather.

Heather's goal was to build a new trauma unit onto her hospital.

My goal is to help Heather achieve hers.

Dixie had done a remarkable job as the committee's public relations director. Thanks to her publicity and promotion of those being auctioned, they had sold all 500 of their $1,000 tickets in the first two weeks. They had a long list of wealthy people requesting tickets. Many of the requests came from the groupies who followed the top-name celebrities being auctioned. Tonight, they would decide whether to keep it exclusive or open the event up to more people.

Roxie's software had separated the ticket requests into "can afford to bid" and "cannot afford to bid" categories. "We must keep out the riffraff," she'd said, smirking.

Trin tried to suppress the grin that covered her face when Heather entered the room. Then Heather smiled at her, and everyone else ceased to exist. Heather took her seat beside Trin, brushing her hand across the blonde's back as she sat down.

Trin called the meeting to order. Roxie reported that they had over two million dollars in their bank account, thanks to ticket sales, Reed's donation, and other generous donors in Iran.

Trin cringed. She didn't like accepting funds from a country that had so little regard for women.

Reed presented signed contracts and releases from those who had agreed to be auctioned.

Dixie gave them a rundown on the publicity she had scheduled for the upcoming month. "Heather and Trin, I have several requests from talk show hosts to interview you. Are you willing to make yourselves available?"

"As long as my schedule allows," Heather said.

"Same here," Trin added.

"I've had inquiries from a couple of national talk shows to interview you both as a couple," Dixie said. "Would it be possible for you to set aside a week for a whirlwind tour of the talk show circuit?"

"Let us discuss that," Trin answered. "We can let you know tomorrow."

"Is that necessary?" Roxie snapped. "I mean, we've already sold out our tickets and have a waiting list. Why send them off together when we need them here?"

"I'm not thinking about ticket sales," Dixie replied. "I'm thinking about donations and accepting bids over the internet."

"The internet?" Father Provoost gasped. "That could be dangerous."

"Nonsense," Dixie blurted out. "I mean, there are ways to set up security and all kinds of background checks before accepting a person as a bidder. Roxie is our resident computer genius. I'm certain she can set up a safe bidding situation for us."

"Yes . . . I could do that," Roxie said as a wicked smile danced on her lips.

"There are companies that specialize in online auctions," Peter pointed out. "They're insured and bonded against hackers."

By the time the meeting ended, they had agreed to locate a larger facility to host the gala, sell 250 more tickets at $2,000 each, and Peter would investigate the possibility of an online auction.

Trin adjourned the meeting and headed for the door, eager to get home with Heather. She rolled her eyes when she realized that Peter Trotter had cornered Heather.

"Heather, I need to talk with you," Peter said, catching Heather's arm and pulling her away from the others.

"Okay."

"I haven't performed a surgery in over a year," Peter fumed. "I understand that it's because you told everyone not to let me operate on patients."

Heather glared at the man. "We can discuss this in my office in the morning. This is neither the time nor the place to have this talk."

"I can't believe it's true," Peter wheedled. "I have such high regard for you."

"It's true. I've had several discussions with you about your sloppy surgical techniques, and honestly, the hospital can't afford any more malpractice lawsuits caused by you."

"Are you serious?" Peter raised his voice.

"As I said, this is not the place to have this discussion. My office, nine in the morning." Heather whirled around, searching for Trin.

Chapter 21

Heather lay on her back reliving her night with Trin. The soft singing coming from the bathroom made her smile. Trin always sang in the shower. Heather listened to the words. She wondered if Trin was just making them up or if someone had written a song about a woman named Heather.

Oh Heather, honey, warm as the sunshine.
Oh Heather, honey, your love is so-oh fine.

Heather would always treasure the way Trin's face lit up when she joined the blonde in the shower.

##

Heather watched Trin secure her gun. "I can't even tell you how my heart stops every time you strap on that gun."

"Believe me, honey, Lucy has saved my life on more than one occasion."

"Lucy? You call your handgun Lucy?" Heather laughed out loud. Trin leaned down and kissed her.

"Are you ready for your meeting with Peter this morning?"

Heather sighed. "As ready as I'll ever be. We're trying to find a job for him that doesn't require the use of a scalpel."

"Why don't you simply let him go? That would effectively end his career. No one would hire him if your hospital fired him."

"Dad has strong ties with Peter's father." Heather told Trin the story of Jarrod's heroic wartime rescue of Eric Hunter.

"Ah, yes. That's a tough one," Trin said, frowning.

Heather backed up to Trin so she could zip her dress and then turned in her lover's arms for a kiss. "I just want to go on record as saying that on a scale of one to ten, you were a nine last night."

Trin's smile widened as she pulled Heather in for one more kiss. "Only a nine?"

"I have to leave you some room for improvement," Heather said as she picked up her bag and laptop. "It makes you try harder. Don't forget we have to select our costumes for the Ball."

"Whose idea was it to turn it into a masquerade ball?" Trin grumbled as she followed Heather out the door.

Peter Trotter was pacing in the hallway outside Heather's door when she stepped from the elevator. She looked at her watch then at Peter. "You're thirty minutes early."

"I know," Peter barked. "I want to get this over with."

Heather unlocked her door, and Peter followed her into her office.

She sat down in her chair, unlocked her lap drawer, and pulled out Peter's thick file. She waited for him to begin the conversation.

"As you know," he mumbled, "a doctor who isn't performing surgeries makes little money."

Heather nodded but said nothing.

"I need to make more money," Peter said. "I'm beginning to have financial problems. You need to schedule at least one surgery a week for me."

"How would you feel about heading up our fundraising division, Peter?"

"What would I be paid?"

"The highest annual salary you made as a surgeon minus the cost of your malpractice insurance." Heather opened his file and double-checked her figures.

"I need double that amount," Peter declared. "I would be in a higher pay bracket if you hadn't banned me from the operating room."

"Peter, you know why you were taken off the surgery rotation." Heather's patience was wearing thin.

"I had a few slips, but that's no reason to take away my livelihood."

"It has nothing to do with your livelihood," Heather pointed out. "It has to do with the number of patients you have crippled and maimed.

"The hospital can no longer afford your malpractice insurance and certainly can't afford another lawsuit because of your ineptness.

"Some of your so-called slips border on criminal negligence. Neither I nor the other doctors on staff will vouch for you in the future."

Peter clenched his fist as he rose from his chair to stand over Heather. "After the sacrifice my father made for Eric, you would treat me like this?"

"Peter, the board is offering you an excellent administrative salary, better than any other hospital pays its fundraising director."

"I'll have my father speak with Eric," Peter roared. "He'll stop this."

"The board's decision is final, Peter. Take it or leave it."

"We'll see about that." Peter stormed from the room, slamming the door behind him.

Chapter 22

"How do I look?" Trin said as she examined herself in the full-length mirror.

"Like I shouldn't be letting you leave the house." Heather tried to catch the breath Trin had taken away. "You are one gorgeous woman, Trinidad Winfield."

"Not to be conceited," Trin said, grinning, "but we do make an awesome-looking couple. Do you think your mother will approve?"

"Ask me if I care," Heather huffed. "That balloon burst a long time ago, when I realized she valued money over people. I'll never forgive her for what she did to you."

"Let it go, honey." Trin bent to touch her lips lightly. "I didn't smear your lipstick."

Heather slipped her arm through Trin's. "I hope my mother manages to stay sober tonight. She can be quite charming when she isn't drinking." *Which isn't very often.*

"Well, I'm glad it's just the four of us for dinner. It'll give me a chance to get to know your parents better."

"You seem to know my father pretty well. He truly likes you, even when you were just a roughneck."

Trin laughed. "Your father is a true gentleman and an excellent doctor. I like him a lot. He reminds me of my dad."

"They're here," Melody announced. "Thank heavens they drove Heather's car and not that awful Jeep Trin drives. I don't want the neighbors seeing it parked in our driveway."

Eric watched his wife and wondered when she had become such a snob. He walked to the front door and greeted both women with a warm hug.

"Wow! I'm not sure my old heart can take dining with three beautiful women at once," he said.

Melody joined them in the foyer and offered each woman a stiff hug. "We are delighted to have you in our home," she said, smiling at Trin.

"Thank you, Mrs. Hunter. I appreciate the invitation."

Melody led them into the study. "Please join me in a drink while Mrs. Hodges gets dinner on the table."

"You two have caused quite an uproar with your auction for the Cattle Baron's Ball." Eric chuckled.

"That's all they talk about at the club," Melody chimed in as she refilled her wine glass. "How ingenious the two of you are and that this will be the greatest Ball of all time."

"As much as I'd like to take the credit," Trin said, "it was Reed Palava's idea."

"You should just be quiet and accept the credit," Melody said.

"That's not our way," Trin quipped. "We'd much rather give Reed the credit."

"But you two are the movers and shakers," Melody insisted.

"No, Mother, it's the entire committee. Every one of our members makes strong contributions to what we're doing."

"Even Peter Trotter?" Melody snarled, taking a long swig of her wine.

"It looks like Mrs. Hodges has dinner ready," Eric said as the housekeeper returned. He gave silent thanks for the woman's timeliness.

"Iced tea for me, Mrs. Hodges." Eric placed his hand over his wine glass. "I'm on call tonight."

"I'd prefer iced tea too," Trin said, and Heather agreed.

"Since I've started with wine," Melody giggled, "I'll just stay with that."

"Dinner was excellent, Mrs. Hodges," Trin said finishing her entrée.

"Wait until you taste her Brazilian flan." Eric praised the woman who had cooked for them since Heather was sixteen.

"Who's your historical character for the Ball?" Trin asked Eric as they settled in the study and Melody insisted on serving the coffee.

Eric chortled. "I'm thinking Doc Holliday."

"What about you, Mrs. Hunter? What's your costume?" Trin tried to hide her surprise as she watched Melody fill her coffee cup with brandy.

"Marie Antoinette," Melody said, beaming. "I always wanted to be queen."

"She was beheaded, Mother. When she was told her subjects were starving and had no bread, her heartless reply was, 'Let them eat cake.' You should pick a historical figure that was more compassionate and popular."

"Perhaps you're right, dear." Melody sat down and sipped her drink before addressing Trin. "How long have you been . . . dating my daughter?"

Here it comes, Heather thought.

"Mother, you know Trin and I have been together almost two years."

"What I really want to know is when are you going to ask my daughter to marry you?"

Trin placed her coffee cup on the end table beside her chair. "I have asked your daughter to marry me. She's thinking about it."

Melody glared at Heather. "Why would you have to think about it? She's a Winfield!"

An uneasy silence settled over the room as Heather tried to control her temper.

Eric cleared his throat. "It's getting late, and Heather has an early surgery in the morning. We should call it a night."

Trin thanked her hostess for a lovely evening and followed Heather out the door.

"Trin, I'm so sorry," Heather blurted out as they fastened their seatbelts.

"Shush." Trin leaned over and kissed Heather. "You have nothing to be sorry for. We only have to answer for our own actions, not those of others. But . . . I would like to know when we might get married."

"I . . ." Heather tried to suppress the image of Trin's hand as she'd sutured it back onto her wrist. "No matter how hard I try, I can't silence that little voice in the back of my mind that keeps reminding me of the dangers of your profession. I . . . I don't want to be a widow, Trin. You're a Winfield. You will always be a Winfield. Winfields are—"

"I don't want you to marry me because I'm a Winfield," Trin said, nibbling her bottom lip. "I also don't want you to refuse to marry me because I'm a Winfield. My name doesn't matter. What matters is, do you love me enough to forsake all others?"

"Yes," Heather whispered.

"Good. Now take me home and let me work on getting a ten."

Heather's laughter was interrupted by the ringing of Trin's cell phone.

##

"Trin Winfield... Yes, I know where that is. Have you called for ambulances?... I'm on my way."

"What's wrong?" Heather tried to hide the fear that was knotting in her stomach.

122

"One of our new rigs in Joshua has been destroyed by explosives. They're trying to cap the flare, and several employees have been burned.

"When we're drilling a new well," Trin explained, "we bring in mobile homes to house our employees. We keep at least a dozen men on site at all times until all the safety protocols are in place and working properly."

Heather made it home in record time, and they dashed into the house. Trin ran to their bedroom and traded her dress for jeans, boots, and a Henley. She grabbed the keys to her Jeep and holstered her Glock.

She was surprised to find Heather had changed, grabbed her black doctor's bag, and was waiting for her at the door. "This will be dangerous," Trin said, grimacing. "You should—"

"Go with you," Heather barked. "People will need my help. Half the battle with burn victims is to make them comfortable to keep them from going into shock." She held up her black bag. "This is full of morphine. I can save lives, Trin."

While Trin drove, Heather called her father. "Dad, there has been an explosion at one of Trin's wells. We're headed there now. About a dozen people are burned. Would you make certain the trauma units are staffed and ready to go when they arrive?"

"There." Trin nodded toward the distant horizon, where the bright orange glow from the blazing gas well lit up the night sky as if the world were on fire.

As they drove closer to the well, a line of traffic impeded their progress.

"Where are all these people coming from?" Heather asked as the air became heavy with smoke and cinders.

"We're evacuating all the homes within one mile of the site," Trin said. "Unfortunately, a 240-unit apartment complex for senior citizens is only a few hundred yards from the well. They all have to be relocated until we cap the escaping gas."

The scene around the blazing well was chaotic. Police and fire departments from Burleson, Joshua, Cleburne, and Crowley were circling the blaze like bees around a magnolia tree.

Trin turned to Heather. "This is a cluster f—"

"Go," Heather yelled over the noise. "Do whatever you need to do. I can take care of myself."

Trin grabbed a hardhat and a high-powered megaphone from the back of her Jeep and climbed onto the hood. She began directing the emergency vehicles to where they were most needed.

Heather pulled her long, dark hair into a low ponytail and ran to the closest ambulance. "I'm Dr. Heather Hunter from Saint Patrick's Episcopal Hospital," she said. "We need to line up all the ambulances and set up a triage area to stabilize the burn victims before transporting them to the hospital where a trauma unit is standing by."

The ambulance driver nodded and ran to the next ambulance to spread the information. Within minutes, the ambulance medics were evaluating the injured and directing Heather to the most severe cases.

The second ambulance she climbed into housed a man burned beyond recognition. He was howling in pain. Heather moved quickly to inject him with morphine to ease his agony and gave him a shot of the strongest antibiotic she had to lessen the chance of infection. She knew she had to intubate him to insure he would be able to breath.

"Doc . . ."—a bloody hand grasped Heather's wrist— "My wife and baby . . . tell them I love them."

When the man's hand dropped away from her arm, he left the skin from his fingers hanging there. She searched the pain-glazed blue eyes of the man and realized it was Swede. "Oh God," she whispered before turning to the ambulance driver. "Get this man to the hospital, now!"

She called Eric and described the extent of Swede's injuries. "Dad, spare nothing on him. We've got to save him. He has a wife and small baby. And, Daddy . . . he's Trin's best friend."

Trin looked up as the last ambulance pulled away with the injured. She searched the faces of the first responders, trying to locate Heather. She finally saw her on her knees, cleaning the wound of a policeman who had been struck by a falling pipe.

The officer moaned as Heather secured a clean bandage to his forehead. She touched his cheek and assured him he was fine.

Trin had never loved the doctor as much as she did at that moment. Dark tendrils of hair had slipped from Heather's ponytail and danced like smoke around her soot-smudged face. Trin thought she had never looked more beautiful.

"Winfield, we've got to divert and flare the well's natural gas stream," the foreman of the company's damage control team yelled.

"Do it," Trin commanded.

"We don't have a lease on the adjoining property, and that's where we need to divert it." The man flapped his arms in frustration.

"Just do it," Trin yelled. "Let me worry about the property owners."

The foreman signaled his team, and they loaded into their trucks and drove a half mile from the well.

"We're running out of water," the fire marshal from Cleburne informed Trin.

Trin rubbed her eyes. "Over there. There's a small lake. Draw water from it."

"But we don't have permission—"

"Now you do," Trin bellowed. "I authorize it."

The rising sun cast long shadows over the five-acres of devastation. Trin thought it looked like some of the bombed war zones she had been in during her Afghanistan tour.

Flames were still spewing from the well and would be until the containment crew diverted the gas away from the wellhead. They would have to wait a few days for the area to be safe enough for a crew to cap the well.

Heather was still on her knees, packing her paraphernalia into her bag. Trin moved to stand beside her.

Heather tilted her head to look up at the tall roughneck, as Trin reached out her hand to pull the doctor to her feet. She clasped Trin's hand as she steadied herself on legs that were weak with exhaustion.

"I need to get to the hospital," Heather rasped. "They'll need my help."

"Honey, you're exhausted." Trin pulled Heather into her arms and held her against her chest. "Let's call your father and see if they need you."

"What about you?" Heather asked as she overcame the desire to lean on Trin. "How long must you stay here?"

Trin shook her head. "I've done all I can do. Everything's as under control as we can get it until we cap the well, and our specialty crew is working on that now."

"Let's go home," Heather mumbled as Trin tucked a loose strand of hair behind the doctor's ear.

##

Heather called the hospital for a report on the injured. Lori gave her good reports on most of the victims. "You should talk to your dad about one of the badly burned men," she said. "Hang on."

When Eric got on the line, his tired voice made the hair stand up on the back of Heather's neck. "Your friend is alive, but just barely."

126

"Do I need to come to the hospital?" Heather's voice wavered. "Can I do anything?"

"No, he's with our top burn specialists. They've put him into a coma to help deal with the severe pain. They submerged him and cleaned his burns. They're debriding him now. Your shot of morphine and intubation is probably what kept him from dying of sheer agony. Your intubation tube is all that kept his trachea from closing completely and choking him to death."

"Dad—"

"Don't worry, baby. I'm sitting with him around-the-clock until he's out of danger. And Heather, I'm so proud of you. All the medics are singing your praises. From all the reports I'm getting, you and your roughneck must be one hell of a team."

"Thanks, Dad." Heather glanced at her exhausted partner. "We are one hell of a team."

"Everyone is going to live," Heather informed Trin as she disconnected the call.

Trin took her hand. "Thanks to you. You're even more impressive than I ever imagined, Dr. Hunter."

She glanced sideways when Heather failed to respond. The exhausted doctor was sound asleep.

##

Heather gradually became aware of her surroundings. She vaguely recalled Trin supporting her as they walked to their bedroom. The sound of Trin singing in the shower made her happy until she remembered the night they'd just lived through. *Swede! I haven't told Trin about Swede.*

"Good morning, my little ragamuffin Trin's lips brushed hers. "You're welcome to the shower."

Heather moved and realized that her body was covered in grit and soot. She opened her eyes. Trin was clean, but her cheeks were red and blistered from the fire. "I have some ointment for your face," she croaked. She cleared her throat and tried to speak again.

"Here, honey, drink this." Trin handed her a bottle of water. "You're parched."

Heather pulled herself to a sitting position and took a sip of the water. Then she drank the rest of it, trying to hydrate her tongue and throat. Her lips were dry and cracked.

"I've never been involved in anything like that," she said. "I could tell by the way you took control that you're used to handling dire situations."

"That was my first for Winfield Oil and Gas," Trin said, shrugging, "but I handled similar situations in Afghanistan." She didn't add that she had caused similar situations for the enemy in that country.

Chapter 23

"We can ride together," Trin said as she watched Heather put on lipstick. "I'll check on our employees while you make your rounds."

"We can visit your employees together." Heather tiptoed and placed a soft kiss on Trin's lips. "Your employees are now my patients." She wiped her lipstick from Trin's lips with her thumbs.

"I'd like that. It'll probably make our employees more confident that they are getting the best treatment possible."

Heather found her black bag. "I'll need to refill this after last night."

Heather searched for the words to tell Trin about Swede's condition. She knew no easy way to break the bad news. She waited until Trin had backed the Jeep from their driveway and placed her hand on Trin's thigh.

"Baby, I need to tell you about Swede before you see him."

She felt the shudder that ran through Trin's body and hesitated, giving the blonde time to prepare herself for the news.

"Swede was the most severely injured man I treated last night." Heather watched Trin's jaw muscle tighten as she clenched her teeth. "He's in a medically induced coma but stable."

"How much of his body is burned?" Trin fought back tears. "Is he wrapped in gauze like a mummy?"

"Eighty percent of his body is burned. Some areas are burned more severely than others. He's wrapped in see-through bandages, so we can watch his progress.

"I want you to be prepared when you see him. He's connected to several machines to keep him alive. We're pumping fluids into him because vital moisture is seeping from his body. It's essential we stop that and balance his hydration."

Heather watched Trin as she mulled the information.

"What are his chances?"

"I'm not certain. I spoke with Dad for a few minutes, but he was called into surgery. We should check on Swede first."

"While he's still alive." Trin's husky voice was barely above a whisper.

Trin stood in the doorway of the intensive care unit and watched as silent tears rolled down the cheeks of Swede's wife, Reba. She couldn't touch her husband; he was too badly burned, his entire body encased in clear plastic bandages. She could only look at him and try to be brave.

Trin walked into the hallway. She leaned her back against the wall and closed her eyes as she tried to breath past the weight crushing her chest. *God, why Swede? He's one of the truly good guys.*

Soft fingers caressed her cheek, and Trin opened her eyes to gaze into Heather's soulful brown ones. "I'm so sorry," Heather murmured. "We're doing everything humanly possible to save him."

"If you save him, what will he be? What will his life be like? Were his eyes affected?" She wanted to fall into Heather's arms and find comfort in the doctor's softness.

Heather seemed to realize her need and pulled Trin into a tight hug. "He may live, but I can't give you any guarantees on his quality of life."

Trin leaned her head on Heather's shoulder and found a semblance of solace in her lover's arms.

Dr. Eric Hunter cleared his throat to make his presence known to the two women locked in an embrace outside ICU.

Trin stood tall, wiping tears from her eyes as she greeted Eric. "Dr. Hunter, thank you for all you and the hospital are doing for Swede."

"Heather deserves the thanks. She's the one who has made certain he has the treatment he needs."

Eric placed a hand on Trin's shoulder. "He isn't out of the woods yet. I'm going to check his chart and look at him. Do you and Heather want to join me?"

As Trin and the doctors entered ICU, Reba tried to force a smile and failed. She burst into tears and threw herself into Trin's arms. "He loved working with you, and look what it got him," she said, lashing out at Trin.

"Reba, I'm so sorry. I would trade places with him in a heartbeat if I could." Trin held the woman and let her cry until her tears became dry sobs.

"I didn't mean to take out my anger on you," Reba said. "I know you loved him too."

Trin quickly corrected her. "*Love* him. I love him."

##

Trin and Heather visited the other Winfield employees. Swede was the only one suffering life-threatening injuries.

"I feel so guilty," Trin admitted as they entered Heather's office. "I keep thinking I should have done something better. Provided additional security. Looked harder for the terrorists who are attacking us. Added—"

"Shush." Heather's lips vibrated against Trin's as she pressed their mouths together. "You did everything you could."

"I don't know what I'd do without you." Trin pulled Heather closer. "You're the only thing keeping me sane right now."

Heather's intercom clicked as the receptionist interrupted them. "Dr. Hunter, Mrs. Southerland is here to see you."

Trin opened the door and ushered Reba into Heather's office.

"I hope I'm not interrupting anything," Reba said.

"No, we were just discussing treatment for our employees," Trin answered. "I'll leave you two alone. I'm sure you have questions for Dr. Hunter."

"You can stay. I'm just trying to figure out my life for the next few months. With the baby and all." Reba fought back tears.

"Dr. Hunter can answer your medical questions," Trin said. "I want you to know that all expenses will be covered by Winfield Oil. Swede will remain on full pay. If you need anything, just call me." She handed Reba a business card. "The bottom number is my personal cell phone."

For the first time, the hint of a smile crossed Reba's lips. "Thank you."

Trin turned to speak to Heather when her cell phone rang. She answered it and began talking to her father as she opened the door. She blew a kiss to Heather and left the office.

"Reba, I want to assure you that your husband is in good hands," Heather said as the door clicked to a close. "We've called in the top burn specialist in the country."

"I have no doubt you're doing all you can do," Reba said. "I have some rather personal questions to ask you. Please give me straight answers. Don't soft pedal it."

Heather's stomach turned. She was certain she knew the subject of the conversation. "I'll give you honest answers, Reba."

132

"You knew Swede before the accident. You know what a virile man he was." Reba stopped talking, as if searching for the right words to continue. "His entire body is horribly burned. I overheard a nurse say that his clothes burned into his skin, and his flesh was falling from the bone."

"It's a common practice to debride a badly burned patient," Heather replied. "We cut away the dead skin to prevent infection and to allow the living tissue to adequately heal."

"The nurse went on to say that all the soft tissue on Swede was incinerated." Reba squeezed her eyes closed to hold back the tears burning behind her lids.

"My question, Dr. Hunter, is . . . is my husband's manhood still intact?"

Heather tried to think of an easy way to answer Reba's question but there was none. "No. The fire—"

"Castrated him?" Reba sobbed.

"Yes."

##

After Reba left her office, Heather said a silent prayer to a God she sometimes doubted but still felt compelled to plead with for divine intervention. Swede would need a miracle.

Her cell phone announced a text message from Trin. "Don't forget we have a board meeting tonight."

"I love you," she responded. She had a desperate urge to hold Trin. Not to make love, but to feel her strength and warmth and know the blonde was safe in her arms. "See you at six."

##

Trin listed her committee members on her laptop as they filed into the meeting room: Reed, Roxie, Father Provoost, Peter Trotter, Dixie Dancer, and Heather. Heather took her place beside Trin.

"We're a month away from the Ball," Trin announced. "We need to go over everything to make certain we've covered all our bases."

Roxie reported they had $12 million in their account, thanks to generous donations from the board members and ticket sales.

Reed verified confirmations from all but five of the A-list celebrities they had invited to participate in the auction. "Everyone is excited about the event."

Father Provoost announced that the Ball had been moved to the Magnolia Ballroom of the Sheraton Hotel to accommodate the additional attendees.

According to Peter, the cost of the online auction was prohibitive on such short notice. "The company said they could have it ready to go for next year, if we give them the go-ahead now."

The board agreed to visit the possibility of the online auction after the Ball was over and they could assess the cost effectiveness of it.

Dixie reported that she had interviews scheduled on national TV stations for Trin and Heather.

"I would like to make one request," Father Provoost said. "Would it be possible to play down the fact that you're a lesbian couple?"

Trin and Heather stared at the priest in shocked silence.

"I've never hidden the fact that I'm a lesbian," Trin said. "I'm not going to hide it now."

Father Provoost addressed Heather. "That is true, but I believe Dr. Hunter has just recently come out of the closet and—"

"That's not true," Heather said, trying to suppress her anger. "I have never hidden my predilection for women. I don't advertise my sexual preferences, but I'm certainly not ashamed of the fact that I'm with Trin."

"Gosh, Heather, does that mean I can wear the T-shirt that says, 'I'm with Her' on national TV?" Trin joked.

"This isn't funny," the priest yelled. "You two could cost us the support of all the Republicans, and they're the people with the money in this town."

Trin stood. "Perhaps you should resign from this board if we make you so uncomfortable."

"No, no." Provoost became more anxious. "I'm just thinking about what is best for the image of the Ball."

Reed tapped her coffee cup with a spoon. Silence fell over the room. "I have never seen Dr. Hunter or Trin be anything but gracious and impeccably behaved. I think it's ludicrous that you would even insinuate that they would behave in a manner that would be detrimental to this board or the Cattle Baron's Ball."

"I'd stake my reputation on them being the best representatives for this board," Dixie added.

"Do we need to put this to a vote?" Trin said, glaring at Father Provoost.

"No, that's not necessary," the priest mumbled. "Obviously, I'm the only one with concerns. Just remember, sin is sin no matter how one sugarcoats it."

"True, Father," Trin glared at the man, "but Jesus didn't die on the cross so you could beat others on the head with it."

Trin waited until everyone left the room, and then she turned to Heather. "What a day. Would you be open to leaving your car in the parking garage overnight and riding home with me? I need you with me."

Heather touched Trin's hand. "Of course I will. I don't want to leave your side either."

Heather held Trin's hand in her lap as the blonde pulled her car out of the garage.

"What did Reba say today?" Trin asked.

Heather related their conversation and waited for Trin to comment.

Trin exhaled slowly. "Poor Swede. If he makes it, their lives will never be the same."

"As you've shown me,"—Heather squeezed Trin's hand—"there are many ways to please a woman."

Trin snickered. "I don't know about straight people. I'm certainly not going to guess about their sex lives. I just know I'm devastated over what has happened to Swede and Reba. Dammit, Heather, I feel so guilty."

"Baby, you weren't even there when the attack happened. You couldn't have prevented it."

"I have to make certain Reba and the baby are provided for and set up a college fund for the child." Trin began listing the things she could do to help compensate Reba and her baby for Swede's injuries. "My mind can't let go of the way she looked the first time she saw her husband in ICU."

Trin pulled through a Burger Barn and picked up their dinner. "Not our most nutritious meal," she said, attempting a grin, "but I don't feel like cooking, and I know you don't."

"Not really," Heather murmured. "I don't have much of an appetite."

Chapter 24

They ate their burgers, quietly discussing the Ball. Both had been shocked at Nathan Provoost's comments.

"You never dated him?" Trin asked.

"Not really. We often were the plus-one for each other at fund-raisers, hospital receptions, church functions. That sort of thing. I've always thought of Nathan as a friend."

Trin frowned. "Did he ever indicate he wanted something more?"

"Of course," Heather huffed, "men always do that, even priests. When I started dating you, Mother did everything she could to force me to consider Nathan as a husband."

They sat for a long time without talking. Heather had never seen Trin so subdued. She realized her fiancée was troubled over recent events and her inability to catch the terrorists targeting Winfield Oil.

The hospital ring tone sent Heather scurrying for her cell phone. She cringed at the thought of leaving Trin alone. She knew the blonde needed her.

She listened as Lori described the reaction a patient was having to the antibiotics they were taking to assure the body's acceptance of a recent skin graft.

Trin motioned toward the bathroom and headed off in that direction as Heather continued to talk. She prescribed another antibiotic and asked if her father was at the hospital.

"No," Lori replied. "He performed two surgeries today. He was pretty exhausted, so I told him to go home, that I would call him if he was needed."

"I don't know how the trauma wing would operate without you." Heather thanked her, disconnected the call, and hurried to join Trin in the hot shower.

##

"I love the way our bodies feel together after a shower," Trin murmured as she turned out the lights and snuggled into Heather's arms. "You feel so . . . actually, nothing in the world compares to how good you feel naked."

Heather held her, stroking her back and cuddling her. She knew Trin needed her strength. A shiver ran through Trin's body as her tears began to fall onto Heather's breasts.

"It's okay, baby," Heather whispered. "Everything's going to be okay."

"He doesn't even look human, Heather."

"I know, honey." Heather pulled her closer as sobs racked Trin's body.

Trin clutched Heather to her like a lifeline and buried her face in the softness between the brunette's breasts.

Heather kissed the top of Trin's head and cooed soothing words. Eventually, Trin's sobs lessened until she fell asleep wondering when Heather had become her rock, the foundation on which she had built her happiness.

##

"I'll take you to your car." Trin placed a sweet kiss on Heather's lips. "Thank you for being there for me last night."

Heather touched Trin's cheek with her fingertips. "I'll always be here for you. I love you."

Trin leaned her forehead against Heather's. "I love you more than you will ever know."

Chapter 25

Reba was in Swede's room when Heather and Trin arrived. The dark circles beneath her eyes were a testimony to her lack of sleep. She smiled when her two friends entered the room.

"He's the same." Reba's voice wavered.

Heather checked Swede's chart. "We need to do a couple of unpleasant procedures this morning," she informed Reba. "Have you had breakfast?"

Reba shook her head.

"Honey, why don't you take Reba to breakfast? By the time you get back we'll know more about Swede's condition."

Trin held out her hand to Reba and pulled the redhead to her feet. "Have you left the hospital at all?"

"No," Reba replied.

"Let's get you out of here and into some sunlight." Trin squeezed her hand and pulled her toward the elevators.

Trin waited until the server took their order then placed her hand over Reba's. "Reba, is there anything I can do? Anything the company can do?"

Reba shook her head.

"What about the baby? Who's keeping her?"

"My parents have her. She's six months old, Trin. Will she ever know her father?"

"I honestly don't know, Reba. We'll do everything possible to pull Swede through this."

"But he won't be the man I married," Reba sobbed. "He won't even be a man."

Trin glanced out the window. She had no answer for her friend. She knew Swede would never be the same.

The waitress served their breakfast and they ate in silence.

"Reba, why don't you go home, take a nice hot shower, and sleep in your own bed. Swede is going to be in the hospital for a long time, and you must live your life as close to normal as possible. You can't sit in that room 24-7. You need to spend time with the baby."

"We named her after you, you know," Reba said, a faraway look in her eyes. "Swede loves you like a sister."

"Little Trin needs you." Trin's soft voice pulled Reba from her thoughts.

"Yes, you're right. Could you take me home? I have no idea where my car is."

"Of course. Let's run by the hospital and see what Heather has to say. Then I'll drive you home."

"He's doing as well as can be expected," Heather informed them as they sat in her office. "You're wise to go home and get some rest. This is going to be a long ordeal."

As Trin and Reba left her office, Reed walked in. "I'm so sorry to hear about your husband," Reed said, hugging Reba. "If there is anything I can do, please let me know."

"That was kind of you," Heather said as Reed sat down in the chair across from her.

"I meant it." Reed shuddered. "I met her at the vending machine while I was waiting for Father Provoost. I can't imagine the horror of having a loved one burned that badly."

"How's your mother?" Heather inquired.

140

"She's doing very well. The doctors still won't release her to travel, but she seems stronger every day.

"But that isn't why I've come to see you. I wanted to let you know that the hotel is sold out. There are no vacancies. My uncle and his entourage arrived today and took the last rooms."

"The hotel will refer people to our overflow hotel." Heather shuffled the papers on her desk. "Why are you working so hard for the Ball's success?"

"Isn't it obvious?" Reed's impish grin made Heather laugh. "I still hope to entice you to operate on my mother."

"Reed, bring her to me. I'll operate on her for free as a favor to a friend."

"I also want to invite you and Trin to dine with my uncle and me tonight. My uncle is Asheed Palava, the general of our army. He would provide protection for you if you agree to visit our country and operate on my mother."

"We'd be honored, but let me check with Trin before I give you a definite commitment." Heather sent a text to Trin and then continued talking with Reed.

Trin texted back, "Fine with me."

"We'd love to meet your uncle and dine with the two of you tonight."

"Oh, not just the two of us," Reed said, laughing. "It will be his entire retinue. So be prepared to party.

"I'll send my driver for you at seven," Reed said as she left Heather's office.

##

"Um, you look so . . . desirable." Trin watched Heather as she slipped on her heels. "I'd much rather stay home and help you get comfortable."

"You have no idea how much I would prefer an evening alone with you," Heather said. She caught Trin's hand and turned her around. "You look like a model. A gorgeous, sizzling-hot model."

"Maybe you could cool me down when we return home," Trin murmured, pulling her lover in for a long, slow kiss.

"Oh my, Miss Winfield, you certainly know how to take a girl's breath away." Heather fanned her face.

"Wait right here," Trin said. She grinned as she hurried into her closet. A few seconds later, she was back by Heather's side.

"I know you agreed to marry me, and I'm the happiest woman in the world, but I'd like to make it more official." Trin dropped to one knee and held out an open ring box. "Dr. Heather Hunter, will you marry me soon?"

Heather gazed into Trin's blue eyes. "Soon?"

Trin nodded. "The sooner, the better."

"Yes." Heather leaned down and took Trin's face between her hands. "I love you, Trin Winfield." The kiss lingered on their lips long after they stepped away from one another.

Trin slipped the ring onto Heather's finger.

"It's the most beautiful ring I've ever seen!" Heather gasped.

"It can't do justice to the lady wearing it," Trin said, her eyes sparkling. "Tonight, when we return home, I want to set a date. Soon!"

"I don't mind, but why the sudden rush?" Heather asked.

"Swede is a painful reminder of how fragile life can be. Marrying you is at the top of my bucket list."

"I know you're the only daughter," Heather said. "Will your parents insist on a big wedding?"

"I'm not marrying my parents," Trin affirmed. "I'm marrying you. All that matters is what you want."

"Right now, all I want is to get the dinner party over and get back home so I can properly thank you for this gorgeous engagement ring."

"Oh, one night won't suffice," Trin teased. "I'm thinking more like every night for the rest of your life."

"You'd get anything you want from me even without the ring." Heather slipped her arms around Trin's neck and pressed the full length of her soft body against the blonde.

The limo arrived right on time and delivered Trin and Heather to the hotel where Reed and two men were waiting for them in the lobby.

The men were perfect specimens of the male gender. They were clean-shaven, with jet-black hair and full, sensuous lips that curved into delighted smiles at the sight of Heather and Trin.

As Reed introduced them, the men bowed and kissed the back of Trin and Heather's hands. "Abid and Fardis are my twin brothers," Reed said.

Fardis touched Heather's ring with his fingertips. "You are committed to someone?"

Before she could reply, a young woman in a business suit joined them. "Reed, your uncle is waiting for you. Dinner is about to be served."

Fardis linked his arm with Heather's, and Abid did the same with Trin. "We will be the envy of all who attend our dinner tonight." Fardis laughed.

Heather was surprised to find her mother, Father Provoost, Roxie, and Trin's parents had also been invited to the dinner party. *Dear God, please keep Mother sober.*

##

Trin checked the place cards and was disturbed when she saw that Heather was seated between Reed's uncle and Fardis. The Winfields were seated across from Heather, and Fardis was next to Melody. Trin was at the far end of the table, away from Heather. She was certain the seating was intentional.

Roxie was seated next to Trin and flirted openly with Reed's brothers.

"I'd be careful if I were you," Trin said. "You might end up in a harem."

"Hmmm . . . a lot of other beautiful women." Roxie winked. "That wouldn't be all bad."

Asheed welcomed his guests and happily discussed the upcoming auction for the Cattle Baron's Ball. "We are looking forward to helping you raise the funds to add not one but two trauma units to your hospital, Dr. Hunter."

Heather graciously thanked him.

The Palava family spent the evening fawning over Heather while Melody basked in the praise the wealthy oil sheikhs lavished on her daughter.

"Melody," Asheed said, leaning close to Heather's mother, "you must help us persuade your daughter to visit our beautiful country. It would be a mission of mercy if she would operate on my dear sister and make her whole again."

"I'm certain that can be arranged." Melody flashed a flirtatious smile and polished off the rest of her wine.

Trin wondered how someone as stupid as Melody Hunter could raise a woman as wonderful as Heather. She was certain Heather's common sense and integrity were inherited from Eric Hunter.

"Don't you think so, Miss Winfield?" Asheed's smarmy voice pulled Trin back to the present conversation.

"I'm afraid I missed your question," Trin replied.

"I said you are a very beautiful woman, and you have visited our country many times and have always returned safely." Asheed's obsequious repeating of his remark was accompanied by a twisted grin. "And you are a known lesbian."

"That's true, but I fear your Supreme Leader values oil deals more than the life of females. I think Dr. Hunter would be making a grave mistake if she decided to go to Iran."

Asheed placed his hand over his heart. "You have gravely wounded me, Miss Winfield. I was certain I could count on you to take my side in this matter. After all, I am the highest-ranking general in our country. I can certainly guarantee Dr. Hunter's safety."

Trin raised her brows. "Um, negotiating with you is like dealing with Sybil—all those personalities. One never knows which personality will show up at the table."

Everyone within earshot chuckled at Trin's remark. Scott Winfield laughed out loud.

"Scott," Lucinda Winfield chided her husband, "don't encourage her. She acts just like you as it is."

Trin excused herself and located the bathroom. She waited a few minutes and called Heather's cell phone. "This is the hospital, Dr. Hunter. We need your services."

Heather wanted to find Trin and kiss her for saving her from the most uncomfortable dinner party she had ever attended.

"I'm sorry," Heather announced to the group after she hung up the phone. "I have an emergency at the hospital."

"Nonsense, dear," Melody slurred. "Tell them to call your father."

Heather glared at her. "He performed two difficult surgeries today, Mother. He's exhausted. I need to go."

She said her goodbyes and thanked her hosts as Trin and her mother hurried to her side. Lucinda hugged Heather. "Congratulations, dear," she whispered. "We're very excited about having a doctor in the family."

Heather couldn't hide her smile as she hugged her future mother-in-law.

##

Heather kissed Trin on the cheek as the blonde fastened her seatbelt. "Thank you for getting me out of there. I was beginning to feel uncomfortable. Even my mother was pushing me to go to Iran."

Trin shook her head. "Believe me, darling, Iran is no place for lesbians. I've never had a problem there because we always go with a diplomatic delegation.

"If I went to Iran alone, they would make an example of me in a minute because it would draw world attention to what happens to lesbians in their country.

"It is amazing that the men are allowed, even encouraged, to rape young boys and girls, but that isn't considered a sin. I'm not certain how they justify it. They simply say it's part of their culture. They're animals."

Heather laid a calming hand on Trin's leg. "Honey, I'm not going to Iran. We don't even need to discuss it."

"On a happier note," Trin said, wrinkling her nose, "my parents are elated that you've agreed to marry me."

"I don't think my mother noticed I was wearing an engagement ring. I'll tell Dad in the morning. He'll be pleased. Mother will go wild and start planning the social event of the decade. I'd really just like to get married without all the fanfare."

"Are you certain? I mean, I could fly us to Las Vegas, and we could get married this week."

Heather frowned. "I'm not wild about Las Vegas, but I'm willing if you're sure that's okay with you."

##

The next morning Heather awoke to the sound of Trin talking on the phone. She walked into the kitchen and poured a cup of coffee. Trin blew her a kiss as she continued to listen to the person on the phone. "That's great. Thank you so much."

Trin hung up the phone and pulled Heather onto her lap. "How would you feel about getting married right here in good old Cowtown?"

"I'd love it." Heather kissed her fiancée. "When?"

"That was the county clerk I was speaking with. We can get our marriage license today, wait three days, and get married here."

"I'd like that," Heather said.

They drove to the courthouse in downtown Fort Worth and applied for their marriage license. Then they headed to the Episcopal church.

"I don't mind an intimate ceremony," Trin said, "but I do want a church wedding. I'm hoping that Bishop Ryker will marry us. Our families make huge donations every year to support God's work."

Heather nodded but didn't reply. She knew there was no way Bishop Ryker would marry two women.

##

Bishop Grant Ryker stood as Trin Winfield and Dr. Heather Hunter entered his office. "The good Lord must be smiling down on me. I rarely have two such beautiful women in my office."

"We came to talk to you, sir," Trin said, shifting from one foot to the other.

"Oh, yes." Ryker smiled. "I have the figures right here." He pulled a budget sheet from a file folder. "This is what it will cost to add a gymnasium to the church. We are so thankful that we're in the running to receive some of the funds raised by the Cattle Baron's Ball.

"Father Provoost tells me you've already raised a tremendous amount of money."

Trin took the budget spreadsheet he held out to her. "Thank you. We actually came to ask a favor of you, sir."

"Anything." Bishop Ryker motioned for them to take a seat in the two chairs in front of his desk, and he settled into his high-back office chair.

"Heather and I wish to get married," Trin blurted out.

"A double wedding," Bishop Ryker said with a smile. "I'm honored that you're asking me to marry you. Who are you marrying, Heather?"

"Trin, sir."

"Of course. Trin, who are you marrying?" Ryker squirmed in his chair as he realized theirs wasn't a simple request.

"Heather and I want to marry each other, and we want you to perform the ceremony."

Bishop Ryker inhaled sharply and ducked his head, hoping the two women didn't see the surprised look on his face. He'd heard rumors about Trin Winfield but never a breath of impropriety about Dr. Hunter.

His mind raced. The Winfields and Hunters donated millions in tithes each year. To lose them as parishioners would be a lethal blow to the church's coffers. Still, to marry two lesbians in his church would go against everything he stood for.

"Heather, I thought you were dating Father Provoost," he managed to say.

"Nathan and I are good friends," Heather said. When she paused and looked at him, her nervous smile nearly made him ill. "But I love Trin."

Bishop Ryker stood and paced the floor. "I'm certain that both of you know how conservative I am and how closely I try to follow Christ's teachings and the Bible."

"With all due respect, sir," Trin said as she got to her feet. "There is not a single place in the Bible that forbids women being together."

"Yes, well, I'm sure that's because men wrote the Bible," Bishop Ryker pointed out. "And while they could easily comprehend men committing sodomy, it was beyond their comprehension that women would prefer other women instead of men. A little vanity on their part, perhaps."

"Exactly," Trin said, pushing on. "The Bible was written by men . . . who take it upon themselves to change it every so often. Sir, I believe love is love. The gender doesn't matter. It isn't about sex; it's about finding one's soulmate. Heather is my soulmate."

Distress filled Bishop Ryker's eyes. "Let me pray about it. May I give you my answer tomorrow?"

Both women nodded and bid the bishop goodbye.

"I think we've presented him with a conundrum," Heather said as she linked her arm through Trin's.

Before they reached the car, the hospital's ringtone demanded Heather's attention. She listened for only a few seconds before replying that she was on her way.

"There's a problem with Swede," Heather explained. "We need to hurry."

Chapter 26

Eric Hunter looked up from Swede's chart as Heather and Trin entered the hospital room. "Dr. Swink just debrided him. His blood pressure and all vitals are dangerously low."

Heather checked the new dressings covering most of Swede's body. "He's still weeping. Did Dr. Swink order additional fluids after the debriding?"

"No, but I think that's essential," Eric said. "I'll take care of it. I need to talk to you about Peter. Will you be in your office later?"

"I'll be here the rest of the day," Heather assured her father.

The door opened slowly as a wide-eyed Reba entered the room. Her gaze moved from doctor to doctor then settled on Trin. "What's wrong? Is Swede . . .?"

"Everything is fine," Trin said as she slipped her arm around Reba's thin shoulders. "We're just having a consultation to make certain Swede is getting the best treatment possible."

"Dr. Swink asked me to step out while he attended to Swede," Reba said. "Is he resting okay?"

"He's on heavy doses of morphine," Heather replied. "He's in no pain."

"Have you had anything to eat today?" Trin asked.

"No, I . . . I forget to eat."

"Yes, you've lost a lot of weight. How long have you been here?"

"Since six this morning." Reba frowned as her stomach growled.

"Let me take you to lunch," Trin insisted. "My vehicle is with the valet. It won't take long to get it and get you out in the sunshine."

Reba nodded. "I'd like that." She caught Trin's hand and clung to the blonde.

"I'll be in my office if you need me," Heather said as she followed her father out the door.

##

"What's Peter whining about now, Dad?" Heather sat down on the sofa beside her father.

"He is furious that you've given strict orders that he is not allowed in the operating room," Eric said. "He says you've made his medical degree and license to practice worthless. In short, he's threatening to sue the hospital if we don't allow him to do surgery."

Heather pulled Peter Trotter's file from her desk drawer. "Let him sue. If the things in this file are made public, he will see more lawsuits than most people ever hear about. He'll probably be imprisoned for medical negligence." When her father didn't respond, Heather continued.

"Dad, please let me fire him."

"I owe Jarrod," Eric mumbled. "Would you recommend him to another hospital?"

Heather stared at her father in disbelief.

"No, of course you wouldn't," Eric grumbled. "Neither would I. At least here we can contain him. Keep him from harming anyone else."

"If I could fix Jarrod, make him whole again . . . then would you fire Peter?"

Eric snorted. "In a heartbeat. I don't like him any more than you do."

"Good, then let's move on to a more joyous subject." Heather smiled. "Trin and I are getting married."

Eric's eyes sparkled. "Congratulations, honey. I am so happy for both of you. I've never seen two people so much in love. I noticed that rock you're wearing, but I was waiting for you to tell me."

"Thanks, Dad." Heather hugged her father.

"You do know what this means, right? Your mother will turn your wedding into the society sideshow of the decade."

"We're eloping."

"You would do that for me?" Eric was gleeful.

Heather joined in her father's merriment. "No, but I would for Trin and me. Neither of us wants a big wedding. Just a simple church wedding. We've asked Bishop Ryker to marry us."

"You know that won't happen," Eric huffed. "And when your mother finds out, you know she won't rest until she's turned your wedding into a social-ladder-climbing showcase for herself."

"I'm not telling her," Heather said. "I wanted you to know, but please don't pass the information on to her."

"Heather, you must tell her sooner or later."

"Preferably later," Heather mumbled. "I'm thinking, after the fact."

"Whatever you do, honey, I wish you and Trin all the happiness this world has to offer."

##

Bishop Grant Ryker prayed all night. He didn't want to waver in his faith, but he also felt compassion for Trin and Heather. Both women were pillars of their community. Both were exemplary Christians. He had no doubt they were devoted to one another and would keep their vows— probably better than most straight couples he had married.

He knew he would face a backlash from his ultra-conservative Christian followers. He knew he had railed against same-sex marriages from his pulpit. If the request had come from anyone else he would have immediately said no. But he personally liked and admired both women. His decision truly had nothing to do with the amount of money their families tithed each year. Money wasn't the issue. A homosexual marriage in the church was the issue.

Bishop Ryker continued to ask God's guidance long after the sun rose. Finally, he had his answer. He walked to the kitchen, put on the coffee, and called Trin Winfield.

"Trin, would it be possible for you and Heather to meet with me in an hour?" Ryker asked. "I have an answer for you, but I want to discuss it with you in person."

"Yes, sir, we'll be there."

Trin rolled over and wrapped herself around Heather, pulling her lover's back tight against her chest. "The bishop wishes to speak with both of us in an hour."

"Umm, then you need to move away from me, lady, or I won't be responsible for what we do for the next hour."

Trin kissed the back of Heather's neck and then rolled out of bed before the brunette could catch her.

"The bishop is waiting for you," the church secretary said as she led Trin and Heather into Ryker's office.

The two women were shocked by the bishop's face. It was obvious he hadn't slept all night. Dark circles accentuated sunken eyes, and puffy skin beneath dark orbs evidenced the struggle he'd had with himself during the night.

"Please sit down. Would you like some coffee?" Bishop Ryker offered.

They declined and sat down in the chairs across from him.

"I have prayed over your request all night." He cleared his throat. "I cannot marry you in the church."

Heather bowed her head, fighting back tears.

"But I would be honored to marry you in a simple ceremony in any other setting and give you the blessings of my office."

"Would you marry us in my parent's home?" Trin asked.

"Certainly," Ryker said.

Trin caught Heather's hand. "That's all we ask, sir. That would be perfect." Heather nodded.

"Do you have time to marry us at five in the afternoon this coming Thursday?" Trin inquired.

"I'll make time," Ryker said, smiling.

Chapter 27

Trin called the committee meeting to order. "Tomorrow is the big day. We either wow the establishment or fall short of the achievements of our predecessors.

"I have a brief announcement to make before we continue. Heather and I were married yesterday."

Heather watched as Trin's announcement was greeted with mixed emotions. Roxie cursed under her breath, and Father Provoost blanched. Everyone congratulated them, despite their personal feelings.

"May we have a rundown on how this auction works one more time?" Father Provoost asked.

"It's really quite simple," Reed said, jumping up from her chair and grinning from ear to ear. "Those participating will have a number pinned to their lapel signifying that they are to be auctioned off at the end of the evening. Whoever wins the bid on an individual gets to spend eight hours with that person. Their eight hours must fall between eight in the morning and midnight, and a chaperone is supplied if one is requested.

"My family's private jet will fly the winner and their prize to New York for dinner and to attend the current hottest show on Broadway."

"This is just wonderful," Peter said, clapping his hands. "Can you imagine the bids we'll get for Trin, Heather, and that actress Regina Redman?"

Both Reed and Father Provoost knew they would be bidding on the beautiful doctor.

Publicity by the church, entertainers' studios, and the national news media had resulted in a sellout. Dixie and Roxie had prevailed on the newly selected hotel's management to donate the ballroom for the night, so the ball would be pure profit.

"Our financial report is staggering," Roxie chimed in. "We have already surpassed some of the past balls in fund-raising."

They discussed every detail of the Ball, and at the end of the evening Trin was satisfied that they had everything under control. "In the morning we will wake up to find the Ball has taken on a life of its own and will take off like a cattle stampede. All we can do is stay out of the way and let the professionals take it from here."

Trin adjourned the meeting, and everyone began discussing their costumes.

"What costume are you wearing?" Reed asked Heather.

"The evil queen." Heather laughed. "I may be positively wicked."

"And I'm going as her white knight." Trin joined the discussion, slipping her arm around Heather's waist. "Every evil queen needs a white knight."

Trin was talking with her brothers, her back to their bedroom door when Heather made her appearance. The quick intake of breath from Monty and Vegas told her Heather was in the room—that and the ever-present tingling sensation she felt when Heather was near.

Trin turned slowly to look at her. Heather stole her breath away. She wore a flowing, floor-length, black skirt, and her blouse plunged low, revealing ample breasts. A riding crop hung loosely from her hand. Dressed as the dark queen, she looked powerful, exciting, and terrifying.

Trin so wanted to see if she could live through making love to her—right now. She fought a battle with her mind and body to keep from pushing Heather back into the bedroom and ravishing her. Fortunately, she won. Besides, her wife wasn't the type of woman one could push around.

"Trin," her brothers chorused, "your wife is gorgeous."

Trin stood staring, her mouth hanging open. She couldn't take her eyes off Heather. She was too beautiful to touch. The heat wave that swept through Trin was unbearable.

Heather moistened her lips with her tongue and tilted her head slightly, holding Trin's gaze. Trin whimpered as her wife slowly walked toward her, swaying her hips like the seductress she was. She slapped her riding crop against the leather of her high-heeled boot.

"You're drooling, darling," Heather said, dabbing the corner of her wife's mouth with her handkerchief.

Trin was mesmerized.

"Darling," Heather leaned slightly against her. "Your brothers are in the room."

"Yes," Trin whispered, never taking her eyes from Heather. "We should go."

"I heard Roxie Royce is planning on spending eight hours with Trin," Vegas teased.

"Oh?" Heather cocked an eyebrow. "In her dreams."

The brothers exited the elevator ahead of their sister and rushed to hold the ballroom door open for them. Heather caught her wife's hand and whispered in her ear. "See anything you like, knight?"

A soft moan escaped Trin's lips as she mumbled, "Everything, my queen."

By the time they arrived at the Ball, Trin had gotten a modicum of control over herself and was almost able to converse intelligently. Everyone was enthralled with the dark woman who was obviously a queen. She wore a mask and didn't look like anyone they knew. Both men and women were writing down her number for the bidding later tonight.

Across the room, Trin held her wife close, whispering words of love and adoration in her ear. Heather loved when Trin was like this. Trin always adored her, but tonight she was like a teenage boy desperately trying to get to first base. Heather refused to kiss her, saying she didn't want to ruin her makeup. Truth was, she loved to hear Trin beg. As they danced, Heather rubbed the handle of her riding crop up and down Trin's leg. Trin moaned loudly.

"Hush," Heather hissed. "If you can't be a good girl, I'll have to dance with someone else."

Trin gripped her tightly. "Don't go that far," she warned.

Heather knew the outfit she was wearing was driving Trin crazy. It covered her from head to foot, exposing nothing except the delicious swell of her breasts in front. There was no place Trin could touch her skin without fondling her breasts. She knew Trin wouldn't do that in public, so she teased her mercilessly.

"I would give anything to kiss the top of your breasts," Trin whispered in her ear. Her warm lips stirred Heather's desire. She knew they were working themselves into a frantic state of lust for each other.

"Shouldn't we cool this down?" she said, kissing Trin's neck.

"I honestly can't, darling," Trin murmured. "You ignited this flame. You have to be the one to control it."

The band ended the song and a man took the microphone. "Ladies and gentlemen. The time has come for us to start our first annual Cattle Baron's Ball Auction. Last year we raised $3 million for the charities. We hope to top that this year. If everyone who has registered to bid will move to the adjoining room, you will find bid paddles and refreshments on the tables. Seats at the tables closest to the stage are reserved for those being auctioned. The second tier of seating is for those bidding, and the third tier is for spectators. First and second tiers, please sit where your numbered placards are."

As people made their way to their respective seating areas, Trin recalled the steps required to bid in the auction. A check or credit card had to be placed on file with the accountants running the auction. A contract had to be signed stipulating the maximum bid one was willing to make. She knew the accountants had already checked with the banks and credit card companies involved to verify the lines of credit.

An hour into the auction, half a million dollars had been raised. Obviously, bidders were waiting for certain individuals to take the stage to be auctioned off. The organizers decided it was time to start auctioning the celebrities in attendance.

A popular TV actress brought $300,000. "I definitely want a chaperone," she whispered to Trin as she walked to meet the winner of her auction.

Loud applause spread throughout the room when Trey Slater strolled onto the stage. The popular movie star inspired a heated bidding war between both men and women. Trin was astounded at how open same-sex bidders were and was amazed at the price they were willing to pay for the handsome actor.

The mayor's daughter finally closed the bidding on Trey with a $500,000 bid. The night wore on as the rich bid wildly on the famous.

"It seems we have the dark queen and her white knight left to auction," the announcer said with a chuckle. "Does everyone know who these two beautiful people are?"

A resounding, "Yes!" came from the crowd.

"Are you ready to bid on them?"

"Yes!" the crowd roared.

The host led Trin to the stage and introduced her. A soft murmur of approval spread through the room.

"I think most everyone knows Trinidad Scott Winfield." The announcer swept his hand toward the white knight. "I believe I heard someone say earlier that Trin is Fort Worth's own rock star."

The crowd laughed.

"So let's start the bidding at fifty thousand."

Several paddles went up. "A hundred thousand," Roxie called.

Trin's price quickly escalated to $1 million. An Egyptian princess was bidding for her because she liked her looks. A movie star was holding her own in the bidding because she wanted to spend an evening with Trin. Roxie simply wanted her and had vowed to have her, unchaperoned. The bidding stalled at Roxie's $4 million bid. The auctioneer goaded the crowd, trying to increase the bid. "Four million going once, going twice . . ."

"Five million," Heather bid, her voice echoing throughout the room.

A hushed silence fell on the ballroom as spectators waited for Roxie to raise the bid. She was certain she couldn't raise that much money quickly, so she excused herself from the bidding.

"$5 million it is, for Trinidad Scott Winfield." The announcer grinned from ear to ear. He wasn't used to seeing this kind of money tossed around at a local charity event. "From the dark queen herself. Do you want to claim your prize?"

Heather gracefully ascended the stage and led her wife back to their table.

"Thank you so much," Trin whispered. "I thought you were going to let Roxie have me."

"Never," Heather growled.

Then the announcer quieted the audience. "And now we have the queen herself. Do you know who she is?"

"Yes!" the audience thundered.

Heather took the stage slowly, gracefully, like a queen moving to take her throne. The gasp from the audience acclaimed the woman's beauty. They were used to seeing her as Dr. Heather Hunter. As a queen she was even more devastatingly gorgeous.

"One million dollars," a man's voice called from the center of the room.

"Two million," Asheed Palava yelled.

"Three million!" a very drunk Father Provoost screamed.

"Four million," a movie producer called.

The bids were coming so fast and furiously that the auctioneer was having trouble keeping up with them.

"Five million," a female voice bid.

"Six million," Asheed responded.

"Seven million," the woman called out.

"Eight million." Asheed nodded.

"Nine million," the woman replied.

A wave of anxiety swept over Heather. She didn't know any of the people bidding on her.

Trin hadn't taken her eyes from Heather's face and immediately noticed her eyes go black with panic.

Trin stood and looked around her. There wasn't enough money in this room to buy eight hours of her wife's time. She glared at Asheed. "Ten million."

"Twenty million!" Asheed yelled.

Silence fell on the room.

Roxie grasped Trin's arm. "Let it go, girl. You can chaperone them."

"Twenty going once, going twice, sold to number 101!" The auctioneer slammed his gavel as Trin jumped onto the stage and offered her arm to her wife. Heather clung to Trin like a shipwreck victim to a lifeboat.

Everyone crowded around them. "Do you realize that sheikh just paid $20 million for your wife?" Monty asked.

"Money well spent." Trin scowled as Heather leaned against her. "We really should go make sure everything went smoothly with those checks." She placed a chaste kiss on her wife's lips and led her to the cashier window.

"Both checks have already cleared, and the funds are in our account," Trin heard the cashier say to Father Provoost, who was standing there. The priest nodded to Trin and Heather and hurried away.

"We just wanted to check and make certain everything went okay with the funds transfer," Trin said, smiling at the cashier.

"Yes, ma'am," the cashier replied. "As I was just telling Father Provoost, both Dr. Hunter and Asheed's checks have already cleared and the funds are in our account."

"He was checking on our payment?" Trin frowned.

"Yes, ma'am," she said softly. "For some reason, he didn't seem to think Dr. Hunter had that kind of money."

Heather excused herself to go freshen up in the ladies' room. She was glad to see she was alone. She stood for a long time, subduing the anxiety attack that had overcome her on the stage. She was truly amazed the auction had triggered this reaction. Perhaps it was the realization that in many Muslim countries, women were auctioned off to husbands. The thought made her sick to her stomach.

She whirled around as the bathroom door opened. A drunk Father Provoost staggered in. "Father," she gasped, "you're in the wrong room."

Moving faster than she had ever imagined he could, he pinned her against the wall.

"You need to leave." Fury welled up in her. The man was a pig, a disgrace to his beliefs and the church.

"I tried to buy you." He slobbered as he unfastened his pants and let them drop around his ankles.

162

"You're out of your mind, you oaf." She tried to push him away from her, but couldn't budge his weight. "Leave now," she commanded.

"Not until I—"

The ladies' room door swung open, and a furious Trin grabbed Provoost by his collar and dragged him to the center of the ballroom with his pants down around his ankles. He tried to walk quickly to get away from the stares but only managed to trip over his pants and fall face-first into the dance floor.

Trin rushed back to the ladies' room as Heather walked out. "Take me home, darling," Heather whispered.

The Winfield family and Eric joined them. "I think it's time to get our resident queen home," Trin informed them as they all held back their laughter at the sight of the drunken priest rolling around on the floor, trying to pull up his pants. Onlookers were trying to help the man to his feet when he uncontrollably urinated on them.

A TV camera was filming the priest for the late-night news. By noon the next day Nathan Provoost's name had become synonymous for hypocrite.

Chapter 28

Heather was standing in front of her full-length dressing mirror when Trin entered the room. She was still wearing her Ball costume, and Trin was still dressed as the white knight. She took a minute to study Trin's face.

Trin no longer had the desperate look she had worn, panting around after her all evening. In its place was the dark, angry look of one whose wife had been accosted. Heather didn't want their otherwise enjoyable evening to end with Trin upset. She loved her too much.

Heather had already pushed her anxiety attack and the priest from her thoughts. The only thing on her mind now was her wife.

Trin walked over to stand behind her, admiring her shape in the incredible outfit she'd worn to the Ball. The top was a blouse that wrapped around and tucked into the skirt, allowing the wearer to easily raise or lower the plunging neckline to expose as much or as little cleavage as they desired. Heather had it loosened now, so that it opened all the way to her waist. It barely covered her nipples. Her breasts strained against the soft, silky material.

Watching Trin in the mirror, Heather smiled as she saw the look in her eyes.

Heather turned slowly to face her wife. "I believe I won you in the auction tonight. That means I own you, darling." She slapped the riding crop against her leg.

"You have always owned me, Your Majesty." Trin wondered why they still had on their clothes.

"I want you to undress me," Heather commanded.

Trin stepped toward her and tentatively placed a hand on her cheek. She leaned down and kissed Heather slowly, softly.

"You're going to make me work for you," she murmured against Heather's lips, "aren't you?"

The vibration of Trin's lips against hers sent a quiver through Heather's body. "Yes," she whispered back, her lips still against Trin's. "Am I not worth working for?"

"Working for, fighting for, dying for," Trin whispered into her ear.

Trin kissed her way down Heather's chest to where the blouse slipped into the skirt, gently touching every inch of exposed flesh. She slowly pulled the blouse from the waistband and slid it back to expose perfect breasts. Trin raised her eyes to stare into Heather's. "May I, Your Majesty?" Trin's voice was deep with desire.

"Yes." Heather closed her eyes as she exhaled the breath she had been holding from the moment Trin had first touched her.

Trin let Heather's blouse drop to the floor and ran her hands possessively down her smooth, silky back, as her lips and tongue paid homage to her glorious neck and breasts. Heather moaned loudly and fought to keep from clutching her hands in blonde hair and pulling Trin hard against her.

Trin continued to caress Heather's breast with her tongue, pulling her closer with one hand while the other hand expertly unbuttoned the endless row of buttons on her skirt. As the skirt fell away, Trin slowly slid her hands down Heather's legs. Dropping to her knees, she kissed the hot flesh between her thighs.

Heather brought the riding crop down on Trin's back, "You're taking too long." Her husky, luxurious voice made Trin's heart beat faster.

"I am just trying to be of service to you, my queen." Trin looked up at her dark eyes. "That was quite a price you paid for me. I simply want to please you."

And she did.

Trin lay on her back, trying to slow the pounding of her heart. Heather raised herself on one elbow and gently traced Trin's full, kiss-swollen lips with her fingertips. "I have never known such pleasure as you give me," she whispered. "The price I paid for you at the auction was a bargain."

Erin Wade
The Roughneck & the Lady

Chapter 29

Trin felt the earth shake before she saw the gas shoot toward the sky. "Cap it!" someone screamed. "Cap it before the whole damn thing blows."

She ducked as an iron pipe swung toward her, and another roughneck roped it into place and wrapped a chain around it. Several men pulled the pipe over the spewing hole. They let it down slowly, careful to avoid letting metal strike against metal. Even the tiniest spark would send them all to kingdom come.

The rig foreman and another man twisted the catch that locked the pipe into place and closed the valve built into it, successfully containing the spewing gas.

Trin joined them at the wellhead. "What happened?"

"Someone tampered with the shaft casing," the foreman said, pointing to saw marks on the metal. "It was a miracle this whole thing didn't go up in flames."

"Secure the site until the police arrive, and I need to see the security team that has been on duty the last twenty-four hours." Trin scowled.

She stomped to the portable building that served as their office on the site and called the local sheriff's department. Within minutes, men and women began streaming into her office.

"Which one of you left your post unattended in the last twenty-four hours?" she said.

Four or five of the men shuffled their feet and looked at the floor.

"I don't need names. I'm not trying to place blame," she said, scowling. "It's a fact that some of you left your

167

security post to go to the restroom, to get a cold drink or something to eat, and there is no excuse for that.

"We have enough people on the security teams to allow for breaks and meals. No one should ever walk away from their post until someone relieves them. You all have cell phones and know how to use them. If you need to leave your positions, call for a relief person.

"The next person to leave their post unattended will be fired. Am I clear? We can't have the personnel on our well sites injured or killed because someone is too lazy to call for help.

"We were lucky today. That might not be the case next time."

##

As she waited for the sheriff's deputies and CSI investigators to finish with the crime scene, Trin penciled in a schedule to visit all the well sites. If she worked hard for fourteen days, she could visit all their locations and meet with the security teams on each site. She would not let anyone else experience the same fate as Swede. Reba's pale face and blank stare crossed her mind.

As she finished her schedule, a text appeared on her cell phone making her smile. "Miss you. What time will you be home?" The text was accompanied by an arousing photo of Heather leaning forward to expose mouthwatering cleavage.

Trin moaned and typed, "About an hour."

"I'll have dinner ready in an hour. Love you."

Trin responded with a heart and prayed the news media wouldn't get wind of today's rig accident. The last thing she needed was a worried wife.

She called the Midland sheriff's office.

"Have you gotten anything out of our terrorist?" Trin asked Sheriff Cliff Douglass.

"No, Trin. He's clammed up tighter than an old virgin's . . . ah, um—"

Trin ignored his discomfort. "I'm going to be in Midland in a few days," she said. "I'd like to interrogate him if you don't mind."

"Be my guest, Trin. Hopefully you can get something out of him."

Trin finished making notes, folded the piece of paper, and slipped it into her hip pocket. *Now to tell Heather I'll be away for a couple of weeks.*

The thought of two weeks without her wife sent a shiver down her spine. She ran through various scenarios in her mind as she drove home. By the time she arrived, she had worked out a solution she was fairly certain she could tolerate for two weeks.

##

"Dinner was delicious, honey," Trin said as she picked up their plates and headed for the kitchen. "Why don't you take your shower while I tidy up and put things away?"

Heather tiptoed to kiss her wife's lips. "Then will you tell me what's bothering you?"

"Yes."

Trin finished up quickly and joined Heather in the shower.

"Humph." Heather grinned. "My prayers have been answered."

"Did your prayers mention making love in the shower?" Trin's eyes twinkled.

"Maybe." Heather moaned as Trin pressed her back against the shower wall.

Chapter 30

The next morning Trin leaned back against the headboard, sipped her coffee, and watched her wife pace the floor. "I should be able to complete my mission in two weeks, honey. It's something I must do. I can't allow someone else to suffer the same fate as Swede. God, Heather, Swede doesn't even look human. He looks like a giant sweet potato."

Heather sat down on the edge of the bed. "I know, baby. I understand why you must do this. That doesn't mean I like it. I just . . . I hate sleeping without you beside me. We've only been together two years, but it seems like I've always fallen asleep in your arms."

"I know." Trin caressed Heather's arm. "I feel the same way. I'll fly home every two days to get my Heather fix."

"I guess that's better than nothing." Heather bit her bottom lip, pretending to pout.

"Don't do that." Trin chuckled. "You know how that affects me, and we do need to work out a few things before I leave."

"When are you planning to start this marathon site visit?"

"We need to wrap up the financial obligations of the Cattle Baron's ball before I can leave town. Tonight's meeting will finalize our intense involvement with the Ball until next year. Roxie will give us a final financial report, and we'll vote on the distribution of funds. We raised enough money for two new trauma units and Father Ryker's gym."

"Have you met Calvin Tremont, Father Provoost's replacement?" Heather asked.

"No, but I do know he's married, so that's good."

"He's been at the hospital," Heather informed her. "He's a nice fellow, very down-to-earth. I think he's going to be an asset everywhere."

"Is your mother speaking to you yet? She was furious over our simple wedding."

Heather suppressed a grin. "No, and it has been so peaceful, but I'm certain it won't last. I never could make her understand that we preferred a simple wedding to a major production with a cast of thousands."

"Yes, all we wanted to do was marry." Trin leaned forward and kissed her wife.

Heather glanced at her watch. "I have a consultation at ten this morning. What does your day look like?"

"I'll be on the phone all day scheduling my security meetings. I'm going to work from home today. Why don't I drive you to the hospital? I need to look in on Swede."

"I'm afraid he isn't doing as well as we had hoped," Heather volunteered. "He's still in a coma, and his burns are so severe that we're having trouble stopping the seepage of fluids from his body."

"Poor Reba." Trin shook her head. "Is she still sitting with him every day?"

"Yes. She reads to him constantly."

"I'm interviewing several people tomorrow to fill Swede's job. I must have a copilot. HR is sending me four people to consider."

"Just remember," Heather teased, "if you hire a woman she must be over fifty, married, and have at least five children."

Trin laughed out loud. "You left out coyote ugly!"

Heather wrinkled her forehead. "Coyote ugly? What's that?"

171

"A Texas term." Trin's eyes danced. "That's when you wake up after a night of hard partying and find a woman sleeping on your arm who is so ugly that you'd rather chew off your arm than wake her."

"You're so bad." Heather smiled as she took Trin's coffee cup and placed it on the night table. "You know what happens to bad girls?"

"Umm . . .?"

"They get a spanking."

"Mm-umm, I really should be spanked!" Trin laughed.

Chapter 31

Trin picked Heather up at the hospital, and they discussed their day on the way to the meeting.

"I called Roxie several times today," Trin said, frowning. "Her secretary said she was out of town on business but would be back in time for the meeting. We already know from our last count that we raised more money than any past ball, but it will be nice to get an exact accounting."

"I'll be glad to wrap this up and move on with our lives. The Ball consumed most of our time," Heather said softly.

Trin pulled Heather's hand onto her lap. "I'm so sorry you had that awful experience with Nathan Provoost."

Heather shrugged. "I thank God every day for sending you to check on me. Otherwise, he might have . . ."

"Then I would have killed him." Trin tightened her grip on Heather's hand. The look of hatred that flashed across Trin's face was terrifying. Heather knew her wife meant what she said. It was disconcerting.

Heather checked out the cars in the parking spaces reserved for the committee members. "Looks like everyone is here except Roxie."

"Roxie's always late," Trin huffed.

In the meeting room, champagne was flowing as Reed and Dixie congratulated everyone on a job well done. Reed hugged Trin and Heather joyously. "I ordered champagne and hors d'oeuvre. I thought we'd have a little celebration and welcome Father Tremont at the same time."

"Excellent idea," Trin said. She cupped Heather's elbow and steered her toward the only new face in the room.

"You must be Trin Winfield and Dr. Hunter." The short, pleasant man held out his hand to Trin. "The bishop was right—you are an impressive couple. I'm Father Tremont, but you can call me Calvin."

"Father, it's a pleasure to meet you and to welcome you to our city." Trin liked the man's firm grip. No dead-fish handshake from Calvin Tremont.

"Father has met everyone else," Reed said, handing glasses of champagne to Heather and Trin. "If Roxie will show her face we can complete our business and visit."

As Trin talked with Dixie, Heather's cell phone dinged in a message.

"It's from Roxie." Heather read the text out loud. "I'm in Malta. Weather has closed airport. So sorry to miss meeting. Please continue without me."

Trin looked around the room. "Did Roxie leave a financial report with any of you?"

Everyone shook their head.

"Then we have nothing to discuss," Trin growled. "Why is she in Malta anyway?"

"Closing an import deal," Reed said casually. "Malta is about 200 miles from Sicily, and the country has an incredible rug manufacturer."

Trin pinched the bridge of her nose and held her champagne glass high. "Here's to the most successful Cattle Baron's Ball in history."

Reed moved to stand between Heather and Trin. "My uncle will be returning home soon. He has completed his business here and wishes to set up a date for his evening with Heather."

Trin furrowed her brow. "I'll be out of town over the next two weeks," she said. "Any time after that is good."

174

"He won't be here that long," Reed informed her. "He was thinking Friday night."

"That's short notice," Heather chimed in, glancing at Trin to check her reaction.

"I can be here Friday," Trin said.

"He didn't pay for an evening with you," Reed smirked. "His date is with Heather."

"True, but I'm her chaperone." Trin glared at her.

"Seriously?" Reed barked. "A thirty-something woman needs a chaperone?"

"That was the stipulation," Trin replied.

"You don't trust my uncle? He donated $20 million to the Cattle Baron's Ball, and you want to chaperone his evening?"

"It's not up for debate," Trin hissed through clenched teeth.

Chapter 32

Sheriff Douglass met Trin at the airport and drove her to the jail. "He's a tough SOB. I'll be surprised if you get anything out of him. We don't even know his name. He's obviously a Muslim."

"Can't hurt to try, Sheriff. I'm at my wit's end. We've doubled security on all our wells, installed state-of-the-art surveillance equipment, and the terrorists still manage to booby-trap our operations. I'm hoping this clown knows something about the cells operating in Texas."

Douglass led the way to the interrogation room. "I'll leave you with him. He's cuffed, so you won't have any problems with him."

Trin stepped into the interrogation room. "How're you doing, Clem?"

He looked confused for a moment. "My name's not Clem." He spoke barely above a whisper. He knew this woman was the one who had crushed his vocal cords.

"Hmmm. Says here your name is Clem Kadiddlehopper." Trin shoved some papers in front of him.

"Name's not Clem," he man growled, shoving the papers back at her.

"Says here it is." Trin continued to needle him. "Anyway, Clem Kadiddlehopper is as good a name as any for a coward. Although that is a long name for a gravestone." She pulled a pen from her pocket and marked through something on the form. "There! Now your gravestone will read Clem Kadiddle."

The agitated terrorist tried to leap to his feet, but the handcuffs fastened to the table jerked him back down. "Not Clem! My name's not Clem!"

"Sure it is." Trin feigned indifference. "It says so on these papers. Clem Kadiddle."

"Ally Abbasi!" The man tried to yell, but only a raspy, "My name Ally Abbasi," came out.

"Humph. Ally, huh? Well, Ally, if you cooperate with me I can get your correct name on these arrest warrants."

Ally narrowed his eyes to mere slits. He knew the beautiful American woman had tricked him. He turned his head, refusing to look at her. He hated her. He began making plans in his mind to kill her. Horrible, agonizing deaths were imagined for her.

After ten minutes of nonstop jabbering, Trin knew she would get nothing else from the terrorist. She stood and walked to the door. "Ally Abbasi? Nah, I'm gonna leave Clem Kadiddle on here." Her laughter filled the room as she closed the door behind her.

"Whoa, you really pissed him off," Sheriff Douglass said, chuckling as they watched Ally through the one-way glass. "Pretty neat trick though. You got his real name. We'll run it through the National Data Exchange System and see if there's any paper on him."

"How long will it take to get a report back from N-DEx?" Trin asked.

"Long enough for us to grab lunch." Douglass smiled.

Douglass was right. When they returned from lunch the N-DEx report was waiting for them.

Douglas whistled. "Jesus! This guy must be a ringleader. He's got his finger in every criminal activity you can imagine." He pitched the report to Trin.

"White slavery, drugs, gun running, airplane hijacking, arson, and warrants for two murders." Trin shook her head. "I didn't realize I was standing so close to such evil."

"You're lucky he didn't shoot you and Dr. Hunter just for the fun of it," Douglass exclaimed.

"At least now you can book him. But Sheriff, put him in lockdown, and don't let anyone talk to him. Most importantly, don't let any other agency take him from you."

"You think someone will come after him?"

"Yes, I'm certain they will, and some of them will be in sheep's clothing. Be particularly wary of our US State Department."

"I think that for right now he'll remain Clem Kadiddle," Douglass said, laughing. "Lost in the system of John Does."

"I'd heard you were very wise," Trin said. "It's a joy to work with you."

Chapter 33

Trin taxied her plane up to the hanger, killed the engines, and called Heather.

She answered on the first ring, bypassing the niceties. "Please tell me you're home?"

"Hello to you too, honey." Trin beamed. "Is it safe to assume you missed me?"

Heather giggled. "More than you will ever know. I'm at the hospital and can't get away. Is there any chance you can run by before you go to your meeting?"

"There's every chance. I'll be there within the hour. I missed you too."

As she drove to the hospital, Trin thought about the meeting she had at four. The Winfield human resources department had narrowed the applicants for her copilot down to four. Although all were very capable pilots she had selected a man named Garret Jennings because of his size. At six-four and over two hundred pounds, Jennings would be a good man to have at one's side in a fight. Most importantly, he had vast experience flying a Dassault Falcon 7X—her plane of choice—and the AgustaWestland AW109 Helicopter that her father favored for close-up inspection of operations.

Once she had settled on Jennings, the HR department had left no stone unturned in their vetting of the man. He was an ex-marine with citations out the wazoo. A true war hero, he had served in Afghanistan at the same base Trin had been assigned. She was surprised their paths hadn't crossed.

She left her Jeep with the valet and bolted to the elevator. She knew she would have to wait until tonight to share quality time with Heather, but right now she wanted her wife in her arms.

Heather was talking to an intern when Trin walked into her office. The expression on her face morphed from troubled to gleeful at the sight of Trin. Trin ducked her head to keep her smile from telling the intern her thoughts. She walked to the window and watched the chopper land on the helipad outside Heather's window. She hoped it wasn't carrying cargo that would require her wife's attention.

"I'll speak with Dr. Trotter," Heather said as she ushered the intern toward the door. "If you have this problem again, come to me immediately."

"Yes, ma'am," the young woman said.

Trin waited for the click of the closing door before turning around. She almost cheered when she heard the deadbolt slam into place.

Then, Heather was in her arms. After a much-needed kiss, they leaned back and looked at each other.

"Dear God," Trin whispered. "You're the most beautiful woman I've ever met."

"Um, do you know that the first time I saw you out of a hospital bed you were looking out a window, watching a helicopter land? My first thought was, 'That's the nicest butt I've ever seen.'"

Heather let her hands slip to Trin's hips and pulled her tighter against her.

"Um, aren't you on call?" Trin mumbled as Heather unzipped her jeans.

"I am, but the way I feel, this won't take long."

"My sentiments exactly," Trin said, moaning.

##

Trin was still trying to catch her breath when a knock sounded at Heather's door. The doctor smoothed down her skirt and buttoned her blouse. "I'm coming," she called out.

"I'm sure they'll realize that when they see the look on your face," Trin said, unable to resist teasing her wife. "I was careful not to destroy your hair."

Heather rolled her eyes and unlocked the door.

"Heather,"—Eric charged into the room—"Oh, am I interrupting something?" He blushed and looked away from his daughter.

"It's okay, Dad." Heather chuckled. "Trin was just leaving. She has meetings this afternoon."

Eric greeted Trin. "I'm glad you're home safe and sound."

"Thank you, sir. I'm glad to be home." Trin backed out of the room. "See you at home tonight, honey."

"Trin?" Eric called after her. "You need to wipe the lipstick from your face before your meeting."

"Dad, you embarrassed her," Heather chided as she closed the office door.

Eric laughed. "Yes, I don't believe I've ever seen a Winfield blush."

"The way you charged into my office, I assume you have something important to discuss with me," Heather said, motioning for her father to sit down.

"Peter Trotter," Eric fumed. "He's made advances to one of our new interns."

"I know." Heather sighed. "I just talked with her. I'll take care of it, Dad. I'm at my wit's end with Peter. Giving him an administrative position and removing him from our roster of surgeons will stop his malpractice suits, but I'm not sure how I can make him keep his hands off the women in this hospital.

"Since I can't fire him, he knows my threats are empty words. The problem is that a sexual harassment suit filed against Peter will also be filed against the hospital."

"Please, Heather, talk to him. I don't know what's wrong with him. His father's such a fine, upstanding man."

"I'm not too sure about that," Heather mumbled.

"What?"

"I said I'll do my best with that." Heather consoled her father. "But you do tie my hands."

Chapter 34

Garret Jenkins was all Trin had hoped he would be: intelligent, witty, fearless, handsome, and as big as a tank.

"There is an aspect of this job you aren't aware of," Trin told Jenkins.

"It can't be too bad," Jenkins effused. "This is my dream job."

"Have you ever considered law enforcement?" Trin asked. "I mean, given your size and intelligence, I'm surprised our government didn't try to hire you during your senior year of college."

"Oh, they did, but I have no desire to work for the FBI or CIA. They're riddled with corruption. I wouldn't mind being in law enforcement, as long as I knew my partner had my back and wouldn't stab it."

"You know who my father is," Trin continued. "But you may or may not know that I'm a federal agent heading up a task force whose sole purpose is to head off terrorist attacks on our oil and gas industry in Texas.

"As my copilot and partner, you'd be expected to serve on my task force."

Jennings was motionless.

"You'd draw a paycheck from the government and Winfield Oil," Trin said, trying to sweeten the offer.

"Weren't you almost killed by some terrorist a few months back?" Garret said. "Where is your last copilot and partner?"

Trin frowned. "When you put it like that, I guess the job isn't that attractive."

"You're avoiding my question," Garret said.

"Yes, I was shot at but had no bullet wounds." Trin hedged, looking for words to describe Swede's fate. She took a deep breath. "Swede, my partner, is more a vegetable than a man. He was horribly burned in one of the well fires set by terrorists. I doubt he'll survive," she said, struggling to choke back her emotions.

Garret stared at her for a long time then jerked his head as if a light had come on in his mind. "I know who you are," he whispered. "I'd be honored to serve with you, Colonel Winfield, in any capacity."

"That's top secret." Trin scowled.

"I know. I just want to say, you were one hell of a sniper," Garret said. "I'll never mention it again."

"Good! How do you know about me?"

"I was the ground troops' commander," Garret said. "Whenever you appeared in camp, we were sent out on reconnaissance with orders to bring back the most accurate information possible on a specific enemy.

"The next day, news would filter in that one of the major players in the jihad had been shot around sunup. You always did your work at dawn."

"Did anyone else connect me to the shootings?" Trin asked.

"No, I only figured it out because you caught my eye, and I was curious about why a beautiful woman like you would be on base. You were covert, so most of the troops never knew you were there."

"Humph," Trin said with a shrug.

"I'd like to take your bird up," Garret said, his enthusiasm growing. "Get the feel of her and see how she responds."

"Do you need to discuss this with your wife?" Trin asked. "Let her know the dangers inherent to this position?"

"No, that would only upset her." Garret couldn't keep the excitement from his voice. "This is my dream job. I won't be able to enjoy it if she's worried."

"Does your . . . uh, er—"

"Wife." Trin filled in the blank for him.

"Does your wife know how dangerous your job is?"

"She does now," Trin snorted. "Let me notify HR so they can take care of all the paperwork and get you on our insurance. We could fly in the morning, if you'd like."

"I'd love to." Garret beamed.

Trin wrote down the address and hanger number where the plane was stored. "I'll meet you there at eleven."

They shook hands, and Trin checked her watch as Garret left her office. She called HR and gave them the go-ahead to put Garret Jenkins on the payroll.

Her next call, to Heather, went to voicemail. *I hope she isn't in surgery*, Trin thought as she prepared to go home.

Trin drove to their favorite smokehouse and picked up a rotisserie chicken. With the precooked chicken she could have dinner on the table when Heather got home.

Heather's heart skipped a beat when she saw Trin's Jeep in the garage. She pulled her car in and closed the garage door. Trin had only been away from home overnight, but it seemed like a lifetime. She gathered her things and stepped out of the car. Trin was in the garage before the car door closed. She took Heather's computer bag and leaned down for a kiss. "It's about time you got home."

"I couldn't get here fast enough." Heather linked her arm through Trin's, getting as close to her wife as possible.

"I have dinner ready. Why don't you shower and slip into something comfortable while I put it on the table?"

Trin placed Heather's things in her office then strolled to the kitchen. She pulled the chilled bottle of wine from the refrigerator and popped the cork. She poured two glasses of the burgundy and carried one into the bathroom, where Heather was slipping into one of Trin's Henley pullovers.

"You have got to be the sexiest woman alive," Trin said, her eyes twinkling as she handed Heather the glass.

Heather sipped the wine. "I'm not really very hungry," she purred. "We could skip dinner tonight, if you'd like."

"I'd like." Trin removed the wine glass from Heather's hand and pulled her into her arms.

"Thank you for last night," Heather murmured as she waved a steaming cup of coffee under Trin's nose.

The blonde's eyes fluttered open, and she smiled as she stretched awake. "Kiss, please?"

Heather placed the coffee cup on the night table and leaned over to kiss her. "What are your plans for today?"

Trin pulled herself into a sitting position, retrieved her coffee, and leaned back against the headboard. "I've hired a new copilot. I'm meeting him at eleven so he can familiarize himself with the plane. Want to go up with us?"

"I'd love to, but I have a surgery at ten. It'll be a long one. Will you be home tonight?"

"Yes, but I have to leave around seven Friday morning in order to be back in time to chaperone your date with Asheed."

"Thank you for that. I know it's an imposition on you, but I don't want to be alone with him on his private jet. He makes me uncomfortable."

"I kick myself daily for letting Roxie talk me into allowing him to win the bid on you."

"It's fine. She was right to do that, and I don't mind as long as you'll be chaperoning."

"I'll be there, honey. Don't worry. Um . . . is there any chance of breakfast to go with this coffee?"

"Go shower. I'll have it on the table when you're finished." Heather brushed her lips against Trin's and took her coffee cup. "Go!"

Chapter 35

Garret admired the Dassault Falcon 7X that had become Trin's home the past few weeks. "She's a beauty, Colonel."

"Thanks, but you can't call me Colonel," Trin replied. "It's just plain Trin. Forget everything you know about me as a soldier."

"Sorry, I—"

"It's for my own safety," Trin added. "The Taliban has a history of searching out and killing known US snipers, so I'd rather remain anonymous."

Garret nodded. "What's the top speed on this baby?"

"Mach 0.90."

"Wow! Almost 700 miles per hour." Garret eyed the endless array of controls in the cockpit. "I flew one of these babies for a corporation but never really opened her up to top speed. I do know it can fly from the Fort Worth Alliance Airport to New York City—nonstop—in about seven hours."

"We bought it for its speed and long-range flight capabilities," Trin explained. "I often fly my father to other countries to conduct business. Of course, I use it to visit our well sites all over Texas."

"I read that the government of Bahrain is considering partnering with Winfield Oil in the production of that large oil and gas discovery off its west coast."

"Yeah, but one never knows with Crown Prince Salman bin Hamad Al Khalifa," Trin pointed out. "I leave the foreign negotiations to my brothers. My bailiwick is the US and Texas."

"You do know that Texas is part of the US, don't you?" Garret teased.

"I did say that like it was a country all its own," Trin said with a laugh. "What I meant was my main focus is Texas."

Garret looked around the runway. Two hangers down from theirs, a monster private jet was being serviced. The tail of the plane displayed the Iranian flag. Garret whistled.

"That's a big mother."

"Belongs to Asheed Palava," Trin informed him.

"Top Iranian general and major supporter of all terrorist groups," Garret noted.

Trin raised a questioning eyebrow.

"I keep abreast of things." Garret shrugged.

"I like trijets," Garret said, running his eyes over Trin's Dassault Falcon. "I'm going to enjoy flying this baby."

"Good, because we leave for Midland/Odessa at seven in the morning," Trin said.

Garret grinned. "I can't wait!"

Chapter 36

Trin and Garret spent the day visiting the well operations around Odessa. Garret was overwhelmed by the size of Winfield Oil's operations. They wrapped up their business, stopped by Sheriff Douglass's office, and headed for the airport.

Trin made her fourth attempt to call Heather, but it went to voicemail. *She's probably in surgery*, she thought.

"Is that Ally fellow the one who shot you?" Garret asked.

"Yeah, he's a tough one. I can tell from his rap sheet he's on the top rung of the terrorist ladder, but we can't get a word out of him."

"I'm surprised you got his name," Garret commented. "Can we send him to Lafaday?"

"Lafaday?" Trin scoffed. "Sounds like a kindergarten."

"It's anything but." Garret grunted as he hefted himself into the cockpit. "It's top secret. Where we take terrorists who have knowledge that will save lives. Lafaday has the means to extract that knowledge."

"Oh, so it really does exist. That's good to know." Trin made a mental note to talk to her father about Lafaday.

"Don't mention it to anyone," Garret reiterated. "If the bleeding hearts get wind of it, they'll want to release the rapists and murderers who are imprisoned there."

Trin was more than pleased with Garret's knowledge of her aircraft. Like her, he seemed to be an extension of the plane. On the way back to Alliance Airport, she turned the bird over to him.

"I'm going to catch a nap," Trin said as she settled back in her seat. "I have a long night ahead of me."

"Business or pleasure?" Garret asked.

"Business. Do you follow the Cattle Baron's Ball?"

"Yeah, your wife was auctioned off to the King of Iran or something like that."

"General Asheed Palava. That was his plane you saw. He won an evening of dining and Broadway with my wife," Trin grumbled. "I'm the chaperone."

Garret laughed. "Good for you. I wouldn't want my wife alone with that wolf. The man's an animal. You know he has a harem?"

"So I've heard." Trin tried to hide her anxiety. She didn't like the thought of Asheed spending time with her wife, even chaperoned. She would be glad when this night was over.

"You must be so excited . . . dinner and theater with a real sheikh." Melody chattered as she helped Heather get ready for her "big date."

"I'm more nervous than excited," Heather said, slipping on her high heels. "I wish Trin would hurry."

"Oh, she's going to meet you at the plane," Melody assured her daughter. "She called me when she couldn't reach you or your father."

Heather checked her phone. "I forgot to take it off silent after I finished my surgery. She's called four times."

Heather looked at her watch as her mother poured two glasses of wine. "I don't understand why we have to be on board two hours early."

"Something about being in line to take off. Here,"— Melody handed her a glass—"this will steady your nerves."

Melody drained her glass and poured another for herself. Heather sipped her wine. It was a little bitter, but she drank it to please her mother.

"Oh, look, Heather. The sheikh has sent a limo for you. May I ride to the airport with you?"

"I'd welcome your company." Heather grimaced. "This doesn't feel right without Trin. I'll be glad to get to the plane and see her."

Melody refilled both their glasses. "Drink this, dear. It will calm you."

Trin skipped down the plane's ramp and looked around for Asheed's plane. She didn't see it. *It's an hour until takeoff,* Trin thought. *I'll check to see which gate it's departing from.*

"You did a great job today," Trin told Garret as they walked inside the terminal. "I'm glad to have you on board."

"I can already tell I'm going to love working with you." Garret shook hands with Trin. "Are you headed my way? We can walk together."

"No, I've got to find out which gate Asheed's plane is departing from. We'll talk tomorrow. I just want to get this date over with. Then maybe you and your wife can have dinner with Heather and me."

"We'd love that. Catch you later, Col . . . um, Trin."

Trin walked to the nearest service counter and inquired about the Iranian jet.

"That plane took off thirty minutes ago," the young woman informed her.

"Are you certain?" Trin barked. "It was supposed to take off an hour from now."

"They did reschedule for an earlier departure time, ma'am. Something about an emergency in Tehran."

Trin's heart stopped. "Tehran? It's bound for Tehran?"

The girl studied her computer screen for a few seconds. "Yes, ma'am. The flight plan they filed shows Tehran as the destination."

Trin hurried to her car as she pushed the cell phone button to call Heather. *Still no answer.* "Calm down, Trin," she said out loud, trying to quell her rising panic.

She called Eric Hunter. He was in surgery. She called Roxie, and it went to her voicemail. She had the same experience with Reed and Melody's phones.

Trin pulled up Find My iPhone and clicked on Heather's phone. The app zoomed in and out on the United States but couldn't find Heather's phone.

Trin decided to go with the worst-case scenario. She might end up with egg on her face, but at least she'd know for certain where her wife was.

Breaking all speed limits and barely avoiding a wreck, she arrived at her office. She unlocked her office door and powered on her computer. The monitor came to life, and she clicked on her Tor Browser to access the dark web. She typed in the address of the Federal Government Database, logged in, and then typed "Hounddog" to access the government's secret database that could track a cell phone anywhere in the world. If a cell phone contained a battery, Hounddog could find it—even at the bottom of the ocean.

Trin shuddered as she watched the software go to work. She wondered how citizens would feel if they knew that the government could track them in a matter of seconds. The ping told Trin it had located Heather's phone. She breathed a sigh of relief as the program zoomed in on her wife's location.

Trin slapped her hand over her mouth to keep from throwing up on her keyboard. She fought back the bile in her mouth and printed out Heather's information. The phone was somewhere over the Atlantic Ocean on a straight course for the African continent.

"That son of a bitch is taking my wife to Iran," Trin cried out.

She set up a conference call with her brothers and her father. "I really need your help, guys."

The three men listened as Trin explained what was happening.

"I'll call the president," Scott said.

"I'm in Iraq," Monty reported. "I can get across the border and put the things you need in a locker at the airport."

"I'm still in Kuwait, but I can get into Iran," Vegas said, seething. "If he hurts Heather, so help me—"

"No!" Trin barked. "He's mine."

Scott was the voice of reason. "Now, children . . . my guess is he has abducted Heather to force her to operate on his sister. Once she has done that, he will return her to us. Let me talk to the president and see how far we get through diplomatic channels."

"You're right, Dad," Trin grumbled. "We'll talk later."

As soon as she severed the connections, she called her brothers back. "Dad isn't on with us," Trin informed them.

"I knew it wasn't like you to give up so easily," Vegas said. "What's the plan, sis?"

"Monty, I'm texting you a list from my burner phone. Please have those items in a locker, just in case we have to go that route. You know how to get the number and combination to me."

"Vegas, please stand by in case I need you."

"You've got it," both brothers chorused.

Chapter 37

Their house felt cold and empty without Heather. She had been gone two weeks. From private sources, Trin had learned that Heather had performed a successful surgery on Reed's mother, and Mrs. Palava was thriving. Surely it was just a matter of time until the Iranian government returned Heather.

The Iranian president had issued a statement thanking the Americans for allowing the beautiful surgeon to visit his country and operate on the matriarch of the Palava family. He declared the operation a success and guaranteed Dr. Hunter's safe return to the US.

Behind the scenes, the State Department was getting a different story. According to Trin's contacts, Asheed had made a private announcement that the American doctor had fallen in love with him and wanted to marry him.

That bit of information had sent Trin through the roof. "She fears for her life if she is going along with Asheed's ridiculous announcements."

Trin kept the news on constantly, watching for any announcement or information about the gorgeous Dr. Hunter. European news stations were enamored with the dark-haired physician who was being trotted all over Iran as the future wife of Asheed Palava. On one occasion it appeared that Heather had skillfully covered a black eye with makeup. She was seated next to Asheed at a state dinner in her honor to thank her for the successful operation she had performed on Reed's mother. Reed wasn't in attendance.

One month segued into two, and Trin was frantic to know that Heather was okay. Reed had disappeared along with Roxie. Father Tremont and her family were the only things holding Trin together.

"Don't do anything foolish," Scott counseled his daughter. "They're negotiating around-the-clock to bring her home."

"They who, Dad? Who, exactly, is working to bring my wife home?"

"Trin, I don't understand how they got Heather on Asheed's plane without you," Scott said, avoiding the question. "She told me she was uneasy about her evening with Asheed. I don't believe she would have willingly boarded that plane."

"Maybe Roxie or Reed tricked her somehow," Trin theorized. "Both of them have disappeared."

##

Trin watched in agony as Asheed Palava walked into a gathering with Heather on his arm. The TV cameras moved in for a closer shot of the couple. Trin pushed the record button on the remote. She knew she would play this scene over and over for some clue about what was happening.

"Tonight I am the happiest man in the world," Asheed declared. "Dr. Heather Hunter has agreed to become my wife."

Trin's stomach did a 180-degree turn but settled as she forced herself to concentrate on everything she was seeing. The room holding the engagement party was huge. Iranian soldiers were stationed every five feet to provide security. A massive crowd filled the room.

Heather and Asheed were visiting with another couple when Heather leaned in to say something to Asheed. Her smile was dazzling, and she seemed happy. Asheed nodded and walked toward the bar.

Heather continued her animated conversation with the couple. She was telling a story and continued to make the same hand motions several times. Each time, the couple laughed out loud.

"Left hand flat, palm up," Trin said out loud. "Right hand fisted with thumb up and resting in the palm of the left hand.

"What's she doing?" Trin continued to vocalize her thoughts as Heather made the same motion again.

"Help me! Damn, she's signing *help me*." Trin squealed. "Help me!"

Her phone rang, and she pushed the button to speak to her father. "Trin, are you watching channel eight?" Scott asked. "I recorded it in case you missed it. Honey, it really does look like Heather is willingly marrying Asheed."

"Dad, play it back. See where Asheed walks away, and she continues talking to that couple? While she's smiling and laughing with them, she's using sign language to contact us. She's signing *help me*."

Suddenly, Vegas's name appeared on her caller ID, and Trin added him to their conversation. "Sis, Heather is on TV, and she's signing *help me*," Vegas blurted out.

"I'll be damned," Scott muttered.

"I'm going after her. Don't try to stop me, Dad!" Trin said before disconnecting the calls.

Chapter 38

Trin made two phone calls and set up everything she needed. She would fly into Tehran with a group of industrialists who were visiting the city to discuss relocating operations to the new capital of Iran, wherever that might be. The location of Iran's capital had moved over thirty-two times during the country's tumultuous history.

Trin studied her face in the mirror. She'd always had long, wavy, blonde hair. She knew it was one of her best features. She pulled a handful of hair away from her head and snipped it with a pair of scissors. She tossed the golden locks into the trash receptacle at her side.

Thirty minutes later she stared at the face in the mirror. It was a face she barely recognized. She looked like a baby chick. An inch of soft blonde hair covered her head.

Too late to turn back now, she thought as she shook the can of shaving cream and spread the fluffy lather onto the side of her head. It took her another half hour to shave her head as smooth as a bowling ball. An Ace bandage wrapped tightly around her bosom made her look flat chested.

She called a friend who made the best illegal passports money could buy. Within eight hours she would be ready to leave the States with two passports for herself and one for Heather.

State Department be damned. She was going to bring her wife home.

##

Trin dug out her passports. One identified her as Bronco Risso of Austin, Texas. The other identified her as Raymond Canton of Toronto, Canada. One showed a bald man wearing a pair of black-rimmed glasses. It would get her from Texas to New York to Tehran. On her return trip, she would depart Tehran for Ontario, wearing wire-rimmed glasses. From Canada, she and Heather would reenter the US on foot. It should be easy to get lost in the tourists returning to New York from their visit to Niagara Falls in Canada.

The flight had been a long one, allowing Trin to get some much-needed sleep. She had a feeling it would be days before she slept again. The delegation passed through Iranian customs without a glitch. Trin's height and bald head made it easy for her to pass as a man. *Now to find the airport lockers.*

Trin entered the lock's combination provided by her brother and found the articles she had ordered: a duffle bag contained a disassembled sniper rifle, high-powered scope, stand, rope, and ammunition. She checked into the airport hotel, picked up her rental car, and then scouted her planned position for the attack.

The water tower was perfect. Located in the suburbs, the tower was far enough away from the oil field to give her plenty of time to escape. She would be long gone before anyone could figure out where the shots had originated. She would get a good night's sleep tonight. Tomorrow would be a big day.

Trin slept late then spent the day exploring her getaway route from her second target. She hoped she wouldn't have to hit it, but that all depended on how quickly the Iranians released Heather.

She knew a second attack would be more dangerous for her because authorities would be on high alert. She and Vegas anticipated a reluctance on the part of Asheed to release Heather and already had explosives planted in an oil refinery on the other side of the city. It was designed to detonate when Trin called the attached phone from her burner phone.

She ate dinner before going back to her hotel. It was well past midnight, and most of the city's residents were sleeping. She kept her mind occupied so she wouldn't think about Heather's fate if she failed.

She carefully reassembled the sniper rifle one more time. With an effective range of over a mile—she would be less than half a mile away—she'd be able to blow up three large oil storage tanks in seconds. The tanks would set off a chain reaction that should engulf the entire oil facility in flames. The rifle's suppressor would make it impossible for those on the ground to determine from which direction the shots had been fired.

She packed the disassembled rifle, stand, ammunition, and rope into a duffle bag she had stolen from the gym across the street. Some good Muslim's wallet and identification were still inside it. She would leave it all for the authorities to find. She smiled when she thought of how the Disciplinary Force of the Islamic Republic would interrogate the unsuspecting owner of the duffle bag, probably even torture the poor devil.

Dressed in black, she walked to the water tower, pulled her leather gloves tighter, and climbed the ladder to the top. She hooked the rope into place, knowing it would facilitate her quick exit from the tower. After all, she could slide down a rope faster than she could climb down a ladder. She reassembled the rifle, scope, and stand. She pushed the magazine clip into the rifle, sighted her first shot, and then waited.

The city began to stir as the sun came up. In the distance, she could see the limos with their security escort making their way toward the oil field. *An added bonus,* she thought.

Trin gave the cavalcade time to get into the facility. It took less than thirty seconds to fire her tiny lethal missiles into three oil tanks and then slide down the rope to the ground.

Moving casually, Trin stepped into an alley and shed the black robe she was wearing. She was now dressed like the international executive she was supposed to be. It was nine in the morning, when she ordered coffee at the restaurant in her hotel.

The TV in the dining room was flooded with scenes from the blazing oil field. The explosion of the three storage tanks had set off a chain reaction that had spread for miles. One after another, tanks and pipelines exploded until the carnage reached the main refinery of Iran. Panic was setting in around the country as every available responder tried in vain to contain the spreading destruction.

Vegas had made his phone call demanding that Heather be put on the noon flight to the US or another oil field would be targeted before nightfall.

At ten, Trin checked out of her hotel and caught a limo to the airport terminal. She mingled with the industrialists, who were aghast that Iran's oil fields were being targeted by terrorists.

She watched as Asheed and four Iranian soldiers escorted Heather into the waiting area. Heather was dressed in the traditional Muslim clothing, with only her eyes and hands showing. *This must be their final insult,* Trin thought. She looked closer to make certain the woman was Heather and was relieved to see it was her wife.

Trin went to the airport phone and had Asheed paged
for a call. The Iranian general scowled as he walked away
from his entourage in search of an airport phone.

Trin walked to the soldiers guarding Heather.
"Restrooms?" she queried them. "I need restrooms."

The men shook their heads and pushed her away from
Heather. Trin could tell by the shocked look on Heather's
face that her wife had recognized her voice.

Trin swaggered down the airport corridor and entered
the men's restroom. Seconds later she slipped into the
ladies' restroom located beside the men's.

"I must use the ladies' room," Heather told the guards.

They shrugged and ignored her.

"If you don't let me go to the ladies' room, I will soil
myself," she pleaded.

The men discussed her request and then pushed her
toward the restroom. As Heather rushed through the
doorway, Trin grabbed her hand, pulled her into the stall,
and locked the door.

"Quickly, change into these clothes." Trin handed her
a skirt, a blouse and a blazer. She stuffed the clothes
Heather removed into her carry-on bag.

Trin checked out her wife. "You've lost weight."

"Trin," Heather whispered, breathless.

"Not now, honey. We have a very small window of
opportunity to get the hell out of here."

She pulled Heather toward the exit and peeked out.
"All clear," she whispered.

She pulled Heather's arm through hers, and they
walked out of the ladies' room and down the corridor,
looking like any man and woman hurrying to catch a plane.

Trin flagged down a tram driver. "I have a fifty if you
can get us to terminal F in ten minutes," she promised the
man.

Heather silently followed her wife's lead and was
amazed at how quickly Trin checked in at the Air Canada

counter and was cleared to board the plane. Trin motioned for Heather to sit in first class and sat down beside her. She pulled the curtain around their seats closing out the world. Only then did she pull Heather into her arms.

They clung to each other as the plane taxied down the runway. They held their breaths as the plane lifted into the sky and wheels retracted into the belly of the aircraft.

Heather caught Trin's face between her hands and pulled her lips to hers. "Thank you for saving my life. I've never been so terrified."

"I've never been so scared," Trin whispered. "I was so afraid I would lose you. I . . ." Tears flowed down her cheeks as she released the agony she had lived with since Heather's abduction. "I couldn't live without you."

"Trin, I'm certain my luggage had a bomb in it. Asheed checked it through customs and onto the plane using his credentials, so it was never examined by anyone. I believe the bomb will explode once the plane is airborne."

Trin's mind raced, trying to decide a course of action. She knew that revealing her identity would endanger the two of them, but they couldn't let a plane full of innocents die because Asheed wanted to kill Heather.

"I knew he acquiesced too easily," Trin mumbled as she dug her federal agent ID out of the secret pocket of her carry-on.

Trin located the flight attendant showed her the government-issued identification and asked to speak with the plane's captain. The woman hesitated.

"You look nothing like this ID photo. You look like a man." The flight attendant studied Trin's face. "A beautiful man."

"It's a matter of life and death," Trin hissed. "And time is running out."

The flight attendant still eyed her suspiciously. "You can't go into the cockpit, but you can speak with Captain Latham via the phone connection." She picked up a handset and keyed in four numbers then handed the instrument to Trin.

"Captain Latham, my name is Trin Winfield. I have just rescued my wife, Dr. Heather Hunter, from the Iranian government."

"Congratulations," the captain said. "I've been following your story on national TV."

"I'm positive the Iranian military has placed a bomb on Flight 8725 bound for New York," Trin continued. "They released my wife, but they also planned to kill her. You must radio and have that plane evacuated immediately."

"Consider it done." The captain was all business as she radioed the Tehran tower. She passed along the information on an open channel so anyone listening could pick it up. She faked losing her signal as the tower demanded she return her plane to the Tehran airport.

Asheed called in reinforcements as soon as he realized that Heather had slipped away from his men. The airport was swarming with Iranian army troops when the news media from several Western TV affiliates showed up at the airport with their cameras rolling.

Asheed groaned as he watched Flight 8725 flood the tarmac with people who ran from the plane to the safety of the terminal. The flight personnel were still on the runway when the plane exploded. They suffered minor injuries as the blast rocked the area. General Asheed knew his days were numbered.

The flight attendant opened the drape pulled across Trin and Heather's seats. "Agent Winfield," she whispered, "the captain wishes to speak with you."

Erin Wade
The Roughneck & the Lady

Trin walked to the front of the plane and picked up the headset. "Winfield here, Captain."

"You were correct," Captain Bonnie Latham said. "The plane exploded on the tarmac, but thanks to you, no one was seriously injured. I wanted to let you know that I'll be questioned about the source of my information. The flight attendant and I will never reveal your presence on this plane. They will check my flight manifest and find nothing that will incriminate you. I will do my best to direct the investigation toward me, so you can make a clean getaway from the airport after we land."

"Thank you, Captain. If I or my wife can ever be of service to you, please don't hesitate to call on us."

"My wife and I appreciate all you do to help keep our country safe," Captain Latham replied. "Good luck, soldier."

By the time the authorities discovered Trin's gun and the duffel bag, she and Heather had landed in Ontario, Canada. As promised, Captain Latham diverted attention away from them and onto herself. The flight attendant feigned ignorance of everything.

They spent the night in the Embassy Suites overlooking Niagara Falls. The next day they crossed the bridge to the US side of the falls with a large group of tourists. By nightfall they were safely ensconced in a beautiful Manhattan apartment owned by Winfield Oil.

Heather lay on her side, studying the perfect face of her wife. She had been shocked by the sight of a bald Trin, but nothing could change the perfect angles of Trin's cheekbones or the depth of her sky-blue eyes. She moved her fingertips to touch the face that had given her the courage to fight through the nightmare of the past months.

Trin's sleepy eyes opened, followed by a lazy smile. "I was afraid to open my eyes," she whispered. "Afraid I was dreaming." Her hand languidly moved down Heather's back and rested at her waist.

"Oh, how I've missed the feel of your hands on me," Heather murmured.

Trin surveyed her wife's beautiful face, slowly shaking her head as if she couldn't believe such a gorgeous creature existed.

They made love, fervently reaffirming their passion and commitment to one another. Trin lay on her back and Heather snuggled into her side, resting her head on Trin's shoulder.

"Do you know who was involved in your kidnapping?" Trin asked. "Was it Reed?"

"No," Heather said vehemently. "Reed was truly horrified to learn her uncle wasn't going to return me. She tried to help me escape and paid dearly for it. I don't know what happened to her. She simply disappeared."

"She showed up at the US Embassy in Turkmenistan seeking political asylum," Trin murmured as she stroked Heather's back. "She's safe for now."

"I knew you would come for me," Heather declared. "I just had to stay alive until you got there."

"Did Asheed . . .?" Trin swallowed back her fear. "Did anyone . . . hurt you?"

"Not really," Heather mumbled. "A few backhands and verbal abuse, but no one molested me, if that's what you're asking. The Supreme Leader wanted me in good condition for the wedding."

"How did they get you out of the States in the first place?"

"I was drugged. Asheed sent a limo, and Mother rode to the airport with me. The last thing I remember is having a horrible row with her because I robbed her of her socialite wedding. I laid my head back to avoid talking with her and fell asleep. That's the last thing I remember."

"I will find out," Trin declared "and when I do, they'll wish they'd never laid eyes on you."

##

Trin was on the phone when Heather walked into the bedroom towel-drying her hair. "I know, Dad…. No, both of us are fine. Heather's a little skinny, but gorgeous as ever. We're going to stay here for a few days before we brave the storm."

Trin listened as her father explained the machinations the Winfield family had orchestrated to make it appear she was in the US. "I've arranged an interview for you with two major news stations, so the world can see you waiting to be reunited with Heather. Monty and Vegas are already in New York. Call them at this number. It needs to look like they are supporting you as you wait your wife's arrival.

"Have you watched the news at all the past two days?"

"No, sir." Trin's sheepish reply made Scott laugh.

"I suppose you had more important matters to attend to," he said. "Can you take down the information you need to contact the stations and confirm the interviews? Every news outlet in the States is clamoring for an interview with you."

Trin wrote down the information and then bid her father goodbye.

"I love the way you Winfields stick together," Heather murmured as she straddled Trin and pinned her to the chair.

"It's good to know my family always has my back."

"You'll have to get a wig before being seen in public," Heather said as she caressed Trin's bald head. "You know, without your glorious hair you're just another pretty face."

Trin laughed and lowered her lips to Heather's. "It'll grow back."

As they ended their kiss, Heather sighed. "Hair or no hair, you still take my breath away, Trin Winfield."

##

"You'll have to remain out of sight" Trin explained as she awaited the arrival of her brothers to make the rounds of New York newsrooms. "It can't appear that I had anything to do with your rescue. The Iranians would retaliate against our oil fields and me.

"The president is making an announcement in a few minutes giving the army full credit for your rescue. It's a win-win situation for all of us—a feather in the president's cap, accolades for the Army Special Forces, and the assurance that Winfields had nothing to do with your return to the States. Tomorrow morning, Monty, Vegas, and I will meet a military transport supposedly carrying you from Europe. A female officer who could double for you will walk down the plane's boarding ramp dressed in Muslim attire and get into a military limo. My brothers and I will have a tearful reunion with her.

"Tomorrow evening you and I will hold a press conference, and all hell will break loose."

Heather tiptoed to kiss her wife. "Sounds good to me. By the way, your wig is perfect. It looks like real hair."

"It is real hair," Trin chuckled. "It's just not mine."

A firm knock on their door announced the arrival of Monty and Vegas. Trin let them in and updated them on the final arrangements Scott Winfield had made to protect his only daughter and her wife.

"Don't unlock this door for anyone for any reason," Trin cautioned Heather as she pulled the door closed behind her.

Vegas and Monty linked arms with their sister as they walked side by side down the corridor. "Ready to throw up the world's biggest smoke screen?" Vegas grinned.

"My wife's home," she said, smiling back at him. "I'm ready to set the world on fire."

##

Trin and her brothers visited four newsrooms, and Trin sat through emotional interviews about how she wouldn't feel safe until her wife was beside her. The stations continually ran the president's announcement about the Army Special Forces team that had extracted Heather from Iran.

The British Broadcasting Company provided extensive footage of the Air Canada passenger plane exploding on the tarmac. The explosion had been blamed on Asheed, and he had been called before Iran's Supreme Leader.

Two of the stations made the extra effort to obtain film footage of the Iranian oil field that was still blazing and questioned if the explosion had been caused by Muslim terrorists protesting the current regime.

At the end of the evening, Americans were bursting with pride for their armed forces and congratulating the president for authorizing the extraction. There wasn't even a whisper that Trinidad Winfield might have single-handedly stolen her wife from the clutches of the Iranian army.

Chapter 39

Trin didn't open her eyes. She was afraid the soft warmness beside her would vaporize like all her other dreams of Heather.

Heather stirred slightly and pushed deeper into Trin's side. She moaned softly as she nestled into her wife's arms and returned to a sound sleep.

Trin didn't move. It was enough to simply lie beside the woman who ruled her world. As she had done a thousand times the past week, she gave thanks for Heather.

"Are you awake?" Heather whispered.

"Are you lying beside me?"

"Yes!"

"Then I'm awake," Trin said, chuckling. "I have dreamed this so many times while you were away only to find I was sleeping alone."

"I know," Heather murmured. "I knew I loved you, but being away from you made me realize that you truly are the most important thing in my life. I guess there is a lot of truth in that old idiom 'absence makes the heart grow fonder.'"

Trin stroked Heather's long, dark tresses. "I love your hair. I'm sorry I don't have any."

Heather giggled. "Believe me, your missing hair in no way diminishes your skills as a lover. As a matter of fact, you're better than ever. You haven't been practicing while I was gone, have you?"

"Only in my mind and with you," Trin grinned.

Their conversation was interrupted by the ringing of Trin's cell phone.

Trin rolled over and picked up her phone. "It's your father. Why don't you call him back? I'm certain he'd rather hear your voice than mine. Tell him we'll be home tomorrow."

"He'll want to pick us up from the airport." Heather smiled as she thought about her handsome father.

"Mine wants to meet us too." Trin laughed. "Let your dad pick us up. I'll talk to Mom and ask her to have your parents over for dinner, so we can answer all their questions at once."

"Brilliant idea." Heather caught Trin's face between her hands and kissed her sweetly. "You're more than just a pretty face."

Heather called her father and arranged for him to meet their plane at the airport. Then she asked the question she had been avoiding.

"Dad, how is Swede?"

"Not so good, honey. He's on life support. Reba wanted to keep him alive until you returned. She thinks you're a miracle worker."

"If only I were," Heather murmured.

"Let's hope my mother is sober tonight," Heather said as she zipped Trin's dress.

"I'm sure she'll be fine." Trin gave her a reassuring smile. "This is the first time the six of us have dined alone together."

"I'm certain Mother will be in grilling mode," Heather grumbled.

"Grilling mode?"

Heather laughed at Trin's expression. "You know . . . she will grill us about everything."

Trin slipped on her heels waiting until the last minute to put on the wig. "This thing is hot," Trin said as she positioned the blonde hair over her bald head. "How do I look?"

"Like a million dollars. You're beautiful."

"Let's go face them." Trin reached for Heather's hand and laced their fingers together.

"I tried to contact Roxie today," Trin informed her wife as she backed from their driveway. "She has disappeared."

"I'm sure someone knows where she is. Why are you trying to contact her?"

"I want to wrap up the Cattle Baron's Ball. A reporter called me today and asked for some final information on the Ball. You know, how much we made, when are we going to dispense the funds? Did we really double the amount raised by our predecessors?"

"All legitimate questions," Heather replied.

"Yes, but questions only Roxie can answer. I guess I could contact the bank and request a copy of our bank statements. My name is on the account too."

"Did you call her parents?" Heather asked.

"No, I should do that. I heard she was on vacation. Maybe they can tell me how to reach her."

Heather inhaled deeply and squeezed Trin's hand. "Here we are."

##

"It is so kind of you to have us all to dinner," Melody Hunter said as she greeted Scott and Lucinda Winfield.

Heather nodded as she hugged Lucinda. "Thank you."

Everyone wanted to know about Heather's experience in Iran. She explained that the surgery she performed was nothing short of a miracle. "The hand had been attached to Mrs. Palava 's leg for over a year. The doctor who performed the surgery did an excellent job. We had to cut off enough of her arm—about an inch—to reattach the

212

hand to it and then sever the hand from her leg and reattach it to her arm. I was blessed to have a talented team of doctors to assist me."

"I'm sure no one wants to hear about blood and gore over dinner," Melody snapped. "What we really want to know is how did Asheed treat you? When he decided to marry you, what did he say? You could do worse than a wealthy prince for a husband, you know."

Everyone stared at Melody in disbelief.

"I'm already married." Heather glared at her mother. "Happily married."

Scott broke the tension as he herded everyone from the dining room. "Why don't we move to the drawing room for an after-dinner drink?"

"Are you getting reacclimated?" Scott handed Heather a glass of wine.

"Thanks to Trin." Heather smiled at her wife. "She's been wonderful.

"I'm trying to put my Iranian experience behind me. Heaven knows I have a ton of work waiting for me at the hospital. I don't know how you kept up with everything, Dad."

"He lived at the hospital while you were gone," Melody grumbled. "Between dealing with the government to get you back home and keeping the trauma room running, he had little time for me."

Heather's smile never reached her eyes. She was used to everything being about her mother.

"A toast." Scott Winfield held his glass high. "To Heather's safe return and everything returning to normal."

"Amen!" Trin grinned as she clinked her glass against her wife's.

"I did talk to Jarrod Trotter," Melody said between sips of her wine. "He assured me that Peter had everything under control."

The quick glance between Heather and her father belied Melody's statement.

The two families visited until Eric realized how late it was. "We must go. I have an early morning tomorrow."

"I do too." Heather headed off her mother's argument about leaving.

Scott and Lucinda walked everyone to the door. As Eric and Melody stepped outside, Scott caught Trin's arm. "I need to talk to you."

Trin took her wife's hand and pulled her back toward the drawing room. Scott closed the door and followed his wife to where the women were sitting.

"Scott, Lucinda, Trin," Heather smiled, "thank you from the bottom of my heart for bringing me home. I don't know what I would have done without you."

Scott beamed. "I'm sure you know we had two choices: either help Trin or let her go it alone. You're our daughter too, so the choice was simple. We would have moved heaven and earth to bring you home."

"I'm sorry your parents can't know of my involvement," Trin said. "It would bring swift retaliation from the Iranians if they knew I rescued you. Not to mention their embarrassment that a woman bested their army."

"You might be interested to know that Asheed has disappeared from the face of the earth. He's either dead or in some dark dungeon somewhere," Scott added.

"But that isn't why I asked you to stay." Scott settled on the arm of his wife's chair. "Trin, the attacks on our fields have increased. We've got to find the terrorists who are responsible for the damage. It's just a matter of time until more of our employees are hurt or killed."

Trin nodded as she thought of how to confront the terrorists. "I'll take care of it, Dad.

"Garret and I will fly to Midland Monday. Is it okay if we take the chopper?"

Scott grimaced. "You've never flown a helicopter."

"No, but Garret has."

"True. He piloted me all over the place while you were MIA. You did a great job hiring him. He's a good man."

"I'm glad you like him," Trin said. "I'd better get a good night's sleep if Garret and I are flying tomorrow."

##

On the way home Heather held Trin's hand in her lap and played with her long fingers. "I love your hands."

Trin smiled. "I love your touch."

"I have a question to ask you," Heather said.

"Anything. I have no secrets from you."

"How did you get the name Trinidad?"

Trin threw her head back and laughed. "You can't repeat this. My parents would kill me."

"Scout's honor," Heather said as she flashed the three-finger Boy Scout salute.

"My parents thought it would be fun to name us after the town where we were conceived. My brothers were lucky. My parents were in the States when they became a reality. Monty's full name is Montana Scott Winfield, and Vegas is Las Vegas Scott Winfield."

"I love your parents. They're so . . . uninhibited."

"Yes, well, by the time I came along they were world travelers and vacationing in places like Australia and Trinidad. I'm just thankful they weren't in Australia when I was conceived. I'd be named Humpybong or Tittybong after some Australian town. Can you imagine what my name would have been shortened to if my folks had named me Tittybong Scott Winfield?"

Laughter filled the Jeep as they considered names Trin might have been stuck with.

"It would be difficult to strike fear into the hearts of bad guys with a name like Titty Winfield."

"You're so funny," Heather said. "I love the way you make me laugh."

"I love the way you laugh." Trin grinned.

Chapter 40

Melody threw the newspaper across the room. The front-page story was about some incredible surgery Heather had performed on the ten-year-old son of a Winfield employee. Lucinda had brought the boy to Heather. A horse had trampled his leg when he was six. It had been broken in several places and healed improperly, making it difficult for him to walk.

In a six-hour surgery, Heather had to break the bones again and reset them so the boy's leg would heal correctly. A photo of the beaming boy standing between Dr. Heather Hunter and Lucinda Winfield almost covered the top half of the front page.

My daughter was too selfish to put me in the spotlight as the mother of the bride when she married Trinidad Winfield, but she can pose for photos with Lucinda Winfield.

Melody poured a tumbler of Jack Daniels and carried it outside to the patio. Although Heather had been welcomed into the Winfield family with open arms, the joy of belonging to one of Texas's wealthiest families hadn't been extended to Melody.

Nothing is more dangerous than a mother bear whose cub has been mistreated, and it was obvious that Lucinda Winfield was still angry about the way Melody had tried to humiliate Trin at the reception.

Although Melody's drunken tirade at the roughneck had rolled off Trin, and her daughter-in-law always treated her with respect, Lucinda wasn't so forgiving.

Lucinda was polite and cordial whenever she crossed paths with Melody, but she never included her in any of the gatherings of her wealthy friends. The dreams Melody had entertained of hobnobbing with the rich and famous hadn't materialized.

She would show them all. She had accumulated enough wealth to turn her nose up at the Winfields and Moncriefs of Fort Worth's hoity-toity society.

Melody glanced at her watch. *Three in the afternoon. Not too early to have a drink.* She discounted the two glasses she had already consumed and stumbled to the liquor cabinet.

The face in the mirror over the bar looked back at her. Were her looks fading? Were there wrinkles where smooth skin used to be? Were those crow's feet at the corners of her eyes? She jumped when the phone rang and sloshed her drink onto the floor. *The maid can clean it up.*

"Hello." she said clearly, trying not to slur her words.

"Hi, honey. I thought you might like to go to that new restaurant on Seventh Street." Eric's voice was light and happy. "I thought we'd invite Heather and Trin to join us."

"That sounds wonderful. What time?"

"Let me call the girls and find out if they're available. I'll call you right back."

Eric arranged the dinner date then called his wife to let her know what time he would pick her up. He was looking forward to a nice, quiet dinner with his family.

##

Trin hung up the phone after talking to the caterer who hadn't been paid. She had spent all day fielding phone calls from various suppliers who had helped make the Cattle Baron's Ball a success. No one had been paid. Bills were ninety days past due, and the smaller suppliers were getting antsy.

For the third time today, she called Roxie's father Bart Royce. He had been avoiding her phone calls all day. Once again, his secretary said he was tied up in a meeting and Trin left her cell number. "Please tell him to call me. I must speak with him," she told the woman.

This is ridiculous, Trin thought as she shuffled through the past-due invoices that had been mailed directly to her instead of Roxie.

She shoved the bills into a file folder and headed for Royce International's headquarters. If Bart wouldn't speak to her on the phone, she would confront him in person. Surely he knew where his daughter was.

Trin was surprised to find Royce International almost deserted. It was usually teeming with activity. She parked in Roxie's reserved spot in front of the door and walked in.

As she strode toward the receptionist, Trin removed her sunglasses and flashed her most disarming smile. "Bart is expecting me," she cooed.

"First door on your right," she said, smiling back.

Trin thanked her. "Is everyone on vacation? It seems a little dead around here."

"No, Mr. Royce has laid off half the workforce." The receptionist eyed Trin again. "I don't want to discuss it in the office. Perhaps you could buy me a drink when you finish, and I'll tell you all about it."

"Perhaps." Trin treated her to the Winfield smile that showcased her dimples.

Trin didn't knock. She walked into Bart's office and closed the door. Bart Royce scrambled out from behind his desk to greet her.

"Trin,"—he cleared his throat—"what an unexpected pleasure. Please sit down."

Trin took the offered seat and got down to business. "Sir, I must talk to Roxie. I've looked everywhere for her, but I can't find a trace of her."

"She's in Guanajuato," Bart informed her, returning to his desk. "She's supposed to be back next week."

"When did you talk to her last?"

"Yesterday," Bart mumbled.

"Did she call you?"

"Yes, she checks in with me every few days."

Trin placed her business card on Bart's desk. "Next time she calls you, please have her call me. It's imperative that I speak to her as soon as possible."

"Is anything wrong?" Bart scowled.

"Just some business Roxie and I need to take care of. If I don't hear from her by tomorrow, I'll have to take care of it myself, and I did want her input."

Bart picked up the Winfield Oil business card. "Is this the best number to reach you?"

"Yes, my personal cell phone number is the one on the bottom."

Bart stood, signaling their conversation was over. "I'll tell her to call you. It was good to see you."

Trin closed the office door behind her and walked back to the lobby. "Ready for that drink?" she said to the receptionist.

The woman wrote a name and address on a sticky note and handed it to Trin. "I'll meet you there in twenty minutes."

Trin smiled and walked toward the door. "My name's Wanda," the woman called after her.

"See you in twenty, Wanda."

Trin settled into a booth at the back of the Alamo Bar and Grill, ordered a Dr. Pepper, and called Heather. Her call went to voicemail. "Honey, I'm having a drink with Bart Royce's receptionist. Trying to find Roxie. I have a mess on my hands."

She left the name and address of the restaurant and added as an afterthought, "If you haven't heard from me by seven, call me and get me out of here."

Trin watched as Wanda made her way to her booth. "What can I order for you?" Trin asked.

"Gin and tonic with a twist of lime."

Wanda made herself at home next to Trin and openly appraised her. "You don't look like the usual floozies that visit Bart. What's your name?"

"Trin Winfield."

"I was sure I knew you." Wanda beamed. "You're the Winfield oil heiress."

Trin shrugged.

"You're married to that Dr. Hunter who was kidnapped by the Iranians." Wanda shuddered. "That General Palava and his men visited our plant. He gave me the creeps." She downed her gin and tonic.

Trin motioned for the waitress to bring Wanda another drink. "Why did he visit your plant?"

"I don't know, unless they make rugs," Wanda said. "But he seemed very friendly with Bart and Roxie."

"Is Royce International in financial trouble?"

"Yeah, I think so. I don't have access to the books, but we're operating with a fourth of the employees we had last year, and one warehouse has been closed and sealed as if it contained the bubonic plague.

"I don't think the Royce's are hurting, though. They're still high rollers. Bart just purchased a new Porsche Panamera. Those babies start at a hundred thousand."

"Do you have any idea where Roxie is?" Trin asked as she signaled for another gin and tonic.

"She disappeared around the same time the Muslims took your wife.

"Say, weren't you and Roxie dating hot and heavy about three years ago? Roxie told me you were getting married. What happened?"

"We never talked about getting married," Trin said, frowning. "We were an item for a while but nothing serious. I lost my hand in an accident, and Roxie dropped out of my life."

Wanda studied Trin's hands. "Which one is fake? They both look perfect to me."

"Neither." Trin chuckled as she flexed the fingers on both hands. "That's how I met my wife. She reattached my hand."

Wanda downed her fifth gin and tonic, and her tongue really loosened up. "I probably shouldn't be telling you this," she slurred. "I think the Royces have gotten into gun running."

"Gun running?" Trin gasped. "Why would you think that?"

"I think that's why the Iranians were visiting our factory. I think they were working on some deal to have Bart smuggle weapons from the US to Iran."

Wanda leaned her head on Trin's shoulder and giggled. "I think you'll have to drive me home."

"What about your car?"

"I leave it here all the time. The owners are good friends of mine."

Trin punched a number on her cell phone and typed in their location along with the text, "Take Uber."

"Uber will be here shortly to take you home," she informed Wanda.

Half an hour later Wanda sat up straight as a beautiful brunette approached them. "Oh my God, have I died and gone to heaven?"

Trin laughed. "No, that's my wife."

"Did someone call for Uber?" Heather said, wrinkling her nose at Trin.

"I did. Wanda's in no condition to drive home."

Wanda wobbled as she tried to stand, and Heather reached out to steady her.

"I'll put her in the Uber, honey," Trin said. "Would you pay our bar tab?"

##

Heather joined Trin as the Uber driver pulled away. Trin leaned down and kissed her wife briefly. "I'm glad you came with Uber. The drive home will be much more pleasant with you beside me."

On the drive home Trin told Heather all she had learned from Bart and his receptionist. "I guess I'll go to the bank tomorrow and take care of the organization's finances. I'm getting all kinds of calls from decorators and caterers who haven't been paid. Roxie's always been a bit flaky, but she's never failed to handle business."

Trin squeezed Heather's hand. "Enough of my whining. What have you been doing?"

"I had dinner with Mom and Dad. He was as delightful as always, and Mother was her usual inebriated self." Heather played with Trin's fingers. "I love your hands. Nice long fingers. Strong hands."

"Are you okay?"

"I don't know, Trin. I'm worried about Mother. I've tried to talk to her, but she won't even discuss the possibility that she may be an alcoholic. She has always been a bit narcissistic, but now she's almost unbearable.

"She pouted throughout the entire dinner because you weren't there. I wish she could find contentment within herself without relying on others to make her feel important."

"Why don't I take her to lunch one day? Give us a chance to get to know each other," Trin said.

"Seriously, you would do that?"

"I would do anything for you, honey. If it will make your life easier or happier, I am delighted to do it."

"You make my life happier and easier." Heather pulled Trin's hand tight against her body. "Thank you."

"Have you ever noticed how a drive goes faster when we're together?" Trin asked as she pulled the Jeep into the driveway.

##

Trin showered while Heather took a call from the hospital. Heather was in bed but still talking on the phone when Trin slipped between the sheets.

Heather trembled as Trin trailed her fingers down her body. Heather hurried to conclude her call and let her cell phone slide from her hand as she rolled onto her side to face her wife. "We've been together three years," she whispered, "and your touch still inflames me."

"Hmmm." Trin smiled her slow, lazy smile. "That's as it should be. Everything okay in the world of scalpels and needles?"

"Uh-huh." Heather pressed closer.

"Is your dad on call tonight?"

Heather undulated against Trin. "Uh-huh."

"How is—"

"Are you going to jabber all night or make love to me?" Heather said as she burrowed under her wife.

"What do you think?" Trin murmured as she pulled Heather into her arms and nibbled at her bottom lip.

Chapter 41

Trin showed the cashier her identification and requested a printout of the Cattle Baron's Ball bank statement.

"Are you certain this is correct?" She gaped at the bank teller.

"That's what the computer shows," the clerk replied.

"May I speak with a bank officer?"

"Yes, ma'am. If you'll have a seat, I'll get an officer for you."

Bank president Laura Crews surveyed the Winfield woman who was thumbing through a bank printout. A visit from Trinidad Winfield was never a good sign. The Winfields had millions in various investment portfolios in Laura's bank. If the bank ever lost their accounts, it would fold. She straightened her blazer and then walked toward the blonde.

"Ms. Winfield, what a pleasant surprise," Laura said, extending her hand to Trin. "Please come into my office."

Laura closed her office door and gestured for Trin to have a seat. "Tell me how I may help you."

"I'm trying to locate the funds raised by the Cattle Baron's Ball," Trin said, wasting no time on small talk. "This bank statement shows the account contains a million dollars and some change. We should have a billion."

Laura took the statement Trin was holding and typed the account number into her computer. She ran through the transactions from the beginning of the year. "Yes, Roxie Royce and you became the signers on the account last year.

It looks like several automated PayPal deposits were made during the year prior to the ball."

"And after the Ball?" Trin asked.

"One deposit for $20 million and one for $5 million. Several for over $100,000."

"Where's the money?" Trin asked.

"I don't . . . it looks like it was transferred to an out-of-state account after the Ball."

"Who authorized the transfers?" Trin scowled.

"Miss Royce, of course."

"Laura, I need to know the bank and account number that received that money." Trin cocked an eyebrow. "Now!"

"Your name is on the account," Laura assured her. "You have a right to know about all transactions."

The bank president scrolled through the account and located the wire transfer that had moved the funds from the Ball's account to an account in Detroit, Michigan."

"What name is on the account?"

"Bart Royce," Laura mumbled.

"Did you say Bart Royce?" Trin gasped.

"Yes."

Bart Royce was backing his Porsche from his parking spot when Trin pulled her Jeep behind him. He couldn't back up or go forward.

Bart jumped from his car and stormed to the driver's side of the Jeep. "What the hell . . . Trin, what's the meaning of this?"

"Get into my vehicle. We need to talk."

"I don't want—"

"Bart, I don't know what the hell is going on," Trin growled, "but I'm pretty sure you can enlighten me. I'm in no mood to pussyfoot around. Now, get into the damn Jeep."

Bart licked his lips and looked around as if checking to see if anyone was watching. Then he climbed into the passenger seat of the Jeep.

"Your office may be bugged," Trin said as she pulled onto the interstate. "I need to know where Roxie is."

Bart snorted. "I told you, I don't know."

"If I have to stop this vehicle to get straight answers, you won't be a pretty sight when I'm through with you."

The anger on Trin's face reinforced her words. Bart swallowed, licked his lips again, and cleared his throat. "I don't know where Roxie is. I do know she's in bad trouble."

"Why?"

"When the Iranians flew here to attend the auction, it was just a cover to allow them to move around freely." Bart cleared his throat again. "Any chance of getting a drink?"

Trin pulled into a Sonic Drive-In. "What do you want?"

"I meant an alcoholic drink," Bart scoffed.

"You can have whatever Sonic serves." The angry look on Trin's face darkened. "You're not getting out of this Jeep until I have the answers I want to hear."

"Large Coke," Bart grumbled.

Trin pulled back on the highway. "You were saying?"

"To avoid scrutiny of their activities, the Iranians used our private plane to fly to Detroit and arrange a deal with a gun dealer there." Bart paused, taking a long pull on his straw. "They ordered several million dollars in arms, with the promise of a $25 million down payment and the remainder when the arms crossed into Canada."

"What did you get out of this deal?"

"Screwed," Bart huffed. "They wanted me to make the deposit payment to avert suspicion from them. They became incensed when I told them I didn't have that kind of money. They . . . they took my Roxie and said she would be returned when I made the payment. They promised to pay me back double the money."

"Where did you get the money?" Trin had a sinking feeling.

"I was desperate. I searched Roxie's office and found her checkbook and account information for the Cattle Baron's Ball. There were millions in the account. Using Roxie's computer so it was identified by the bank's software, I made a wire transfer from the Ball's account to my warehouse account in Detroit. They're supposed to wire the money into my account, and I'll replace the funds in the Ball's account and get Roxie back."

"You transferred out much more than you needed to cover the Muslim transaction," Trin noted.

"I may have taken enough to pay off some of my debt," Bart mumbled.

"How long ago did you make the down payment on the arms deal?"

"Three months ago," Bart said, his voice barely above a whisper. "I've tried to contact them but failed. Asheed has disappeared from the face of the earth. I have no idea who to talk with. I'm just hoping someone contacts me."

"When they do, call me immediately," Trin said. "Don't try to deal with these bastards alone. Roxie's life is at stake."

Trin was certain Bart wasn't telling her all he knew. She drove him back to his car. As he opened the door to get out, fingers of steel wrapped around his wrist and Trin jerked him back to her.

"If you're lying or withholding valuable information from me, neither heaven nor hell will have a place for you to hide from me. Are we clear?"

Bart made a strangling sound and nodded. Trin released him and shoved him from her Jeep.

Chapter 42

Still thinking about the information she had gleaned from Bart, Trin drove to the hospital to check on Swede. She had visited her former employee and best friend every day, and there had been no change.

As she turned onto Eighth Avenue, her phone rang. Sheriff Douglass's number popped onto her screen, and she pushed the button on her steering wheel to answer the call.

"Hello, Sheriff."

"Trin, you need to get here as soon as possible." The tension in the voice of Midland's top lawman was palpable. "We're getting chatter about destroying the Winfield oil and gas operations in the Permian Basin and your fields in Beaumont. I don't have enough men to fan out and cover the areas in danger."

"Have you spoken with the Beaumont sheriff?" Trin asked.

"He's on vacation, and his second-in-command is scared to make a decision on his own."

"I'll try to line up some Texas Rangers," Trin said. "We'll be there before dark. Let's interrogate Clem again and see if we can get anything out of him."

As Trin drove toward the hospital a plan began to form in her mind, and she called her secretary. "Missy, file a flight plan for Garret and me to the Midland airport. Call Garret and ask him to meet me at the airport in an hour. Contact the rest of the team and tell them to meet us at the Midland sheriff's office at eight in the morning. Oh, and we'll be taking the helicopter."

Trin left her Jeep with the hospital valet. "Keep it here. I'll be back in less than an hour."

Trin sprinted up the stairs to Heather's office on the second floor. She tapped on the door as she opened it to announce herself.

Trin loved the way Heather's eyes always lit up when she entered a room. "God, I'm glad to see you," Heather said as she moved from behind her desk and embraced her wife.

Heather's lips were always so soft, so sweet. "You taste like cherries," Trin said, nibbling at the full, bottom lip that always drove her insane.

"Umm . . . and you taste like—"

Loud alarm bells began clanging, and Heather jerked from Trin's arms. "Swede!" she yelled as she ran from the room.

Trin followed Heather as she ran down the hallway toward the burn unit. Doctors and nurses were everywhere, and Reba lay crumbled on the floor, crying.

Trin sat down beside her and pulled Reba into her arms. "It's okay, sweetie," she cooed.

"He's gone, Trin," Reba sobbed. "Swede's dead."

Trin bowed her head and squeezed her eyes shut, fighting back tears. When she opened her eyes, she was staring at a pair of shoes she knew were Heather's. She didn't want to slowly scan perfect legs, up past the flat stomach and ample breasts to the face of an angel, but she couldn't stop herself.

Heather's eyes were black with misery. They answered all Trin's questions. "He's gone," Heather murmured.

Reba wailed louder, and Trin held her tighter. She held Reba like she wished Heather was holding her right now.

As the personnel in Swede's room began to clear out, Trin got to her feet and pulled Reba up with her. She gave up a silent prayer when she saw Father Tremont and his wife, Rebecca, walking toward them. The Tremonts had become a solid source of strength for Reba. Reba fell into Rebecca's open arms.

##

Heather gripped Trin's hand as they walked back to her office. "I'll talk with Father Tremont and help with the arrangements."

"Bill everything to Winfield Oil," Trin mumbled, still trying to keep from crying.

Heather opened her office door, and Trin followed her inside. "Baby, I'm so sorry," Heather said, locking the door and pulling her wife into her arms. Trin melted into her and cried like a baby.

As the flow of tears lessened, a hard resolve filled Trin's heart. She would find who was responsible for the fires. Someone was going to pay with their life for killing Swede.

Heather led Trin to the sofa, where she again cradled her in her arms. Trin wanted nothing more out of life than to bury herself in the warm safety of her wife's arms, but she knew she couldn't stay. She had work to do.

"I'm here for you, Trinidad," Heather whispered in her ear. "I'll always be here for you."

"I have to go." Trin exhaled loudly and wiped her eyes. "I have to go to Midland tonight."

"Why?"

"I'll be back tomorrow night," Trin promised. "Sheriff Douglass has requested my help."

"It's dangerous, isn't it?" Heather tried to talk around the lump in her throat. "I . . . I can't lose you, Trin. Please be safe."

"I will, honey. I'll see you tomorrow night."

231

Chapter 43

"What's up?" Garret asked as he buckled himself into the helicopter. "Why the chopper?"

"Sometimes I like to get closer to the ground than I can in the plane," Trin said, adjusting her headset.

"Trin, we've been airborne fifteen minutes, and you haven't said a dozen words. Is everything okay?"

"No, there's a lot that isn't okay. My best friend died today."

Garret took a deep breath. "I'm sorry to hear that."

"The terrorists have kidnapped a friend and are planning to attack Winfield Oil's operations in Texas."

"This is beginning to sound more like Afghanistan than the United States," Garret said.

"I won't ask you to do anything dangerous, Garret. I don't want another death on my conscience."

"I'm a big boy, Trin. I knew signing on with you wouldn't be a walk in the park. You can count on me for whatever you need."

"Today is going to be pretty calm. We're just going to interrogate Ally—or Clem, as I like to call him." Trin chuckled. "It drives him crazy."

Sheriff Douglass met them at the airport. You two want a bite to eat before you talk to Ally?"

"No, sir," Trin replied. "We want to move as quickly as possible."

When they arrived at the sheriff's headquarters, Ally Abbasi was already in the interrogation room. He smirked when Trin entered. Garret and Douglass watched through the one-way mirror.

"I have a list of questions to ask you, Clem." Trin dropped a two-page typed list onto the table in front of Ally.

Ally spit on the list and grinned maliciously at Trin.

"I also have a long list of things I'm not allowed to do to you," Trin huffed. "I can't waterboard you, cut you, choke you, burn you, freeze you, hit you, or shoot you. Man, my hands are tied, aren't they?

"I'm going to give you one last chance to answer my questions." Trin paced the floor.

"I need the location of all your cells in Texas. I need the list of planned terrorist acts against Texas citizens and companies.

"I need to know the names of the individuals responsible for the attack on the Winfield wells in Joshua. I know your cells are running drug operations, arms deals, and white slavery camps. I want the locations of those.

"Where is Roxie Royce?"

Ally smirked and shrugged one shoulder. "Thousands will die, and there's nothing you can do about it. Your bleeding-heart politicians have tied your hands for a few Muslim votes."

Trin controlled the urge to bury her fist in the man's face. "I know who you are, where you rank among terrorist leaders. I know you speak English fluently, so why don't you save both of us a lot of trouble and give me the information I need?"

Ally's evil cackle brought a smile to Trin's face. "I had a feeling you wouldn't cooperate," she said. "You leave me no choice but to transfer you to federal prison in Fort Worth."

For the first time, fear flickered in Ally's eyes.

Trin leaned into his face and whispered, "Yeah, I'll have you all to myself on the ride back to my town."

She walked to the door. "Sheriff, could you join us, please?" she called into the hallway.

Sheriff Douglass stepped away from the one-way mirror and sauntered into the interrogation room. "Is there a problem, ma'am?"

"I just need you to sign this transfer order." Trin handed Douglass a folded paper. "I want to take Clem to Fort Worth with me."

Douglass scanned the form and pulled a pen from his shirt pocket. "Looks like everything's in order. We'll be glad to get rid of him."

"No! No! You can't give me to her. She will kill me."

"Nah, Agent Winfield won't kill you," Douglass said, glaring at Ally. "You'll just wish she would."

##

Sheriff Douglass double-checked Ally's restraints. His wrists were secured with reinforced handcuffs, and his feet were chained together. A thick cable ran from the shackles on his feet, up his stomach, and fastened to the manacles binding his wrists. Garret led the prisoner by a long chain attached to the center of the cable running down Ally's body.

"Don't you want his hands cuffed behind him?" Sheriff Douglass asked.

"No, that might break his arms or pull them out of socket." Garret climbed into the chopper, and Ally planted his heels, refusing to step up into the helicopter. "You can either use the step and get in, or I'll drag you in myself," Garret said. He cocked his head and counted to three. At the count of three, Garret yanked on the chain, slamming Ally against the side of the chopper, and dragged the terrorist into the aircraft. Blood ran down Ally's face.

"Garret," Trin chided, "I think you caused his nose to bleed."

"He hit it against the chopper trying to get in." Garret shrugged.

Trin jumped into the passenger seat beside Ally, pulled the door closed, and fastened her seatbelt. Garret flipped the switches to start the rotors moving as Trin hooked the end of Ally's chain leash to a huge S-hook and placed a headset over his ears.

"Can you hear me?" she asked, watching to see if the man's eyes snapped toward her. They did.

"Good. Now I'm going to position your mouthpiece right in front of your lips, so we can hear you when you start talking."

Ally spit at the mouthpiece then jerked backward as the chopper lifted into the air.

Once the aircraft had cleared the trees, Garret leveled it and headed toward the most secluded of the Winfield oil fields.

Trin unrolled a long strip of masking tape and securely taped the headset onto Ally's head. "A couple more wraps and this thing will stay on through a tornado," she said, smiling.

"You might want to mumble something," Trin said. "Just to make certain I can hear you when you scream that you're ready to talk."

"That's not going to happen," Ally growled, giving her the sound test she wanted. She nodded.

"Do you know what happened to me today?" Trin asked.

Ally glared at her in silent hatred.

"My best friend died because of one of your terrorist attacks. He had a wife and a small baby.

"Then I discovered your folks have kidnapped a friend of mine. I want to find her—alive."

Ally's eyes darted around the chopper then back to Trin.

"Last chance, Clem. Are you going to answer my questions, or do I cut the Gordian knot?"

"Go to hell, bitch!" Ally croaked as he swung both fists toward Trin. She ducked and pulled the lever on Ally's door.

"After you," she yelled as she shoved him from the chopper.

The man's raspy scream almost deafened her as he plummeted toward the earth. A strangled "Oomph" let her know he had reached the end of the chain.

"You can start talking any time you want," Trin suggested, "and I'll pull you back inside."

Only cursing and growling returned through her headset.

"Garret, see those cell phone towers? See if you can run the poles with Ally. I'm betting sooner or later you will tear off his head."

"Nah, boss, I can probably fly fifty miles weaving in and out between those things without bashing in his head."

"You can't do this," Ally sobbed. "Your . . . your government won't allow it. Aaahhh!" the man squealed as Garret flew him straight toward a tower, weaving right at the last minute to avoid planting him in the metal.

"My government will never know," Trin cooed. "They don't really like cowards like you who kill innocent men, women, and children."

Ally shrieked as Garret swung his body away from a tower just in time to keep from ripping him to shreds.

Garret laughed. "How about a bet, boss? I bet you fifty bucks I can make it through fifty of these towers without tearing him to pieces."

"I'll take that bet," Trin said. "Even if I lose, I'll be a winner."

"I-I'm freezing," Ally rasped.

"Aw, that's too bad. We have hot coffee. You can have some if you answer my questions." Trin's voice was deep and deadly.

"Bitch!" Ally screamed until he was hoarse as Garret weaved him in and out between power lines and steel girders.

Finally, she'd had enough. "I'm tired of this," Trin said. "Just wrap him up in some power lines. We'll swear he jumped from the chopper. Give me a count down so I can release him just before he hits, or he'll wrap us up too."

Garret made a big circle and then headed for a cluster of power lines. "Counting down from ten, boss.

"Ten, nine—on target, boss—eight, seven, six—get ready to release, boss. Five, four, three—"

"I talk! I talk!" Ally's gravelly voice came through the headsets. The chopper tilted veered off, barely missing the lines.

"Now," Trin growled. "Start talking now. There won't be a countdown next time. Just my signal to behead you on the electric lines." She motioned for Garret to turn on the tape recorder connected to their headsets.

Garret headed the helicopter back toward Midland as Ally sang like a mockingbird. He gave cell locations, names, places where guns and explosives were stored, and dates for attacks planned on various Winfield sites.

"And Roxie Royce?" Trin asked. "Where is Roxie Royce?"

Trin listened in disbelief as Ally gave her the last bit of information she wanted.

"Why don't you take the controls and I'll pull him back in," Garret suggested.

"I can haul him in, but thanks for the offer."

Trin pulled Ally up slowly, fighting the demon that was whispering, "Just unhook him and let him fall."

"You're close enough to pull yourself in," she informed Ally as his head appeared.

"I can't. I'm too weak," he snarled. "Give me your hand."

"Not in this life, dude," Trin scoffed. "You can either pull yourself in or take your chances on losing a limb when we sit this bird down on the ground. Which is going to happen pretty quickly."

Ally scrambled to pull himself inside as Garret began flipping switches to set the chopper down on the ground.

"Well?" Sheriff Douglass asked as Trin jumped from the chopper.

"We have everything we need. Let's keep him in solitary confinement until we run the sting."

"How'd you do that?" Douglass asked as he hauled Ally out of the plane. "He doesn't have a mark on him."

"It's complicated." Trin chuckled.

Coordinating with the Texas Rangers and other Texas law enforcement agencies, the sheriff, Trin, and Garret spent the entire night arranging to sweep the Muslim terrorists' locations the next day. Careful that no one escaped on technicalities, Douglass had a judge sitting in his office signing arrest warrants as fast as the sheriff's office presented them to him.

The Texas Homeland Security office was happy to be involved in something other than turning back illegals at the Mexico border. The arrests were a big coup for them.

Chapter 44

Heather dropped her spoon and forgot about stirring her coffee as she watched the news reporter running to keep up with Trin's long legs.

"Ms. Winfield, is it true that Texas law enforcement agencies have arrested almost three hundred terrorists?"

"Yes," Trin replied. "Thanks to Sheriff Cliff Douglass, we were able to pull off one of the largest sweeps of international terrorists Texas has ever seen. He coordinated everything and made it happen."

Video of SWAT teams crashing through doors to confiscate billions in cocaine and heroin played nonstop, followed by raids on brothels where women and young children had been forced into prostitution.

Officers lying in wait captured gangs of terrorists as they tried to carry out early dawn attacks on Winfield Oil installations across Texas. Using video and photo identification to arrest the criminals in the acts guaranteed a conviction.

Heather fought the desperate urge to call Trin just to hear her voice and say, "I love you." She knew Trin was up to her ears in alligators. She tamped down her anxiety and waited until she could hold her wife again.

"She's incredible," Eric Hunter said as he joined his daughter in the hospital cafeteria. "Did you know this was going to happen?"

"I knew she flew to Midland in response to Sheriff Douglass's call, but I had no idea it was of this magnitude." Heather's hand shook as she picked up her spoon to stir her coffee. "I worry about her all the time, Dad."

Eric covered his daughter's hand with his. "You have to find a way to handle it. I can't have my top surgeon's hands shaking."

"I know." Heather sighed. "I just need to see her and know she's okay."

Eric cleared his throat and squirmed in his chair. "Do you know where your mother was last night?"

"I . . . no, Dad. Wasn't she at home?"

"I was on call last night and came in to operate on a young man who was pretty torn up in a motorcycle collision. I returned home around three this morning, and your mother was gone. I called her cell phone, but it went to voicemail.

"She called me a few minutes ago to tell me she had spent the night with you because you were worried about Trin."

"Oh," Heather whispered. "I . . . I'm sure she has a good reason for . . . misleading you."

"You mean lying to me?"

"Dad, I don't know what to say. Is she at the house now? Why don't you go home? I'll hold down the fort here. You need to talk to her."

"Heather, I know your mother has her faults, but I love her. I don't want to lose her."

"Go, Dad. I'll call you if I need you."

Lori Rogers carried her breakfast tray toward Heather. "Do you need to be alone, or would you like some company?" Lori asked as she watched Trin Winfield answer reporters' questions.

Heather didn't take her eyes from the TV screen. "Please join me."

"She's one impressive woman," Lori said, nodding toward the TV. "I envy you."

Heather chuckled. "She certainly takes my breath away—in more ways than one."

"You two have gone through a lot since that day they carried her in here on a stretcher with her hand in an ice chest."

"Yes." Heather smiled. "I thought she was a man until the day I released her. Dad had taken over her treatment, and I never saw her after surgery."

They watched as camera crews followed Trin and Garret to the helicopter. "She'll be home in a couple of hours." Heather's wistful tone made Lori smile. "She hasn't slept in two days. She'll be exhausted."

"Who's the hunk with her?" Lori said, rolling her eyes playfully.

"Garret Jenkins. He replaced . . . Swede."

Lori patted Heather's arm. "I'm so sorry about Swede. You know he's better off now."

Heather nodded. "I can't help thinking that could have been Trin."

As if on cue, Heather's cell phone rang, and Trin's beautiful face filled the screen. "It's her!" Heather squealed like a teenager. "Hi, baby. Are you okay?"

"Tired and missing you," Trin's weary voice replied. "I'll be home in a couple of hours. Is there any chance—?"

"I'll be there, baby," Heather assured her. "Be careful."

Heather ended the call and looked hopefully at Lori. "Please tell me we have no emergency surgeries coming down the pipe."

"Not a thing." Lori grinned. "It looks like your gorgeous wife took care of the terrorists for the time being. Go, welcome her home."

Chapter 45

Heather downloaded a novel onto her Kindle and relaxed on the sofa while she waited for Trin. Her heart skipped a beat when she heard the key in the lock. She was at the door by the time it opened. She pulled Trin into her arms and held her tight.

"Are you okay?" Heather asked as she finally released her wife and stepped back to scrutinize the blonde.

"I'm fine, honey. A little tired and sick of this flipping wig." She pulled the blonde tresses from her head and tossed them on the sofa. "I'm sorry. That thing is so hot. It's worse than wearing a rug on my head."

"Are you hungry?" Heather asked as she tiptoed to kiss her wife. "I have your favorite casserole in the fridge."

"All I want is a hot shower and to fall asleep in your arms," Trin replied, returning the kiss.

##

Heather lay awake for hours holding her wife in her arms. When Trin cried out in her sleep, Heather held her tighter and murmured soft, reassuring words to her. She stroked Trin's back and gently traced the outline of her face with her fingers.

When Trin's tense body began to relax, Heather brushed her hand across her soft, downy hair and whispered, "I love you, Chicken Little."

Trin melted into the softness of her wife as she nestled her face between Heather's breasts. Trin slipped deeper into a dreamless sleep, and Heather soon followed her.

##

Heather awoke facing her wife. The worry lines in Trin's brow had disappeared. Her tight lips had softened into a slight smile, and her clenched jaw had relaxed, giving her face a sweet, angelic look.

Heather traced the angles of her wife's face with her fingertips, admiring the high cheekbones and full lips. She softly kissed the barely visible dimples that deepened when Trin smiled. "I love everything about you," she whispered.

"Even my hair?" Trin entwined her long legs with Heather's. "I dreamed you called me Chicken Little."

Heather laughed. "That was no dream." She tousled Trin's soft, curly hair. "I said, 'I love you, Chicken Little.'"

"Prove it," Trin whispered, rising above her.

"I thought you'd never ask."

##

Heather's head rested on Trin's chest. She listened to the rapid strumming of her wife's heart and hugged her closer. "Thank you."

"Umm, believe me, the pleasure was all mine." Trin trailed her fingers up and down Heather's back. "All mine."

Heather giggled. "I would argue that point, but you just keep believing it."

"Is that offer of my favorite casserole still good?" Trin laughed as her stomach growled for food.

"Of course. Let me preheat the oven." Heather slid from her side of the bed and pulled on one of Trin's T-shirts.

Trin wolf whistled as she watched her wife walk toward the door. "Damn, you are the sexiest woman alive."

Heather glanced over her shoulder and squealed as Trin bounded from the bed and ran toward her. After several smoldering kisses, Heather caught her breath. "It'll take about five minutes to preheat the oven and forty minutes for the casserole to cook."

Trin followed her into the kitchen. "Let's preheat the oven, put in the casserole, and see if we can find a way to occupy ourselves for forty minutes."

"I have a few ideas." Heather's salacious grin made Trin's heart beat faster.

"I thought you might," Trin said. "You doctors are so inventive."

"You should call your parents," Heather suggested as she turned on the oven and pulled the casserole from the refrigerator. "Your mom was worried sick."

"Let me grab my phone."

Trin returned to the kitchen dressed in shorts and a T-shirt. She was talking to her mother on the phone. She sat down on the stool at the kitchen island.

Heather slid the dish into the oven and moved to stand between Trin's knees. She grinned as she fondled her wife, who was desperately trying to keep from gasping in her mother's ear.

"I must go, Mom. Heather has dinner on the table.... Yes, we'll see you and Dad tomorrow."

Trin tossed her cell phone onto the counter. "Oh, you are evil, Dr. Hunter, and I love it."

"You have forty minutes to show me how much you love it." Heather giggled.

"Oh, the pressure." Trin mumbled as she pulled Heather further between her legs and wrapped her arms around her.

##

Their dinner conversation was light. Each had something earth-shattering to tell the other but didn't want to ruin the moment.

244

"Did you find Roxie?" Heather said, finally pulling them back to reality.

Trin frowned. "Not yet, but I think I know where she is."

"Is she okay?"

"I don't know."

"Can you tell me about yesterday?" Heather asked.

"I can, but you can't repeat anything I tell you." Trin refilled their tea glasses. "If you do, I'll have to keep you locked in the closet and only let you out when I come home."

"That wouldn't be all bad." Heather giggled as she held up three fingers. "Scout's honor, my lips are sealed."

Trin gave Heather a blow-by-blow description of the events that had culminated in the arrest of several terrorist cells. When she finished, Heather talked about her concern for her mother and father.

"Where was she?" Trin asked in response to the news that Melody had lied about spending the night with her daughter.

"I don't know. I haven't spoken to Dad since then. All hell broke loose in your world, and I came home to be here when you arrived."

"I thank you for that." Trin leaned across the corner of the table and kissed her wife. "I needed you in every way imaginable."

"I know, baby," Heather said, caressing Trin's cheek with her fingertips.

The hospital's ringtone rattled Heather's cell phone. Trin inhaled deeply. "I have to take it," Heather said apologetically.

"I know."

Heather placed the phone to her ear and listened intently as Lori described the situation.

"How did he get into the operating room? What happened to Dad?" Heather bombarded Lori with questions as she gathered her things and headed for the door, Trin at her heels. "I'm on my way."

Trin opened the passenger door so Heather could continue talking. By the time Heather concluded her call, they were halfway to the emergency room.

"What's happened?" Trin scowled.

"Dad's been in a car accident. Peter is operating on him."

"Jesus Christ!" Trin shouted. "That's like being operated on by the grim reaper."

"Exactly!"

Melody and Jarrod Trotter were in the hallway outside the waiting room as Heather flew by. Trin stopped beside her mother-in-law. "What happened?"

"We were in an awful car wreck," Melody said between sobs. "A driver broadsided us and caved in the passenger door on Eric. He was unconscious when the ambulance brought him in."

Trin could smell the alcohol on Melody. Just the fumes from her were enough to intoxicate bystanders. "You were driving?"

"Yes." Melody wailed louder and gripped Jarrod's hand. "Thank God, Peter was on duty."

"Yeah," Trin growled. She didn't even want to think about how Heather would react if something happened to Eric.

##

"God bless, you're finally here," Lori blurted out as Heather held up her hands for the sterile gloves. "He's locked me out of the operating room. The nurses attending don't know what to do. He's already made an incision in your father's back. I've called hospital security."

Heather broke out in a cold sweat. She knew Peter was inept enough to cripple her dad. "Turn on the sound system so I can talk to him," Heather instructed.

"Peter, it's Heather. Thank you for getting things started, but I'm here now, and I'd like to take care of my dad."

Peter cackled. "You don't think I'm capable of operating on Eric?"

"Of course I do. I just want to assist you. You don't have a standby doctor to help you if anything goes wrong."

Peter looked around him as if surprised there was no backup surgeon in the operating room. "I don't need help. I can do this."

"Can you tell me his condition?" Heather tried to keep him talking as one of the nurses edged toward the double doors leading into the operating room.

"He may have a severed spine," Peter reported calmly. "I won't know until I get in there and have a look."

"What do his X-rays show?"

"I . . . I don't know," Peter mumbled.

"You did take X-rays or an MRI, right?" *Please, God, don't let him cut into my father.*

Peter stared at her face in the small window of the emergency room door. "X-rays?"

"Peter, you aren't flying blind, are you?" Heather almost threw up at the thought of the butcherer slicing into her father.

Suddenly a stream of blood shot straight up from the operating table. "Oh dear God!" a nurse screamed.

"Stop it! Stop it!" Peter howled. "One of you clamp that off."

"It's an artery!" an assisting nurse yelled as another nurse hit the automatic button to open the doors.

Heather heard the *click* as the doors slowly swung open—a moment that lasted an eternity.

Although it was against all hospital procedures, security entered the operating room and dragged Peter out as he screamed profanities at Heather.

Heather was already in position, clamping arteries and checking to see what damage the loon had done. In a matter of minutes, she had stopped the blood flow and began suturing the arteries and muscle back together. She checked to make certain Peter hadn't inflicted any more damage and then closed the incision he had made in her father's back.

"You arrived just in time." Lori's shoulders slumped as she leaned against the wall that was holding her up. "I don't know what I'd do if something happened to Eric."

"He's going to be just fine." Heather closed her eyes and gave thanks that her father was going to be okay. *Now to find out what happened and deal with Peter.*

Trin had been sitting beside Melody in the waiting room for what seemed like hours when Heather, another physician, and Lori entered the room. The trio had their heads bent close together, obviously in an animated discussion. As Trin waited for an opportunity to get an update on Eric, Garret and two Texas Rangers strode through the door.

Garret hurried over to where Trin and Melody were seated. "What happened?" Garret sniffed and jerked his head back as the smell of whiskey filled his nostrils.

"Heather's father was in an automobile accident," Trin informed him. She stood leading Garret toward the two Rangers and explaining the situation. "I think they've given Peter a sedative to quiet him and have him secured in the psych ward.

"I need one of you to get Peter's father home. He's the gentleman in the wheelchair."

Trin leaned against the wall as her wife continued to consult with Lori and the other physician. Heather was so professional, so confident, so perfect. Trin tried to suppress the tremor that ran through her body as she thought about how her wife had held her and comforted her the night before.

I'll do the same for her tonight, she thought as she rejoined Melody.

"I need to get out of here," Melody grumbled, fanning her face with a magazine. "This place depresses me. I need a good stiff drink."

Trin snorted. "Your good stiff drink is what landed Eric on the operating table of a madman. I'd think you'd stay sober long enough to find out how your husband is."

Melody glared at Trin. "You can't speak to me like that. I don't care if your last name is Winfield. I'm going through a rough time. I need something to calm my nerves."

"With all due respect, Melody, your drinking almost cost a fine doctor his life tonight."

"Someone take me home!" Melody shrieked. "I can't stand it any longer. I must get out of here."

Heather looked up at her mother then finished her discussion with Lori and the doctor.

"I'd like to sit with Dr. Hunter, if it's okay with you," Lori said.

"I'd welcome that," Heather replied. "I'd planned on staying with him, but I'd feel safe with you watching him. I'd better take Mother home with me."

Chapter 46

Trin logged onto her computer and signed into the bank account for the Cattle Baron's Ball. To her surprise, all the money was back in the account. It had been deposited the previous day.

She changed the username and password on the account so no one else could access it online. She wondered where the funds had come from but couldn't trace the wire transfer. On a hunch she dialed Roxie's cell phone.

"Hello, you gorgeous hunk of woman," Roxie purred, using her sexiest voice. "Did you miss me, lover?"

"I'm not your lover," Trin growled.

"You were once upon a time. You could be again," Roxie cooed.

Trin snorted into the phone. "I don't see that ever happening. Where the hell have you been? What's going on with the funds from the Ball? And how the hell did Asheed manage to kidnap my wife?"

There was a long moment's hesitation before Roxie's innocent reply. "I've been on vacation, and I don't know what you're talking about regarding the funds. Is there money missing? And last I checked, keeping up with your wife is not my responsibility."

"Your father said—"

"You scared my father to death," Roxie said. "He thought you were going to kill him. Whatever he said was a lie to get you to leave him alone.

"You can't go around threatening people just because your name is Winfield."

"Where are you now?" Trin asked.

"My apartment. Want to come over?"

"No. I've got important things to attend to." Trin ended the call.

What the hell is going on? she thought. *We break the back of a major terrorist cell and Roxie suddenly reappears?*

Trin's intercom buzzed. "Ms. Winfield, Reed Palava is here to see you. She doesn't have an appointment."

Trin bounded to the door and threw it open. Reed looked like she had been to hell and back. Trin caught her elbow, escorted her into the office, and shut the door.

"Reed, are you okay?"

Reed collapsed into the nearest chair and began to sob. "Trin, I'm so glad you and Heather are okay. I'm so sorry about what happened to Heather."

"What do you mean?" Trin circled her like a big cat waiting to strike.

Reed cried louder. "What my uncle did to her. I tried to get her out of the country but I couldn't. I had to hide in your American Embassy to save my life. He would have killed me.

"I had no idea he'd become enamored of her, and . . . I never meant to put her in harm's way. I tried to save her. Please believe me."

Reed covered her face and wailed into her hands. "I swear I tried."

Trin was confused. Heather had told her that Asheed had only hit her. Reed was indicating a sexual assault. Trin clenched her fist. "Do you know where Asheed is?"

"No, he was stripped of his rank and placed under house arrest while the government investigated the explosion of that passenger jet on the runway, but he escaped. I pray he hasn't made his way to America."

"Why would he do that?" Trin already knew the answer but wanted to hear it.

"Heather, of course. He's obsessed with her."

"Reed, how did Asheed get Heather on his private jet? She would never go willingly, and she doesn't remember getting on the plane."

"We all helped him. She was drugged. I had no idea he was going to keep her. I was told Heather would operate on Mother and be returned to the States within a week.

"I . . . I am happy that she was able to restore my mother to perfect health. She's a wonderful physician."

"Have you been with Roxie?"

"Roxie Royce? No. Why would I be with her?"

"Both of you disappeared when Heather was kidnapped, and both of you have shown up today. Please don't insult me by telling me it's a coincidence."

"I just arrived in the US yesterday from Iraq," Reed said. "I've been given political asylum in America. I've been holed up in the American Embassy in Turkmenistan. Check with your State Department. They'll confirm it."

"What are your plans?" Trin asked.

"I must hide until Asheed is apprehended. He will kill me. He was furious when I tried to get Heather out of our country."

"You really do think he's here in the States?"

"I'm certain he is. That's why I've come to you. Asheed has spies in your government. I don't trust anyone but you."

##

Trin arranged to place Reed in a safe house until Asheed was apprehended.

She called Heather and was informed that she was in surgery. She sent Garret to the hospital to guard Heather. "I'll be there as quickly as possible," she told him. "Alert hospital security to be on the lookout for the man in the photo I'm texting you. I need to make a few more phone calls."

She wasted no time putting out an all-points bulletin on Asheed Palava. She called her contacts at Homeland Security and the State Department. A call to the Texas Rangers resulted in a team of Texas's finest to share guard duty with Garret. She knew Heather would be safe.

For the next two hours Trin paid all the debts of the Cattle Baron's Ball online. When she finished, she was pleased that they had raised enough funds for two additional trauma units for the hospital and a gymnasium for the church. She knew Heather and Father Ryker would be delighted. She giggled to herself as she thought of the ways her wife would thank her. *A handshake from Father Ryker would be adequate.* She laughed out loud.

Chapter 47

Trin arrived at the hospital to find Heather in her office politely arguing with Garret. Two Rangers stood guard outside her door.

"You're not arguing with your protectors, are you?" Trin leaned down to kiss her wife.

"Trin, I don't need guards with me everywhere I go." Heather frowned.

"Asheed is here in the States," Trin whispered.

The look of terror on Heather's face made Trin's heart stop. "It's okay, honey. We'll guard you 24-7 until he's apprehended."

Heather moved closer to Trin and gripped her hand. "What if he comes after me?"

"I've notified your hospital security and have Asheed's photo plastered all over this place. A team of Texas Rangers will be with you at all times, and I won't leave your side."

"I'll be with her. You go home and get some sleep," Trin told Garrett. "We've got everything covered."

"I'll be back in the morning," Garret said over his shoulder as he left the office.

"Not necessary," Trin called after him.

"For me it is." Garret waved as he disappeared around the corner.

"Walk with me to check on Dad," Heather said, "and tell me what's going on."

Trin told her of the reappearance of Roxie and Reed. She related the conversations she'd had with the women. "Reed is terrified of her uncle, so I put her in a safe house."

"And Roxie?"

"I don't know what's going on with Roxie, and right now I don't care. You're my main concern."

They stopped outside Eric's room to finish their conversation. They could hear voices on the other side of the door.

"Uncle Jarrod and Mother are here," Heather said with a half-hearted smile as she pushed open the door.

"How's my favorite patient this afternoon?" Heather beamed at her father as she turned on the computer beside his bed. She leaned over and kissed him on the cheek.

Eric laughed. "Your favorite patient is ready to get back to work."

"No, I'm keeping you here for at least two days." Heather wrinkled her nose at him. "I know you. You won't follow the doctor's order of complete bed rest. So, we'll just monitor you ourselves."

She scanned the entries on Eric's chart and then turned to her father. "Roll over and let me check the incision."

"Heather . . . ." Eric stopped short of whining. "I'm your father."

"It's not like I'm changing your diaper, Dad." Everyone laughed. "I just want to check on my handiwork."

"I hope you don't expect me to sit here night and day," Melody carped. "It's boring here, and my bridge club meets tonight. I must keep my beauty shop appointment."

"I don't expect anything of you, Mother."

Before Melody could respond, Jarrod reached out and caught Heather's hand. "Heather, I need to talk to you about Peter."

Suddenly, Melody and Jarrod were both whining at once, pulling at Heather.

Trin watched as exhaustion passed across her wife's face. "Out, everyone," Trin commanded as she pushed Jarrod's wheelchair into the hallway and returned to escort

Melody from the room. "Go keep your beauty appointment. I'll sit with Eric."

"Oh dear God, thank you, Trin," Eric exclaimed once the others were gone. "I was beginning to lose my patience with their grousing. You need a reward or something."

The look of pure adoration on Heather's face was reward enough for Trin.

"Jarrod wants me to reinstate Peter."

"No, Dad! You can't," Heather said. "He was going to cripple you. I think he hates you. He blames you for his father's paralysis."

"Jarrod did save my life," Eric mumbled.

"Peter is sexually harassing the nurses and interns. Dad, he's a disaster. He is dangerous. Besides, Dr. Canton is still doing a psych evaluation on him. Dad, the man may be capable of murder."

A knock on the door preceded the entrance of Lori Rogers. "Am I interrupting anything?"

"Just a father-daughter standoff," Trin said, laughing. "Maybe you can be the impartial decision maker."

Lori grinned as she held up her hands. "No way. I just came on duty and wanted to check on our patient."

"Dad wants to keep Peter on staff," Heather huffed, practically stomping her foot.

"I don't want to," Eric said. "I just feel I owe his father."

"Why don't you discuss it when both of you aren't so stressed." Lori's voice of reason made both Eric and Heather smile.

"Have you two had dinner?" Lori asked Trin as the food-service cart was rolled into Eric's room.

"No." Heather tried to hide a yawn.

"Better yet, why don't you two go home and get a good night's sleep," Lori insisted. "I'll keep an eye on Eric."

"I can't leave you—"

"Heather, you're going to have to carry the load for you and your dad," Lori reminded her. "You can't do that without sleep. You'll be under a lot of pressure carrying the workload on your own. We can't afford to have an exhausted surgeon operating on people."

Eric agreed with the trauma nurse.

"Where's Melody?" Lori asked.

"Playing bridge!" Heather growled. "My mother's priorities are a little skewed."

Lori shrugged. "Go. I'll keep your father company."

Chapter 48

"Garret will be at the hospital when I drop you off," Trin informed Heather over breakfast. "I've got one final thing to take care of, and I'll be free of this terrorist mess."

"Is it dangerous?"

"No, just a little mopping up that needs to be done and some paperwork. Nothing life-threatening, honey.

"Did you ever get in touch with your mother?" Trin did the Texas sidestep, smoothly changing the subject.

"No, I called early this morning while you were showering. It went to voicemail."

"Do you want to run by her house and make sure she made it home okay last night?"

Heather scowled. "If you don't mind. I don't know why she isn't answering."

They pulled into the circular drive in front of the Hunter home. "You can wait here," Heather said, patting Trin's hand. "I'll be right back."

Trin watched as Heather stood in the doorway talking to Melody's maid. The conversation was a short one.

"Mom's already gone to the hospital to check on Dad," Heather said, climbing back into the passenger seat. "I'm glad. Sometimes I fear she doesn't appreciate my father."

Trin dropped Heather off and headed to the Fort Worth sheriff's office. A SWAT team was waiting in Sheriff Hudlow's office.

"Did you pick up the search warrant?" Trin ask Hudlow.

"Got it right here." The sheriff showed her the form that would give them the right to search every building and barrel at Royce International. "The ATF fellows are out back smoking."

"Let's do this." Trin pulled on her Kevlar vest and walked to her Jeep. "Want to ride with me, Sheriff?"

"Sure." As Hudlow raised his foot to climb into the Jeep, a singsong voice called out his name, stopping him in his tracks.

"Jesus," Hudlow growled as he placed his foot back on the ground and turned around.

"I just want to make sure my department will get credit for this raid," ATF Agent Shaylor Copeland said as he pranced toward the sheriff.

"Whatever, Copeland," Hudlow grumbled. "Truth is, Trin here brought the case to us. If anyone deserves an attaboy, it's her."

Copeland narrowed his eyes as he raked them over Trin. "You're the agent over the oil and gas agency, ain't you?"

Trin nodded. "I don't care who gets credit. I just want to move fast before it's too late."

"I'm fine with you getting the credit," Hudlow added. "You and your men can take point. We'll follow you into the warehouse."

"Um, we're just here to back you up, Sheriff. We won't be taking point, but we do want the credit."

Hudlow snorted. "Of course you do."

"That settles it." Copeland tried his best to swagger as he walked away.

"Flaming Cheerio," Hudlow snarled. "He isn't worth killing. I don't know why we got stuck with him."

"Um, Sheriff, lesbian here." Trin pointed toward herself.

"I don't care what you are," Hudlow huffed. "You're a damn fine person and a hell of a good law enforcement officer. That little pissant isn't worth a twit on a raid. You watch, he'll show up after it's all over."

259

"Good. He won't get in our way." Trin shoved the Jeep into drive and headed to Royce International.

"I don't think there'll be any danger," Trin told Hudlow as they sat on the hill overlooking Royce International. "I'm pretty sure the firearms are in that building at the back of the property."

"My deputies and your agents will be in place when you bring out the woman."

Trin left the sheriff with his officers and drove to the office door of the operation. "Wanda, where is everyone?"

Wanda jerked her head toward Bart's office. "They're holed up in there with those Muslims."

"Come with me." Trin took her hand and grabbed her purse as she pulled the woman out the door.

"Not that I mind being manhandled by you," Wanda said, giggling, "but what's going on?"

"We're going to raid Royce International. I want you out of harm's way." Trin pushed her into the Jeep and pressed the button on the walkie-talkie that connected her to Sheriff Hudlow.

"I need three men with me here to arrest whoever is in the office. You, your men, and ATF hit that warehouse fast.

"Stay down." Trin pushed Wanda onto the floorboard and then joined the men heading inside the offices.

Trin knocked on Bart's office door as she pulled her Glock from its holster. "Bart, Trin Winfield here. May I come in?"

When she received no response, she opened the door a crack and looked inside the office. Bart was facing the door, and three men were seated in chairs across from his desk.

"Oh, I'm sorry. I'm interrupting your meeting." She pushed the door open and shoved the muzzle of her Glock into the back of the man closest to her. The other officers fanned out and handcuffed all the men without resistance.

"Trin, what the hell?" Bart struggled as he was handcuffed. "What's the meaning of this?"

"It means I think you're an arms trafficker," Trin said as her walkie-talkie came to life and Sheriff Hudlow's deep baritone crackled over the line.

"Trin, we've rounded up all of them. A baker's dozen of them," Hudlow said. "And Trin, there's enough firepower in here to arm a good-size army."

Trin stepped aside and called Dixie Dancer. "Get over to Royce International immediately. We're making a big arrest. You'll want to be the first reporter on the scene. Oh, and Dixie, don't talk to anyone but Sheriff Hudlow. This operation is his baby. ATF will try to take credit for it. Don't let them."

Trin was always amazed by how quickly Dixie could get to the scene of a news story. Her news caravan pulled up as deputies were marching the criminals to the police vans.

Trin grabbed Sheriff Hudlow's arm and took him over to Dixie. "Sheriff, you know Miss Dancer. Talk to her."

Before he could do so, a woman's shrill voice pierced the morning air. "I'll have your badge! Do you know who I am? I have friends in places so high you'll have a nosebleed from answering to them. Get your hands off me.

"Trin! Trin! Tell them to release me," Roxie yelled as she spied the agent. "There has been a terrible mistake."

Trin took the bleached-blonde's arm and led her off to the side. "Roxie, the sheriff has enough on your dad and his buddies to put them away for life. You need to turn state's evidence to get a deal. Otherwise you'll go down with them."

"Are you insane?" Roxie hissed.

"I can make it happen and get you into witness protection."

"You've lost your mind, Trin Winfield. I'm not snitching—"

"Roxie, I've seen what happens to lookers like you in prison. It's not pretty." Trin leaned down and whispered in her ear. "You won't just be somebody's bitch. You'll be everybody's bitch. They'll pass you around for favors like a pack of cigarettes or a chocolate bar."

Roxie hesitated.

"They won't care whether you're on your back or your stomach," Trin whispered as if sharing a secret. "When I drive away, you're dead meat."

Trin turned toward her Jeep.

"Wait, Trin. You've got to help me. I'm not really involved in this. Bart made me help him."

"Roxie, we know you negotiated the deal and brought the arms into the States. You need to tell Hudlow everything, including your part in it."

Roxie nodded. "Can you take these cuffs off me?"

"That's up to the sheriff. I'll get him over here as soon as he finishes his interview with Dixie."

"Trin, you could save me." Roxie looked up at Trin coyly.

"Like you saved my wife from Asheed?" The bitterness in Trin's voice was alarming.

Roxie recoiled. "I . . . I thought I was helping Reed's mother. I had no idea he would . . . ."

Sheriff Hudlow finished his interview and joined them. "Thanks, Trin."

"My department appreciates your cooperation, Sheriff. We all know the story that gets out there first is the one everyone runs with, whether it's true or not. No matter how many reports Copeland writes giving himself credit for the bust, everyone will know you're the man who took down this cell."

"You know Roxie Royce," Trin said, pushing Roxie toward Hudlow. "She's going to give you all the evidence you need to put everyone you arrested today away for a very long time. Then I want to put her into witness protection. Can you swing that?"

Hudlow snorted. "You can put her in the movies for all I care. As long as she helps me clean up Tarrant County and rid us of the evil these men represent."

"I'm off to see the doctor." Trin grinned as she headed for her Jeep.

Wanda was still hiding on the floor of the Jeep. "Can I get up now?"

"Yes, you're safe. Is that your car?" Trin motioned toward a blue Ford and Wanda nodded.

"I'll walk you to your car," Trin volunteered as she helped the secretary from the floor of her jeep."

Chapter 49

Trin pulled into valet parking as Melody was stumbling from her Bentley. She pitched the attendant her keys as she caught her mother-in-law's elbow to steady her.

"Are you on your way to see Eric?" Trin asked as she pushed the elevator button.

Melody concentrated on steadying herself in the high heels she was wearing. "Yes. Is Heather at work?"

"I think so," Trin said.

As they stepped from the elevator, Melody stumbled and dropped her purse. Her cell phone, makeup, and coin purse scattered all over the hallway. Trin handed her the purse and started retrieving the contents.

"I'm going to Eric's room," Melody hiccupped. "Just bring that stuff to me."

A twisted smile worked its way across Trin's lips. Her mother-in-law was really a piece of work. She gathered Melody's things, picking up her cell phone last. It occurred to her that Heather could track her mother with her cell phone. She accessed the phone and downloaded Find My Phone from the apps store. It only took her a minute to link Melody's phone to hers. She would do the same with Heather's phone, so her wife could keep track of her mother. It was just a matter of time before Melody's lethal concoction of arrogance and alcohol killed her or an innocent bystander.

Trin delivered her mother-in-law's things to her, visited with Eric, and set off to find her wife.

Heather was sitting in her desk chair, staring out the window at the Care Flight chopper. The TV on her wall was playing. She didn't hear Trin enter.

"Hey, pretty lady." Trin eased around her desk and touched her lightly.

Heather shook her head and turned away from her wife, trying to compose herself.

Trin dropped to her knees and used her fingertips to pull Heather's face to look at her. "You're crying. Is Eric okay?"

Heather sniffled, reaching for a tissue. "Dad's fine."

"Another patient?" Trin knew Heather was emotionally invested in all her patients.

Heather shook her head and gestured toward the TV, where nonstop news coverage was congratulating Sheriff Hudlow for breaking the terrorist cell in Tarrant County.

Trin watched the parade of criminals to the police vans.

"Will I always find out you were in a life-and-death situation on the newscasts?" Heather's voice was barely above a whisper.

"Honey, I was never in any danger. Not a single shot was fired," Trin assured her. "That was planned and beautifully executed."

"Maybe this time," Heather mumbled. "But I won't always be there to put you back together."

"Heather, honey." Trin laid her head in her wife's lap. Although Heather stroked her hair, Trin couldn't feel it through the wig. "You're not going to leave me, are you?"

Heather moved her hands down to Trin's shoulders. "I love you so much, Trin. I could never leave you. I live in constant fear of losing you to a madman's bullet or an oil rig accident. People like you keep my world safe, but who protects you?"

"I'm surrounded by people who are trained to protect one another—me included. I admit that before I met you I was a chance taker. I was pretty sure I was invincible until you had to sew me back together. I'm not that woman anymore.

"I don't take chances. I think things through before acting. My main goal each day is to make it home to you at night. I plan to grow old with you by my side, honey." Trin chuckled. "I mean *really* old, like ninety-nine-plus."

"Promise?" Heather dried her eyes.

"Scout's honor."

Heather caught Trin's face between her hands and lowered her lips to the blonde's. Trin's kisses were always earthshaking. Her lips moved seductively against Heather's. Her tongue touched Heather's lips and searched for Heather's. Heather leaned harder against her wife. "Let's take this to the sofa," she whispered.

##

Trin inhaled deeply, trying to catch her breath. "I can't breathe," she gasped. "You always leave me breathless."

Heather giggled and shifted to lie flat on her wife's stomach. She too was taking deep, gulping breaths.

"Do you ever take a vacation from the hospital?" Trin asked as she lazily stroked her wife's back. "Like an extended vacation?"

"Do you?" Heather countered.

"No, but I would to be alone with you uninterrupted."

"How long are you thinking?" Heather pulled back and watched Trin's face.

"Six months?"

"Doing what?"

"What do you think?" Trin chuckled.

Heather laughed out loud. "Oh, you do think you're a machine, don't you?"

"Where you're concerned." Trin hugged her tighter. "We could rent a sailboat and sail the East Coast. There's so much history there. So many places I haven't seen in my own country. We could fly to Maine, rent a boat, sail down the coast to the Florida Keys, and fly home."

"You've given this some thought, haven't you?" Heather kissed the soft spot on Trin's neck.

"I have. Our time together has been one emergency after another. I'd like some time alone with you. For you, there will always be another emergency, and for me there'll always be another bad guy. I want to get away from it all for a while."

"I'll have to wait until Dad is a hundred percent and hire a surgeon to fill in for me. And I've got to do something about Peter and Mother."

"Oh, I put a tracker on your mother's phone," Trin said. "Now you can keep up with her."

"I don't even want to know how you did that," Heather grinned. "I thank you for it. When Dad's better I want to convince her to enter an alcohol treatment center."

"You'll have to convince her she has a problem first," Trin mumbled.

"I know."

A knock on Heather's office door interrupted their planning. "Did you lock the door?" Heather whispered.

"No!"

"Just a minute," Heather yelled as they scrambled to straighten their clothes.

Heather smoothed her hair as she opened her office door. It was the hospital's chief of security.

"I was told Agent Winfield was with you." The agent peered past Heather and caught sight of Trin's back.

"Yes, she is." Heather looked over her shoulder to make sure Trin was presentable before inviting him in.

Trin fastened the last button on her blouse and turned to face the man. "Is everything quiet on the home front?" She grinned.

"Yes, ma'am," the security chief said, hiding a smile. "I wanted to let you know that we have stationed two men at every entrance and exit of the hospital. Photos of Asheed are plastered all over the facility. There is no way he will get into the hospital."

"That's good to hear." Trin thanked him and walked into the hallway with him, giving Heather a chance to reapply makeup and comb her hair.

##

Trin spent the following week checking flight schedules and arranging to lease a sailboat in Maine. She stayed at the hospital to watch over her wife and had set up in the small office attached to Heather's. She wouldn't feel safe until Asheed was captured. He'd been spotted in the US, so she knew he was a very real danger.

Her father had balked at the mention of a six-month vacation but relented when he realized that Trin had never taken time from her job. "We didn't take a honeymoon either," Trin had added. "Vegas has wrapped up the new rig he's been on. He said he'd love to spend some time in Texas working with you."

Trin was grinning like the Cheshire cat when Heather walked into her office. "I've cleared my six-months off," she said, lifting Heather off her feet in a bear hug.

Heather giggled. "Put me down. You do know you've made me the talk of the hospital, right?"

The innocent expression on Trin's face was laughable. "What did I do?"

"Oh, let me count the things," Heather said in a singsong voice. "Here are some of the comments I've heard about you: 'Trin is constantly locking Dr. Hunter's door.' And 'Dr. Hunter's lipstick is all over her face.' Or how about 'stealing kisses in the corridor when she thinks no one is looking.' Should I go on?"

"No." Trin hung her head like a bad little girl and then kissed Heather soundly. "Honey, I'm just so excited. I can't wait to have you all to myself."

"Umm, I'm working on it." Heather returned the kiss. "Dad is almost a hundred percent and chomping at the bit to get back to work.

"We interviewed the doctor of our dreams yesterday. As soon as Human Resources finishes the background check we'll make her an offer she can't refuse."

"She?"

"You're not going to be the jealous type, are you?" Heather teased.

"I could be . . . under the right circumstances," Trin grumbled, her eyes twinkling. "Please tell me she's ugly."

"Nope, she's gorgeous."

"Married?"

"Single."

"Straight? You fail this question and you're getting close to the right circumstances."

Heather laughed out loud. "Definitely straight!"

"Whew, okay, you can hire her."

"I've fired Peter. Of course, Jarrod is livid and dealing Dad misery.

"Mother has reluctantly agreed to go into rehab. All the times her cell phone showed she was at the Anatole Hotel in Dallas, she was competing in a bridge tournament there. So, I guess she isn't running around on Dad. I think all my fires are put out."

"Did I mention I adore you?" Trin pulled Heather into her arms again.

Chapter 50

Trin listened to Heather's soft breathing. She tightened her arms around her wife, careful not to awaken her. One more day and they would leave for Maine. She blew out the breath she was certain she had been holding for a month.

"I'm awake." Heather nuzzled her neck and nipped her collarbone.

"Um, I was trying to let you sleep," Trin murmured.

"I'm too excited to sleep." Heather kissed the top of Trin's breast. "Six months alone with you is a dream come true. No hospital emergencies. No terrorists blowing up your oil fields. Just you and me, doing whatever comes to mind."

Heather nibbled Trin's nipple.

"You just made something come to my mind," Trin squeaked.

"Then you should act on it," Heather cooed.

##

Later Heather lay on her back. She loved listening to Trin in the shower. She always sang the same little tune:

"Oh Heather, honey, warm as the sunshine.
Oh Heather, honey, your love is so-oh fine."

Heather laughed when Trin added a verse she had never heard before:

"Heather, honey, give you all my money

and I'll take you around the world.
Heather, honey, it may sound funny,
but I want you to be my girl."

She closed her eyes. *No doubt about it. I'm Trin Winfield's girl*, she thought.

"Do you have to go into the hospital today?" Trin ask as she ran her fingers through the three inches of hair that now covered her head.

"Just to sign off on the new hires and one patient consultation. "You look so cute in that haircut. It's finally long enough to grasp."

"Yes, I noticed you clutch it in your fingers and steer my head where you want it." Trin leaped on the bed and crawled toward Heather on her hands and knees.

"No-o-o-o!" Heather squealed as she rolled out of bed. "Save that for the boat. We have a lot to do today."

Trin fell over on her side, clutching her chest. "Arrgg! Shot through the heart!"

##

They arrived at the hospital to find Eric, Peter, Jarrod, and a greasy-looking man in a wrinkled suit waiting outside Heather's office. "Damn, this can't be good," Trin mumbled.

"Dad, what's going on?"

"Heather, this is Rand Roberts, Peter's attorney. Mr. Roberts, this is Dr. Heather Hunter and her wife, Trin," Eric said.

"You're lesbians?" Roberts's sleazy grin almost slid off his face.

"What can I do for you, Mr. Roberts?" Heather said, ignoring the puffy paw Roberts extended for a handshake. She unlocked her office door and led the group inside.

"You can reinstate Mr. Trotter."

"I don't see that happening," Heather said.

"Then we'll have no choice but to sue the hospital," Roberts smirked.

"You'll have to get in line behind the malpractice attorneys who are suing Peter and the hospital for his ineptness," Heather said. "So, it should be a year or so before we see you again."

Roberts's smirk slid off his face. "What do you mean?"

"I mean we will never settle and never reinstate Peter Trotter." Heather clenched her fist. "If you have visions of a fat settlement you will share, you'd better find another client."

Heather turned to Peter. "We did file a complaint against you with the police when you injured my father. We haven't pursued it because . . . well, honestly, we felt sorry for Uncle Jarrod because he has had to carry you all your life. I will be pressing charges today, so unless Mr. Roberts is a criminal attorney, you'd better find yourself a good one. We have it all on video. Good day, Peter."

Trin touched the button on her phone that immediately brought hospital security to escort Peter and his attorney from the premises.

Jarrod rolled his wheelchair to Heather. "Please, Heather can't you find something for him to do." We can't live on my disability."

"Uncle Jarrod I'm at my wits end. "He' so—"

Her sentence was interrupted by the intercom. "Dr. Heather Hunter, report to the emergency room immediately. Dr. Heather Hunter, report to the emergency room immediately."

Heather ran down the hall, shedding her jacket as she went. Trin caught it and stayed right on her heels. Eric and Jarrod followed.

"I don't usually do emergency room," Heather puffed as she pushed the double doors open and accepted the white hospital jacket from an intern.

"It's your mother," the intern said, pointing toward a gurney in the corner.

"Oh God!" Heather gasped.

Melody was covered with blood and appeared to be unconscious. The ambulance attendant was removing an IV from her arm.

"What happened?" Heather asked the man stepping between him and Melody.

"You cheated on me!" The man said, wrapping his arm around Heather's throat. "Did you think I would let you go so you could run back to your bitch woman?"

Garret slid to a halt beside Trin. "What the hell? I thought you had this under control. Good thing I ignored your directive to stay home."

"Yeah, I'm glad you suck at following orders. You go left. We'll take the first shot we see. Don't hesitate," Trin whispered.

Garret nodded, unholstered his Glock, and moved slowly away from Trin.

"Where is she?" Asheed demanded. "Where's the slut that thinks you're her wife?" He scanned those gathering around him. He saw no one resembling the blonde-haired beauty on Heather's Facebook page.

"She's at home," Heather said, croaking out the words as Asheed tightened his arm against her throat. "What have you done to my mother?"

"Nothing she didn't deserve," Asheed crowed. "She drugged you and turned you over to me, you know?"

Heather couldn't believe what she was hearing. The thought of her mother handing her over to Asheed made her sick. She threw up and Asheed jumped back. Garret fired but missed. He dove behind Jarrod Trotter's wheelchair as Asheed fired at him. Jarrod jumped up and ran out the door.

273

Trin tackled Heather and they rolled away from the Muslim murderer. Asheed's eyes darted around the room and settled on Melody. He jerked her from the gurney and pulled her in front of him as Trin leveled her gun to fire.

"No!" Heather screamed.

Trin pushed Heather behind her and rose to her knees.

"Drop your gun," Asheed demanded. "Drop your gun or I'll blow her brains out."

"Humph," Trin snorted. "That wouldn't be much." She got to her feet.

"I mean it," Asheed growled as he pushed the muzzle of his pistol against Melody's temple.

"Kill her," Trin said. "I'd be rid of her. She's been nothing but a pain in my ass from the day I met her."

Heather leaned against her wife's back. She trusted Trin, no matter what she did.

"If you want to get out of here alive," Trin reasoned, "let her go. Shoot her and the next sound you'll hear is my bullet ripping through your skull."

"I want Heather," Asheed shrieked. "I want her. Give her to me and no one gets hurt."

"Ain't gonna happen, buddy," Trin snarled.

Asheed squinted his eyes and studied Trin. "You! You are her bitch. Why the boy haircut?" Then a light came on in Asheed's eyes. "Ahh, you stole her from me. You destroyed our oil refinery. You are to blame for all of this."

A cunning look crossed Asheed's face. "I've had her, you know. How does it feel to know your woman has warmed my bed?"

"Disgusting," Trin said as she put a bullet between his eyes.

Chapter 51

"That was hectic," Heather said hoarsely as Trin drove away from the police station.

"At least we were all cleared of any wrongdoing," Trin said, weary but relieved. "I was afraid we'd be forced to cancel our vacation."

Trin caught Heather's hand. "Did you see Jarrod hightail it out of that emergency room on his own two legs?"

"Yes. I kept telling Dad there was nothing wrong with him. He was just pretending paralysis to insure his inept son a job."

"He's held your dad hostage all these years when there was nothing wrong with him."

Trin thought for a moment. "So, your mother was the one who drugged you and made it possible for Asheed to take you to Iran."

"I think I've always know that," Heather said, fighting back tears. "I tried to convince myself it wasn't true. She thought she would become someone important to the Palava family if she helped Reed's mother get her surgery. It probably would have all worked out for the best if Asheed hadn't become so obsessed with me."

Trin pulled the Jeep into the garage and pushed the button to close the door. "Want to shower with me?"

"Always."

##

Trin doubled-checked their luggage to make certain everything was ready to go. "Mom, Dad, and Vegas are on their way to pick us up," she reminded Heather.

"Dad and I said our goodbyes earlier," Heather said. "I have everything packed in our checked luggage except for a change of clothes and our makeup. I'm packing those things in the carry-on."

"All we have to do is wait." Trin shrugged as she sat down on the sofa. "My folks will be here any minute to take us to the airport.

Heather sat down in her lap. "I want to clear the air on something." She hesitated for a minute before continuing. "Asheed did not sleep with me."

"I know." Trin kissed the end of her wife's nose.

"How do you know?"

"I asked you right after my daring rescue," Trin said, grinning, "and you said he had not molested you. I believed you. I saw the look in his eyes. It was the nastiest thing he could think of to rile me. He would kill his own wives if someone raped them, even if they couldn't stop it. I knew he was lying."

The blaring of a horn in their driveway made Heather jump. Trin pulled her in for a soft, sweet kiss and then released her. "Sounds like my brother is at the wheel."

The ride to the airport was enjoyable. Heather loved the family she had married into and they loved her. Vegas razzed them about needing six months alone. "What are you going to do for six months?" he teased his sister.

"All the things you wish you could do," Trin bantered.

Lucinda chided her only daughter. "Trin! Behave yourself."

"He started it, Mom," Trin defended.

"They've been like this since Trin was born," Lucinda said to Heather. "But I wouldn't have them any other way."

"Neither would I," Heather said honestly. "I wouldn't change a thing about your daughter."

The Winfields walked them as far as airport regulations would allow before hugging them goodbye.

Heather linked her arm through Trin's. "I love you, Trin Winfield, and I've got six months to show you just how much."

"Just what the doctor ordered." Trin pressed Heather's arm tighter against her side. "You'll find I'm a very good patient."

##

The three Winfields returned to their car. "My sister is really something," Vegas noted. "She makes a brother proud. I'd like to work with her sometime, Dad. I mean, if our assignments ever cross paths."

"Good," Scott said. "When she returns, the two of you are going undercover on our flagship rig in the Gulf. Something strange is going on out there in the water."

The End

If you have enjoyed this book I would be very grateful if you would consider taking a moment to write a brief review on https://www.amazon.com/dp/B07FNDNJ3F

the review can be as short as you like. As a self-published author, honest reviews are the most powerful way to bring my books to the attention of other readers. Reviews also help encourage the Amazon system to include my book in the "Also bought" and search results. Thank you, Erin

Learn more about Erin Wade
and her books at www.erinwade.us
Follow Erin on Facebook
https://www.facebook.com/erin.wade.129142

**Other #1 Best Selling Books
by Erin Wade**
Too Strong to Die ⸲
Death Was Too Easy ⟍
Three Times as Deadly ⤳
Branded Wives ⟍
Living Two Lives ⌐
Don't Dare the Devil ⸲

Erin Wade writing as D.J. Jouett
The Destiny Factor

Coming in 2018
Wrongly Accused
Shakespeare Undercover

Coming in 2019
Assassination Authorized!
Java Jarvis
Dead Girl's Gun
Doomsday Cruise

Below are the first five chapters of *Wrongly Accused*. I hope you enjoy them. *Wrongly Accused* will be released in October 2018.

Erin Wade
The Roughneck & the Lady

Chapter 1

"I can't believe you're doing this to me." Richard Wynn screamed at his now ex-fiancée. "Two years I've invested in you and now you tell me you don't love me. Give me the damn ring. At least I can get my money back on it."

Doctor Dawn Fairchild removed the engagement ring from her finger and dropped it into his hand.

"Please, Richard, I've tried. I just don't love you like I should. You deserve more than a loveless marriage."

Richard downed his scotch and motioned to the waiter for another one.

"You're getting drunk," Dawn mumbled.

"You're damn right I'm getting drunk. My world just went up in smoke. It's someone else, isn't it. You've fallen in love with that Latin Lothario in the emergency room. I saw the way he can't keep his eyes off you. Are you letting him put his hands on you too?"

Richard tossed down his sixth scotch of the night and ordered another one. "You're just like all the other doctors who think they're God. You think you can control life and death, break hearts or mend them, which ever strikes your fancy. You think you are the judge and jury.

"You'll pay for this Dawn. If it's the last thing I ever do, I'll make you pay for this."

"Richard, there's no one else in my life. You know I can't condone what you're doing at the hospital. I think it borders on illegal."

He staggered to his feet. "Come on, I'll take you home. I'm sick of being with you."

"I should drive you home," she said. "You're too drunk to drive."

Dawn paid the check then supported Richard as he weaved his way to the valet. His car was one of the last left on the lot as the restaurant prepared to close for the night.

"Dr. Wynn, I've already brought up your car," the smiling valet held out Richard's key fob.

Dawn grabbed the fob. "I'm driving. Dr. Wynn isn't feeling well." She maneuvered Richard into the passenger's seat, fastened his seatbelt then slid behind the wheel of the Mercedes.

She tried to close out the tirade Richard was launching at her. She was certain he had invented some of the profanities he was spewing.

"Pull over," Richard yelled. "Pull over now. I'm going to puke all over my car.

Dawn pulled the car to the curb and watched as Richard bolted from the car vomiting all over the sidewalk in front of an elite men's apparel shop. He threw up until he began to dry heave, then slid to the sidewalk, resting his back against the store's wall. He massaged his temples.

She got out of the car and maneuvered through the stomach contents Richard had regurgitated. When she stood in front of him, he looked up at her and burst into tears. "Please don't do this to me, Dawn. I love you."

She held out her hand to help him stand. He got to his feet and leaned against the wall. "Feel better now?" She asked.

He breathed in deeply then exhaled loudly. "Much. I'm sorry I didn't mean to go off on you like that. I know you're just trying to be honest with me. I've known for long-time things weren't right between us." He wiped his mouth on the sleeve of his suit jacket then walked to the car.

She watched him as he slid into the driver's seat, then joined him. "Are you certain you can drive?"

"Yeah, I'm good."

He pulled the car away from the curb and accelerated to make it through the intersection. The squealing of brakes and the screeching of metal against metal were the last sounds Dawn heard before sinking into total darkness.

"Please help me! Please someone help me." A woman's voice cried out in the darkness.

Dawn heard the plea for help through the fog and pounding in her head. She unbuckled her seatbelt and opened the car door. She stumbled toward the woman's voice. The woman was on her knees bent over another woman lying on her back. She was crying into her cell phone. Dawn knew without touching the prone woman that she was already dead.

Dawn placed her hand on the other woman's shoulder. The wail of an ambulance told her the woman had called 911. The woman looked up then looked around. "Where did you come from?"

"The other car," Dawn choked.

The ambulance and police arrived at the same time. Dawn was hustled into the emergency vehicle as another ambulance arrived at the scene.

So sleepy, she thought as she stretched out on the ambulance cot. The attendant pulled a sheet over her.

Chapter 2

Valarie Davis pulled the collar of her coat tighter around her neck to ward of the bitter November wind. The priest handed her a single rose and nodded toward the coffin that filled the gaping hole in the ground.

"Toss it on the coffin," Val's mother whispered. Val obeyed and watched the red petals separate and cover her sister's casket just as Mary's blood had covered the pavement.

She spent the rest of the day consoling her parents and accepting condolences from relatives and friends. She wanted to get back to work to get her mind off the incidents of the past week.

"Val, look who's here," her mother dragged her high school boyfriend toward her.

"I'm so sorry about Mary," Detective Bobby Joe Jones mumbled as he shook her hand. "I wish I could do something to make it easier for you."

"Just make sure the person who did this pays," Val hissed.

The next person to console her was her secretary Lillian Cribs. "I'm so sorry about your sister."

Lillian was an excellent secretary, but she left a lot to be desired in the tact department. "Boss, we've got an influenza outbreak. When are you returning to work?"

Val cocked her head to the side and glared at Lillian.

"I'm just asking," Lillian snorted. "How else will I find out?"

Dawn Fairchild awoke in a room that was very familiar to her; the intensive care unit of All Saints Hospital where she practiced.

"About time you woke up, Dr. Fairchild." Martina a friendly Spanish nurse smiled at her. "You've been in la-la land for over a week."

"What am I doing here? What's wrong with me?"

"You're here because we have no empty rooms," the nurse said, "and there's nothing wrong with you but a concussion."

Dawn struggled to sit up and almost fainted when nausea and the pain between her eyes forced her to lay down.

"May I see my chart?" Dawn motioned toward the laptop Martina was using to enter information.

"Sure," Martina turned the rolling table, so Dawn could see the report.

Dawn studied the information attached to her name. "I see no reason for me to be here," she smiled. "I'm discharging myself."

"I'll take care of the paperwork," Martina said. "I'll leave it at the nurse's station. Don't forget to sign it."

"Dr. Dawn Fairchild?" A man dressed in a neatly-pressed suit stepped into the room.

"Yes," Dawn replied as she continued to search for her civilian clothes.

"I'm Detective Bobby Joe Jones," the man introduced himself. "I'm investigating the death of Mary Davis."

"Mary Davis," Dawn processed the name and could find nothing familiar in her mental data banks. "I'm afraid I don't know a Mary Davis."

"She was the young woman involved in the accident you were in seven days ago."

Dawn swayed and lowered herself onto the hospital bed trying to stop her head from spinning. The memory returned like the reoccurrence of a horrible nightmare. Fog, dizziness, blood everywhere and a gorgeous brunette calling for help as she sobbed over a dead girl.

"Yes, yes! I remember." Dawn took a drink of water to alleviate the dryness in her mouth. "That was awful. I . . . I couldn't help her."

Detective Jones gave the blonde doctor time to gather her composure than pulled his notebook from the inside front pocket of his jacket.

"According to the traffic report, you were the driver of the other vehicle involved in the accident."

"No," Dawn shook her head as if clearing the cobwebs. "Dr. Richard Wynn was driving. We were in his car."

Jones studied his notes, then flipped the page. "According to Dr. Wynn you were drive. He said he'd had too much to drink and that you drove him home and took his car to your place."

"That isn't true," Dawn sighed. "I was driving when we left the restaurant because Richard was inebriated but he became ill and demanded I pull over, so he could throw up. After he vomited he forced his way behind the wheel and took over driving the car."

"The car belonged to Dr. Wynn?" Jones started writing in his notebook.

"Yes."

"The valet at the restaurant said you took Dr. Wynn's keys and insisted on driving."

Dawn took a long time to answer. She was beginning to have a bad feeling about the detective's questions. "Yes."

"Dr. Wynn says you dropped him off at his home and took his car. He says he was not even in the car at the time of the fatal accident."

And there it is, Dawn thought. *Fatal accident.*

"I was in the passenger's street. Richard was driving. Surely someone at the scene of the accident must have seen him."

"The only people at the scene of the accident were you and the two women in the other car. One of them was dead on arrival and the other said you were the only one in the car that T-boned them."

And just like that Richard has made me pay, Dawn closed her eyes. He killed a woman then ran away leaving me to pay for his crime.

"There must be some way to prove Richard was driving," Dawn sobbed. "Security cameras at the scene, his finger prints on the steering wheel, some one must have seen him returning home on foot."

"I've run down everything you just mentioned," Jones frowned. He didn't like the idea of the beautiful blonde being incarcerated with hardened criminals. "I found nothing to support your story. Only two security videos on the corner were working and they didn't record the accident. Fingerprints belonging to you and Dr. Wynn were lifted from the steering wheel. That only proves that both of you had driven the car. The best thing you have going for you is there was no alcohol in your system at the time of the accident."

"The most damning information comes from the valet who heard you insist on driving and witnessed you drive away and the sister of the victim who swears you were the only one in the car.

"You ran a stop sign and broad-sided the passenger side of the car, killing Mary Davis."

Detective Jones pulled a pair of handcuffs from somewhere. "Dr. Dawn Fairchild you're under arrest for vehicular manslaughter. You have the right to remain . . .."

This can't be happening. How could the Gods be on Richard's side?"

"In Texas the penalty for vehicular manslaughter is two to twenty years," Libby Howe informed her best friend and client. "We can go to trial or plead guilty and throw yourself on the mercy of the court."

"I can't plead guilty, Libby. I could lose my license to practice medicine."

"I can probably get it reduced to a misdemeanor," Libby thought out loud. "You could lose your license if the judge declares it a felony, but you're okay if it's treated as a misdemeanor. I'm pretty sure I can make that happen."

"Libby, I won't plead guilty. I'm innocent. I didn't kill that girl. I don't care what her crazy sister says, I've been wrongly accused."

Valerie Davis watched her sister's killer as she followed her attorney into the courtroom. Val could tell the blonde doctor was nervous. *Who wouldn't be?*

The trial lasted two days. Two days to destroy a woman's life. The prosecuting attorney presented his witnesses in chorological order leading jurors to the death of Mary Davis.

The valet testified that Dawn was the one driving Richard Wynn's car. Richard swore Dawn had dropped him at his home before continuing to her house. Valerie Davis was the most convincing of them all as she described Dawn getting out of the other car.

Before giving closing remarks, attorney Libby Howe recalled Valerie to the witness stand.

"Remember you are still under oath, Miss Davis," Libby reminded her. "On the night your sister was killed in the automobile accident, are you positive, beyond a doubt that you saw Dr. Dawn Fairchild get out of the driver's side of the vehicle that struck your car?"

Val locked eyes with the beautiful doctor and hesitated before answering. For one split second, she admitted to herself that she had only become aware of the other woman when Dawn had placed her hand on Val's shoulder. "Yes, I am positive."

The jury returned a guilty verdict.

"Court will reconvene at eight in the morning for sentencing," the judge declared.

Dawn fought back the hot tears that threatened to run down her face. Anger flooded her body as she stood and screamed, "Valerie Davis you are a liar."

Val's gaze locked with Dawn's. She had never seen such loathing in anyone's eyes in her life. Dawn Fairchild hated her with a passion.

The bailiff slapped the handcuffs on her and led Dawn from the courtroom.

##

Dawn surveyed the prison that was to be her home for the next two years. Federal Medical Center, Carswell (FMCC) was a U.S. federal prison in Fort Worth, Texas for female inmates of all security levels with medical and mental health problems. It also housed 600 minimum-security female inmates.

The facility sprawled across eighty acres near the southeast corner of Lake Worth and was home to over 1,400 prisoners.

As a teenager, Dawn had heard horror stories about the prison. It was Fort Worth's dirty little secret. Women inmates were often raped by prison guards and denied medical treatment. Belligerent prisoners committed suicide under questionable conditions.

During her residency at Harris Methodist Hospital, she had heard about a new prison administrator who was turning the facility around. She prayed the stories about the current operations of the prison were true. Otherwise she knew she was about to be dumped into the cesspool of all prisons.

Chapter 3

Dawn kept her eyes down avoiding eye contact with the prisoners who made salacious remarks to her as the guards led her to her new home, a six by eight cell.

I can do this for two years, she thought sitting down on the hard bed in her cage. *I'll keep my head down, do my time and get out.*

"Hi, I'm Niki Sears," a scrawny young woman stuck her hand through the bars. She pulled it back when Dawn made no move to touch it. "What are in her for?"

"Vehicular manslaughter," Dawn mumbled.

"Drugs," Niki shrugged. "I'm a drug addict."

"How long have you been in here?"

"Twelve months," Niki grinned flashing a snaggle-toothed smile. Twelve more months and I'm outta' here."

"You've been in here twelve months and you're still using drugs. I'd think you'd be clean by now."

"I am," Niki smirked. "That doesn't mean I wouldn't take a hit of anything if I had a chance"

"Did the hospital give you something to help you withdraw?" Dawn couldn't suppress the doctor in her.

"Yeah, a cell with nothing but a paper sheet. I'm sorry to say I ate it, used it for toilet paper and tore it into small pieces to make a nest in the corner."

Dawn studied the skeletal woman. She was certain Niki must have been beautiful at some point in time. Her green eyes had a haunting look and her lips were the perfect Cupid's bow. She had no eyebrows and her nose had been broken. Missing teeth and a scar down the left side of her face reflected the hard life Niki had chosen.

"Listen," Niki whispered. "Keep your head down and your mouth shut. Try to be as unobtrusive as possible. They'll come after a looker like you."

"They, who?"

"Gotta' get my beauty rest," Niki scoffed. "It also helps to pretend to be crazy. They don't bother crazy."

"They, who?"

Niki appeared to be asleep.

Chapter 4

For the thousandth time Val picked up her cell phone to call Mary. Mary! Her best friend. Her confidant. Her rock. Mary had always been the one to make her laugh and see things through rose-colored glasses instead of the dark grey of Val's world. Mary had convinced her she could make a difference.

Val shuffled through the stack of files on her desk. She knew she was making a difference, but God it was so slow. She had inherited the mess from hell when she accepted her present position two years ago.

An Harvard graduate with a double major in law and medicine, she had quickly made a name for herself. Her rise in the ranks had been phenomenal. Her battles had been hard fought and usually won. Losing her sister was a battle wound that might never heal.

One stupid woman not paying attention and poof, just like that Mary's life was snuffed out. Val had heard that Dr. Dawn Fairchild had been transferred to a prison out of state. That was good. Texas prisons were notoriously hard on prisoners.

Still it's a shame, Val thought. *Dr. Dawn Fairchild was one gorgeous woman. It's amazing how three lives were destroyed in the flash of an eye.* "And you lied," a little voice tormented her.

##

Dawn followed Lucky—a trustee inmate—who had been assigned to show her the routine. She wanted to ask Lucky where she got her name but remained silent. *No one has ever learned anything with their mouth open*, she thought.

"What are in for?" Lucky asked as she led her to the kitchen.

"Something I didn't do."

"Yeah, they all say that," Lucky snorted. "Me, I'm in for murder. Plain and simple. My girlfriend cheated on me and I slit her throat with a kitchen knife."

Dawn didn't respond. *Silence is the safest response. What I really want to do is run screaming from this hell hole.*

Lucky chuckled. "Don't worry, I'm not a killer. I just don't like cheaters.

Dawn gulped and followed the six-foot Amazon to the next room.

Lucky showed her the layout of the kitchen then took her to the laundry room. "Don't come in here alone," she warned Dawn.

"This is where bad things happen to pretty women." She trailed her fingers down Dawn's arm.

Oh God. Please don't let this happen. Dawn stood still maintaining eye contact with Lucky.

"You're going to need a protector in here," Lucky murmured. "A pretty woman like you. They'll gang up on you if you don't belong to someone."

"Lucky," Niki shoved her way through the double doors leading into the laundry room. "There's a fight in the kitchen."

Lucky's eyes darted from Dawn to Niki. "Stay with her, Niki. Don't let anything happen to her."

"Should we call the guards or someone to break up the fight?" Dawn asked as Lucky left the room.

"Nah, there's no fight. I was just trying to stop Lucky from staking her claim on you."

"Oh," Dawn squeaked. "Thank you."

"I was her bitch until I stopped complying with her demands," Niki shrugged. "Then she beat me up, knocked out my front teeth, and threw me back into the shark tank. Traded me for a pack of cigarettes. I haven't always looked like a skank. This place has a way of changing women. I'll keep you safe as long as I can, but I'm not very strong." Niki shrugged her shoulders. "And Lucky is a hulk."

"What do you expect of me?" Dawn whispered.

"Nothing." Niki said. "Just, if you get out of here alive. Please, get me out too."

"I will," Dawn promised.

"I've been instructed to take you to the assessment center," Lucky blasted into the room. "Niki you need to get back to the library. You must to be there when it opens."

Niki nudged Dawn toward the double doors. "I was just telling Dawn that you're someone important here. She's lucky to have you showing her the ropes."

Dawn was surprised at the way Lucky preened over Niki's compliments. Niki continued to praise Lucky all the way to the assessment center. Dawn waved bye to Niki and her friend winked at her. Niki knew her way around the prison and its inhabitants.

Dawn squirmed in the hard-straight-backed chair as the woman across from her studied her file. "You're a doctor?"

"Yes, ma'am."

"What's your specialty?"

"I'm a surgeon and a pretty good diagnostician." Dawn tried to be brief and to the point.

"Humph," the woman slid the papers back into her file. "How would you feel about working in the hospital here?"

"I'd be happy to help in any way I can." Dawn wondered what kind of archaic equipment the facility would have.

"Fill this out. I'll pass your request on to the Warden."

"My request?"

"If you want to work in the hospital, you must request it. If not, I'll have someone escort you back to the cafeteria."

"Yes, yes, I'll fill out the request."

##

"How was your first day?" Niki whispered as they leaned against the bars between them.

"Scary."

"Did they assign you a duty?"

"Not yet. I think they're going to use me in the hospital."

"God, I hope so." Niki sighed. "That would get you out of harm's way. You'd be housed in the hospital instead of this place."

The clanging of iron doors announced the arrival of the guards for their last check of the night. "Pretend you're asleep," Niki pulled her sheet over her and turned her face to the wall away from the guards.

Dawn did as she was told and held her breath as two guards stopped in front of her cell. "Hey, blondie, you awake?"

Dawn didn't move. One of the guards clanged his nightstick between the bars. "You awake."

"What the hell do you want?" Niki sat up.

"Nothing you've got," the female guard huffed. "Go back to sleep, skank."

"She's sleeping," Niki yelled. "She's worn out. Leave her alone."

"What's going on down there?" A voice from the other end of the cells echoed through the unit.

"They're messing with your woman," Niki screamed as Lucky sprinted to their cells.

"Is there a problem here, officers?" Lucky asked.

"No. We were just making sure she's okay," the female guard answered. "You," she pointed at Niki. "You're a trouble maker."

"Everything's good here," the male guard growled. "Let's move on. You need to get back to bed Lucky."

The three walked away bantering about the blonde.

Dawn waited until the steel doors locked then scooted to Niki's cell. "Oh God, Niki I've never been so scared in my life. Thank you."

"Sooner or later they'll get to you," Niki cautioned. "Don't fight, they'll only hurt you more to teach you a lesson."

##

A strangling sound pulled Dawn from a deep sleep. Her body was rigid as she tried to identify the noise. *Choking! Someone is choking Niki.*

Without thinking Dawn rushed to the bars between their cells and started screaming. Two figures were bent over Niki.

"Help! Help! Somebody help her! They're killing Niki."

A loud pop and bright light filled the unit as other prisoners began yelling. The two muggers ran from Niki's cell and disappeared through the door at the end of the alleyway.

Lucky and two guards Dawn had never seen before ran to Niki's cell.

"Jesus Christ," Lucky yelled, "She's been stabbed."

Dawn watched as blood flowed from Niki's stomach. "Let me help her?" Dawn begged. "I can help her."

The two guards looked at one another. "She's a doctor," Lucky yelled. "Let her help Niki. I'll get a stretcher."

By the time Lucky returned Dawn had located the cut artery and pinched it off to stop the bleeding.

"Lift her onto the gurney," Dawn directed. "I'll hold the artery until we can get her to the hospital otherwise she'll bleed to death."

The four of them rode the elevator down to the first floor and Lucky led the way to the infirmary. "This is closer than the hospital, Doc. Everything you'll need is in here."

Dawn located the clamps and looked around for suture. She was surprised to find the infirmary well stocked with swaged needles prepackaged with the needle attached to the thread. She carefully cleaned the wound then neatly sutured the artery back together. She located a punctured intestine and sutured it. She cleaned out the leakage from the intestine to keep Niki's stomach cavity from becoming infected. She checked to make certain the nicked artery and intestine were the only damage done by the would-be killers. She removed the clamps watching to make certain her sutures held as blood pumped through the veins, then she closed the wound.

Niki moaned. "That hurt like hell, Doc."

Dawn patted her patient's hand. For the first time she realized that she had performed a major operation on a patient that wasn't sedated. Her admiration for the pitiful woman on the gurney went way up.

"You must have a pain threshold that's off the charts," Dawn praised Niki. "You never made a sound."

"I didn't want to startle you," Niki groaned. "You had your hands in my guts. Is there any chance of getting some pain meds? I'm really hurting."

"I'll take it from here," the hospital doctor touched Dawn's arm. "I watched what you did. You're one hell of a surgeon. I'll make certain the Warden moves you to the hospital housing when we finish here. I'm Dr. Lance Reynolds, by the way."

"Dr. Dawn Fairchild," she shook his hand.

##

Dawn looked out the window and realized a new day was beginning. *I've survived two days*, she thought. *Taking it one day at a time.*

"You want some coffee," Lucky caught Dawn's elbow and steered her toward the doctor's lounge.

"That sounds great. Will they put a guard on Niki? Whoever tried to kill her is still loose."

"Did you get a good look at them?" Lucky filled two cardboard cups with hot coffee.

"No, it was too dark, but I bet Niki knows who did it. Will there be a full inquiry?"

"Probably, our new Warden is a bitch about this sort of thing. She'll go ballistic and you can bet heads will roll. I'm just glad they didn't go after you."

"Will I meet the Warden?" Dawn asked.

"I doubt it," Lucky shrugged. "She's not a real hands-on administrator but she knows how she wants things to run and if the people under her don't do as they're told, she fires them"

"Have you met her?"

"Yeah. Once a month she holds a luncheon for the trustees. We get to eat with her and answer her questions. She even answers ours."

"What does she look like?

"She's a knock out. The kind of woman you'd give your soul to spend one night with. Like you."

Dawn grunted. "You really are a silver-tongued devil, Lucky."

Chapter 5

Dr. Reynolds immediately arranged for Dawn to transfer to hospital duty. "She's too good to leave with the animals." He informed Assistant Warden Ray McDonald. "She really knows her way around an operating room and I could use the help."

Dawn settled into the routine of managing the infirmary. She had convinced Dr. Reynolds that she could train Niki to assist her. "She's very smart and has a degree in biology."

"She's also a drug addict," Reynolds countered but had given in and granted her request.

Dawn shared her room with Niki since rooms in the medical suites were scarce. Niki had lived up to Dawn's expectations and was thriving in the new surroundings. Both woke an hour early every morning to work out in the hospital gym. "We don't want to get soft," Dawn said. "Besides we need the endorphins to make the day great."

Niki took to exercise with the same zest she had taken to drugs. "Our workouts make me feel like a million dollars. Tell me about endorphins again?"

"They're hormones secreted by the brain and nervous system. They're peptides which activate the body's opiate receptors, causing an analgesic effect, almost like drugs. They have several physiological functions."

"Humph, go figure," Niki groaned.

"I've spoken to the dentist on staff," Dawn said one morning. "He has agreed to cap your teeth that are broken and replace the missing ones."

"They can do that?" Niki beamed. "They can make me look normal again?"

"Yes, but Niki, I want you to take a good look at yourself in the mirror and know that the reason you are here, the reason you look like you do now is because of drugs. You must never do drugs again."

"I promise," Niki pledged. "I feel that God has given me a second chance and I'm not going to mess it up. Dawn, I don't know why you did this for me, but I appreciate it."

"You risked your life for me,"

Loud screaming in the hallway and people scurrying in all directions drew Dawn's attention to the door as it was shoved open and two guards carried in a neatly dressed woman. Blood was oozing across the white blouse she wore.

"That loon on the fourth floor shanked her," the guard explained. "She's hurt bad, Doc."

Niki helped the guards lift the woman onto the exam table as Dawn washed her hands and slipped on surgical gloves. The shank was still buried in the valley between the woman's breasts. Dawn tried to ignore the perfect breasts as she wiped the blood from them.

"Doc it's the Warden." Niki stood slack jawed staring at the injured woman as if she were the second coming.

"Niki, call the anesthesiologist. We've got to move quickly to stop the bleeding when I pull the shank out of her chest."

A hand gripped Dawn's arm. "Please don't let me die!"

The blood in Dawn's veins turned to ice water. She moved to stare into the woman's face. "You! You're the Warden?"

"Yes," Valerie Davis choked.

Dawn leaned closer so only Val would hear her words. "I should let you die, but I won't because I've never killed anyone in my life."

"You're one lucky woman," Dr. Lance Reynolds removed the sutures from Warden Davis' incision. "You won't even have a scar. "Dr. Fairchild is a hell of a doctor.

"She's a surgeon, you know. I don't know what she did to land in here, but you're lucky she was here. She saved your life."

"She hasn't followed up with me on my surgery," Val's stoic expression emphasized her disapproval.

"She asked me to take over your follow-up treatment," Reynolds said. "She said she didn't think an inmate should be treating the Warden."

"I'm sure that was said tongue in cheek," Val huffed.

"No, I believe she was sincere," Reynolds mused. "She has been an incredible asset to our hospital. She's a very dedicated doctor.

"I can't tell you how glad I am to have someone of her caliber," Reynolds said. "You know I'm old enough to start drawing my pension and social security. I'd really like to retire before some nut shanks me. Is there any chance Dr. Fairchild would stay on here after she serves her time?"

"I doubt it," Val snorted. "I don't think we could pay her enough money to get her to work for me."

I hope you have enjoyed this preview of *Wrongly Accused* scheduled for release in October.

Erin Wade

Erin Wade
The Roughneck & the Lady

Made in the USA
Columbia, SC
14 November 2018